NARROW GAUGE TO MURDER

NARROW GAUGE TO MURDER

CAROLYN THOMAS

COACHWHIP PUBLICATIONS

Greenville, Ohio

TO MAGGIE

Narrow Gauge to Murder, by Carolyn Thomas
© 2018 Coachwhip Publications

Published 1952
No claims made on public domain material.
Cover image: Rockies © Mark Byzewski

CoachwhipBooks.com

ISBN 1-61646-439-9
ISBN-13 978-1-61646-439-4

I

Two roads led from Granger to Glory Cloud, Colorado, and whichever one you traveled, you were convinced you should have chosen the other. Any time you climb nearly five thousand feet in ten miles you're bound to notice a certain abruptness and spine-tingling quality in the route. At least if you are no more used to mountain driving than I was that May twenty-fifth when I arrived in Glory Cloud.

That morning we were following the Coyote Canyon road, and in my ignorance I was sure the other way—the Alpine road—would have been preferable. But when eventually I saw the Alpine road I discovered that any advantage one might have over the other was debatable. A roller coaster could have taken lessons from either.

Of course, I was a mere tourist. These roads didn't faze the natives. I glanced at my companion and pilot, Mrs. Amanda Plumb. When the man at the Granger bus station said there was no public transportation to Glory Cloud, and suggested I get a lift with the woman who carried the RFD route, he hadn't mentioned Amanda's driving.

There had been nothing wrong with the streamliner that had deposited me in Denver early that morning. And the bus from Denver had been crowded and slow, but nothing to complain about. But this 1937 Ford with delusions of being a mountain goat, driven by this hardy character with delusions of immortality—oh, brother! I hung on to the door handle and wondered whether I should have followed my family's urging and spent the summer at home.

But I couldn't have stayed home all summer. Those two days after I'd polished off my examinations had been sufficient. I was fond of my family and they were fond of me, but there were too many points where we failed to see eye to eye. They were all in favor of higher education for females, but they thought there was no sense in carrying that sort of thing to extremes—working for an M.A., spending time with such unorthodox characters as that reformer, Jan Polenski. It baffled the hell out of them when I refused to join a sorority. Phi Beta Kappa was all very well, but did it hold dances where one met nice eligible young men?

Now I was cheered to think that, despite my family's dim view of me, I must have made a hit with the Amazonian Amanda. The man at the bus station had warned that getting a ride depended on the adroitness of my approach. And I learned later that if Amanda didn't like you, it was against regulations to give you a lift.

I unriveted my eyes from the tortuous road and scanned Amanda Plumb more closely. In her late forties or early fifties. Skin deeply tanned, lined and weather-beaten, blue eyes faded by long exposure to mountain sunlight, but no gray in the curly, dark-auburn hair. And her physique! The only word for Amanda's five-foot-nine, one hundred and eighty-five pounds of brawn and muscle. She could have served as model for an heroic statue —"Pioneer Woman." I could imagine her cast in bronze, rifle in one hand, infant in the crook of the other arm and several young ones clutching her skirts.

Not that I ever saw Amanda in a skirt. Always she wore blue jeans, a plaid shirt, a man's battered felt hat, stout, high-laced boots. The boots suggested an unpleasant question.

"Are there rattlesnakes around here?"

Amanda jammed on the brakes before a mailbox on a post. No cabin was visible.

"Always rattlers in the hills," she said flatly.

Seeing my shudder, she grinned, added:

"Not where you're going, though. No rattlers in Glory Cloud."

"Why not?"

"Too high. It's near ten thousand feet. They don't like it much above seven thousand."

I wondered about our present altitude. I knew Granger was five thousand and we'd been going up, up, up, right from the town limits. If Amanda's driving hadn't been so unnerving, it would have been a spectacularly beautiful ride.

The road was dirt, with a sprinkling of gravel, barely two cars wide. It wound around hairpin curves and snaked along precipitous drop-offs from which I looked far down and saw the tiny white thread that was Coyote Creek. The steep mountainsides above and below the road were heavily wooded with pine and beneath the shelter of the trees snow still lay on the ground. At one point where the canyon narrowed I looked across to the abrupt rise beyond the creek and noticed a flat, shelf-like clearing halfway up.

I pointed. "That looks like a road over there."

Amanda glanced over and away. An indefinable emotion shuttered her face.

"Old roadbed of the narrow-gauge railroad," she said.

"I'm glad I happened to notice it. Mr. Dahlberg is going to deal with that in his book."

No reply.

"Dahlberg's my major adviser," I went on. "At the university. He'll be out here himself before long. When he gets through reading papers and making out grades. But you probably know him already. He was in Glory Cloud last summer."

"Yeah," she said, "I know him. A trouble-making son of a gun."

"Dr. Dahlberg is a distinguished man," I said coldly. "Anything he writes is definitive. He's writing a book on narrow-gauge railroads in the west, and he will devote special attention to the Granger, Glory Cloud & Western."

"Sounds just like him," Amanda snorted. "Digging up things better left alone. A trouble-maker!"

I didn't care to walk the rest of the way so, with difficulty, I held my tongue. And in all fairness, I knew that my admiration for Axel Dahlberg, amounting virtually to hero worship, interfered with objectivity. That he was brilliant was beyond question; that he antagonized people and enjoyed doing it was equally established.

Seeking a sedative change of subject, I said:

"Tell me something about Glory Cloud. I know it's a ghost town, but what is it a ghost of?"

"How do you mean?" Amanda asked irritably. "It was a boom and now it's a bust, that's all."

"What boomed it?"

"Gold," she said. "The Glory Cloud mine was the first big bonanza around here and it was opened up about 1890. I reckon you could say the town of Glory Cloud was in its heyday for the next twenty years. When I was a kid my pa worked in the mines and did a little prospecting on the side and we lived up there. It was quite a place then."

"What happened?"

Amanda shrugged. "What always happens. The veins pinched off. Oh, there was still gold in them—there's gold in 'em now—but it cost too much to get it out for what it was worth. Things started going downhill. Work in the mines fell off, people drifted on to look for fresh diggings—lots of them just locked up their houses and walked away. Must have been about 1926 they finally closed the mines."

"And they've been closed ever since?"

"Pretty much," she said. "Back in '34 the government did something—devalued currency, they called it—that made gold more valuable for a while and the Glory Cloud mine was reopened. But it was never worked so hard as before, and when the war came it was shut down again. All the gold mines were shut down."

"So now Glory Cloud is just a summer resort."

"I wouldn't exactly say that," Amanda grinned. "If you think you're headed for any place like Estes Park, you're due for an awful shock. A few die-hards stay the year round, and a few summer people come back every year because they own cabins. And there's the old Glory Cloud Inn. It does a pretty good business during the tourist season. But you couldn't hardly call Glory Cloud a summer resort."

We had just climbed an especially steep grade and now there was a weathered sign, Quartz, at the roadside. We stopped at a line-up of some twenty mailboxes. Most of the owners must have lived in hidden folds of the hills. Quartz consisted of a half-dozen houses scattered above and below the road on the hillside. Fifty yards back from the mailboxes was a tavern in a brown frame building.

Branching left from our road wandered an even less promising trail toward a destination indicated by a rude arrow: Bitter Creek. To my question, Amanda replied that Bitter Creek was a tungsten mining community and that it, too, had known its boom days, but that the mines and mills were closed down now and few people were left.

Just above the road fork an old bridge crossed Coyote Creek. Closely paralleling the narrow road to Bitter Creek, but on the opposite side of the stream, was what must have been another stretch of roadbed for the narrow gauge, perhaps a spur from the main line.

The road beyond Quartz made everything before look tame. We started a series of switch-backs that took my breath as Amanda whipped her battered steed around them with utter unconcern. I was too jittery to talk, but Amanda was warmed up now.

"Where you fixing to stay in Glory Cloud? At the perfessor's?"

"Hardly," I replied. "His divorce is still pending and he'll be batching it. Glory Cloud isn't *that* broad-minded, is it?"

She grunted.

"I'm going to stay in the Barlow cabin. You know where that is?"

"Sure. Right across from the post office. Pretty big place for just one person. You in the chips?"

"Far from it. The Barlows are friends of Mr. Dahlberg and they aren't going to use it this summer—they're going to Europe. So he wrote and asked them to let me have it for the season. They were glad to have the place occupied and I'm paying merely a nominal rent."

Granger had been balmy and spring-like, with jonquils and tulips blooming and the grass greening up, but as we continued to climb we retreated into winter. The sun vanished and the sky was a leaden gray. Now there was more snow to be seen than bare ground and there were occasional patches of ice on the road. The high, thin air was not refreshingly cool; it was downright cold.

It depresses me to be cold and I thought that was why my first sight of Glory Cloud filled me with dismay. The village looked bleakly inhospitable that day, the whole scene inimical. Ten thousand feet is high enough, but Glory Cloud was surrounded by mountains that were higher, with the awesome range of the Continental Divide looming to the west. The settlement should have looked cozy, nestled in its little clearing, but instead the massive, overshadowing white peaks made it forlorn and insignificant. The dark green of the pine forest all around was crowding in on the hamlet, gradually taking back its own.

I shivered. "When does spring come in these parts?"

"This is that two-season country you've heard about," Amanda Plumb replied. "Fourth of July and winter."

She jolted to a stop beside a mailbox and I looked up to see a gaunt-framed old man, wearing a mackinaw and corduroy cap hurrying toward us from a shack half-hidden among the pines.

"Hello, Charlie," Amanda called. "I got your cornmeal."

Charlie had few teeth left, but his eyes twinkled and his smile was the warmest thing I'd seen for five miles.

"Good for you, Amandy," he said. "What'd you have to pay?" She told him and he counted out the money from a drawstring pouch: nickels, dimes and pennies.

Driving on, Amanda shook her head. "Poor old Charlie. Time was, he had more money than he knew what to do with. Prospected one of the richest veins in these hills. Now he don't have enough to buy a set of store teeth. Don't know how he'd live if it wasn't for his old age pension from the state."

"What happened to his money?"

Amanda shrugged. "Same old story, I guess. Easy come, easy go."

She rocked around a sharp left turn onto what seemed the main drag, stopping before a two-story log building. A wide porch ran across the front and above shallow steps leading to the porch hung a weathered sign: Glory Cloud Inn. 1893.

"This is it," Amanda said. "You are now in the heart of the city."

The top half of a wide Dutch door stood open, but there was nobody around. Amanda explained the inn wasn't yet open for the season.

"You can probably get dinner here, though. Just let Sarah Walker know ahead of time. A darned good dinner too, if you can afford a buck and a half."

She was rummaging in the back seat, collecting mail and packages. She didn't see the lower part of the front door open and someone emerge. He was a tall young chap in tan G.I. shirt and slacks and he came softly down the steps, unheard by Amanda who was still leaning over the back seat. His quick wink made us old conspirators. Gravely silent, he gave Amanda a sound pinch on the most exposed part of her anatomy.

"Cut it out!" She jumped and whirled, angry color flushing her leathery face. "Who the—! Oh, it's you! Fresh!"

She gave him a playful cuff that would have sent a slighter man sprawling, but she was obviously flattered.

"Here, take this stuff," she scolded. "What kind of a way is that to behave? What will this young lady think of such go-ings-on? Miss Rawson, meet Jeff Calhoun. He's supposed to work here!"

"Hi," he said, giving me the fast once-over. He must have approved of what he saw because he grinned cheerfully and kept looking.

"Hello," I said, while Amanda continued berating him, thrusting sacks and boxes into his arms. There was a lot to un-load because she had brought groceries and supplies for the inn. It seemed that Sarah Walker, the inn's proprietor and owner, be-lieved in saving her own gasoline as much as possible.

I thought Dad would have been more resigned to my summer in Glory Cloud if he had seen this counter-attraction to Jan Po-lenski. Poor Dad just couldn't realize Jan's and my friendship was purely intellectual.

But my reaction to Jeff Calhoun couldn't be termed one hundred percent intellectual. A gal who's five foot, six, has an eye for six-footers with sturdy shoulders and slim hips. Jeff Calhoun was probably a few years older than I, with unruly black hair and such heavy black brows and long black lashes that the intense blue of his deep-set eyes came as a shock. His wide mouth showed both humor and sensitivity. It showed a certain amount of temper, too, but I didn't see that at first.

My opinion of Glory Cloud was rising rapidly. But then a shrill voice from the inn jarred me.

"Well, does it take all day to bring in the mail? There's work to be done in here, young man!"

A middle-aged woman stood in the open door, hands on generous hips, elbows askew. She wore an old sweater and skirt topped by a clean apron and her head bristled with wire curlers. Her face had a faded prettiness, obscured at present by a scowl.

As he turned, Jeff Calhoun chuckled and winked at me again.

Amanda Plumb started her jalopy, then paused and asked:

"Say, do you want to eat here tonight?"

"Why not?" I replied.

Amanda called, "Hey, Sarah. Can you feed another head tonight?"

Sarah Walker, still scowling, was looking over the mail. "Oh, I suppose so."

"Okay," Amanda said, "you've got a reservation."

As we jolted away I remarked, "She didn't sound very keen on the idea."

"That's just Sarah's way. She likes to pretend the customers are an awful nuisance and that she's doing you a favor to take your money."

The majority of the houses in town stood along this east and west main drag, but they all looked vacant and closed. Two blocks west of the inn we made a right turn by a small frame schoolhouse and drove a short block north, stopping in front of a white shingle house which a large sign proclaimed to be the Glory Cloud Post Office.

This house, too, was unoccupied. In front stood a line of boxes and Amanda explained that the handful of year-round residents got mail in those during the nine months the post office was closed. She nodded toward a sprawling log cabin across the road.

"End of the line. That's the Barlow cabin. Got a key?"

"It's supposed to be over the door." With unexpected reluctance, I climbed out of the car and collected my gear. The car wasn't much and Amanda Plumb had her shortcomings as a companion, but I had grown used to them both. I realized how alone I would be when she drove off.

This short block over from the main street had put us in the suburbs. The houses were more widely scattered; except for the unoccupied post office there wasn't a cabin nearer than half a block. Some distance west of this corner the road dead-ended, and up there, where the tall pines took over, stood several cabins, but no smoke came from their chimneys. Half a block east of my corner and across the road was a gray frame bungalow where smoke was rising.

The clammy chill of the gray day filtered into my bones, and I longed to ask Amanda to enter the cabin with me. It looked secretive and withdrawn, with its shuttered windows. But I hesitated to play a fluttery female with the self-sufficient Amanda. She was turning around in the road, chugging off with a casual wave.

So what was wrong with me, standing there with teeth in my mouth, dreading to enter a perfectly good cabin? I lugged the two big bags up to the front stoop, put them down, groped over the door for the key.

It was there, and I slipped it into my pocket. More efficient to bring up everything from alongside the road before unlocking the door. That was just common sense.

True enough, but common sense didn't enter into my undiluted joy as I collected the last piece of luggage and glanced up to see an elderly man coming down the road from the west. He was striding along briskly, militantly erect, and as he came closer I saw the white hair under a felt hat and the bushy white mustache. He appeared as delighted to see me as I was to see him.

"Good afternoon, young lady," he beamed. "Welcome to Glory Cloud. Let me give you a hand. Tuckerman's my name,

Dr. Herman Tuckerman. Always happy to aid a fair maiden in distress."

I took his outstreched hand. He must have been pushing seventy, but he had a real grip and a lively sparkle in his bright blue eyes.

"I'm Gail Rawson. I'm not sure I qualify as either a fair maiden or as one in distress, but I'm glad to see you."

He took the key and unlocked the door while I explained again how I happened to be occupying this cabin. The mention of Dahlberg didn't elicit any cracks this time, but the genial old doctor looked sour. What had Axel done here last summer to get everybody down on him?

The door opened directly into the kitchen, an arrangement that struck me as quaint, till Dr. Tuckerman explained the cabin had originally been a prospector's one-room dwelling. When the Barlows purchased it for a summer place they added on rooms here and there, so that the final result was higgeldy-piggeldy, but surprisingly charming.

The kitchen was large and cheerful with yellow checked gingham and sunny oilcloth. Directly opposite the door by which we had entered, another door led into the living room. In the south wall of the kitchen was a large window with a yellow plastic-topped table and chairs beneath it. On the opposite side of the room, beside the sink, was a door leading into the bath and beyond the bath was a bedroom.

I noted with approval the large electric refrigerator and the conveniently-placed hutch, gay with pottery. But my glance recoiled from the object Dr. Tuckerman was dealing with.

"What's that?" I said sharply.

"It's a cookstove, young lady. A regular, old-fashioned cookstove."

"Am I supposed to cook on that thing?"

"Best food in the world is cooked on a stove like this, Miss Rawson. I know women who wouldn't have anything else. What's more, you'll be glad for the heat it throws out. We have brisk nights in Glory Cloud all summer."

I stared at the black monster and I saw myself wasting away on a diet of raw food. I was already too slim.

While the doctor continued his good work I inspected the rest of the lay-out. A living room in knotty pine with a big fireplace at one end flanked by bookshelves; across the room from the fireplace a broad window. Comfortable furniture, Navajo rugs, snowshoes crossed over the mantle, an assortment of old guns on the walls, a coat closet—empty. I approved.

Beyond the living room was a large glassed-in porch, apparently a sort of dormitory. Two double beds were out there and other decrepit furniture, including a massive old wardrobe more than six feet tall. It was empty. Nor was there anybody under either bed. At one end a door opened to the outside, but it was locked and appeared seldom used.

Returning to the living room, I opened the door into the bedroom. A large, pleasant room with two empty closets. A second door in the bedroom led through the bath back into the kitchen.

By now the stove was giving out a heartening glow, and old Tuckerman was carrying logs and kindling to the fireplace. I thought I had worked off my nerves by the exhaustive survey, but I jumped at a knock on the kitchen door.

A bright-eyed little old lady stood there, holding a dish wrapped in a hand-embroidered napkin. She wore a tired fur coat and a green bandanna tied babushka-fashion under a sharp little chin.

"I'm your neighbor, Luella Greenfield. Mrs. J. Reed Greenfield," she announced. "I thought I saw someone get out of Amanda's car and then I saw your smoke so I knew I was right." She put down her dish, held out a small, wiry hand.

"My, aren't you a pretty young thing! You look tired, though. Our Colorado mountain air will fix you up. Are you going to stay all summer? I suppose you're a friend of the Barlows. I knew they weren't coming out this year— Why, Herman! I didn't know you were here."

Dr. Tuckerman, appearing from the living room, looked self-conscious.

"Just helping the young lady get settled," he said stiffly.

Mrs. Greenfield pulled off the bandanna, patting at sparse white hair knotted at the back of her neck. Her rosy color heightened and the blue eyes grew even brighter.

"Isn't it lucky I brought along plenty of stew! I'll wager you haven't had your lunch yet, either, and it's almost two o'clock. I was just getting ready to eat when I saw that Amanda had a passenger and I thought, 'Now, whoever that is will be cold and hungry and won't have any groceries on hand. I'll just take my nice beef stew over for a friendly gesture.'" She turned to me, "You know Coloradoans are the friendliest people in the world, my dear."

I murmured appreciation, but I reflected that if she had seen me alight from Amanda's car, she must also have seen Dr. Tuckerman joining me.

"As a matter of fact," he began, "I had a sandwich at Fay's, but—"

Luella Greenfield was only momentarily dashed.

"Oh well, what's a sandwich for a big, strong man? You've been working too. I'll set the table here and put out these buttered rolls and—"

It was good beef stew, rich and hot and spicy. While we ate I learned a lot about Luella Greenfield, but not so much about Dr. Tuckerman. He hadn't impressed me as tongue-tied, but he didn't have a chance against the competition.

I learned that Mrs. Greenfield was a native Coloradoan and proud of it. That years ago she had lived in Glory Cloud when her husband was station agent for the narrow-gauge railroad, but that now her home was in Pueblo. That the gray bungalow down the road was hers and that after moving to Pueblo the family had used it for summer vacations. That since her husband died and her children married Mrs. Greenfield spent the entire summer in Glory Cloud, arriving early in the spring.

I learned further that two of Mrs. Greenfield's enthusiasms were fancywork and culture. That is, Culture. When I stemmed the flow long enough to mention Dahlberg's name, she twittered with delight. Such a wonderful man! So cultured! Such a worth-while addition to Glory Cloud's little summer colony.

However, she was no fool. A marathon conversationalist, and completely touched on that subject of Culture, but she had a quick, dry wit and a salty way of commenting on life and people. She also, I gradually realized, had her cap set for Dr. Tuckerman, but he was wary. I wondered who Fay was.

I had promised myself a nap before dinner and it was after three when I got rid of my good Samaritans. The living room with its crackling fire was cosier than the bedroom; I dropped on the davenport and passed out.

I got to the inn a few minutes after six to find Dr. Tucker-man and Luella Greenfield already there. Also a serenely gracious woman with stunning gray hair; also a middle-aged man, wearing rimless glasses and an eager-beaver expression. But Jeff Calhoun was not in sight and I wondered whether my hasty attempts at glamour were to be wasted.

When I'd roused from my nap it had been after five; the room had been almost dark except for the dying fire. Only time for a quick overhaul—Amanda had warned me that Sarah Walker was a bearcat for punctuality. But I brushed my pageboy vigorously and applied fresh lipstick. And I opened a bag, dragging out gray flannel slacks and a cherry-colored Angora sweater. There was that about having long legs and slim hips—slacks were definitely okay for me and I might as well make the most of it. What was it Jan had said, in his belittling way that made it seem a criticism? He'd told me I was the Lauren Bacall type. I couldn't see it, but it sounded good.

That evening Dr. Tuckerman took me under his wing. The little group awaiting dinner was clustered around the massive stone fireplace, perhaps for psychic warmth since there was no fire in it.

"This is the young lady I was telling you about, Fay," the old doctor said. "Miss St. Vincent, Miss Rawson. And this, Gail, is Milton Evans. You'd better watch sharp or he'll sell you an insurance policy." Tuckerman chuckled quietly, but Evans' dutiful laugh sounded forced.

Tuckerman patted the chair beside the one he'd vacated and picked up a highball glass. "How about some internal warmth for you, young lady? Just a little nip to sharpen your appetite for Sarah's fine cooking. Relaxes the nerves too, eh Milt?"

Quick irritation flickered across Evans' face and his beady little eyes glittered, but his smile was smoothly condescending. He rose to re-fill his own glass, saying unctuously:

"Of course, I'm no medical man. I'm just a poor tired businessman. But my physician was in perfect agreement when I explained to him the consensus of modern medical opinion in regard to alcohol. You probably don't know, but—"

Dr. Tuckerman's mouth was wry as he mixed me a highball at the homespun bar on a card table while Evans proceeded to tell the doctor what he probably didn't know about developments in medicine. Sampling my drink, I noted that Luella Greenfield, spruce in a giddy silk print, had no glass and that disapproval was plain on her sharp little face. A teetotaller. She was shaming us idlers, her fingers busy at an elaborate bit of embroidery.

My glance moved on to Fay St. Vincent, toying with her ladylike glass of sherry. Before seeing Fay's clothes I'd been reasonably content with mine, but now I mentally consigned the gray slacks and cherry sweater to the rummage sale.

The green gabardine slack suit Fay wore was flawlessly cut and tailored. That outfit had cost money. And she was as well built for slacks as I was, though she must have been fifty-odd years to my twenty-four. Tall and slim, she had a high-bridged aristocratic nose and fine gray eyes. Her hair, a silvery blue-gray, was worn in an upsweep which should have looked ridiculous with sports clothes, but didn't on her. The upsweep was studded with tiny silver-mounted combs and she wore dozens of heavy silver bracelets. Fay was one of those rare women who can look and act the great lady in any setting and bring it off. Was it my imagination that invested her smile with a faint aura of romantic tragedy?

"Herman tells me you've taken the Barlow place, my dear," she said sweetly. "That's nice—you'll be my nearest neighbor, at least till the summer people come."

I inquired about her location and learned it was beyond the dead-end of the road west from the post office, back among the pines.

"Fay likes privacy," Luella Greenfield put in tartly. "Sometimes."

Dr. Tuckerman flushed angrily and Milton Evans looked slyly amused.

"*Touché!*" he chortled. "That's French. It means—"

"We know what it means, Milton," Fay said coolly. She turned her unruffled composure back toward Mrs. Greenfield. "Now Luella, you know Papa built our cabin there years ago."

She smiled again at me. "Herman didn't tell me what brings you to Glory Cloud, dearie. We're delighted to have you, of course—a little young blood is stimulating for us oldsters."

"Oh now, Fay," Milton Evans protested heavily, "haven't you heard the saying that you're only as old as you feel? Why, you and Luella and Herman all look like mere kids. And here I am, younger than any of you, a near-nervous wreck, packed off by my doctor for a rest-cure. You probably don't know—"

Fay's eyebrows were disdainful, her lilting voice icy. "We live right, Milton," she said lightly. But Evans looked affronted out of all proportion to the banality.

Ignoring the byplay, I answered Fay's question.

"I'm killing all kinds of birds with one stone. Partly I'm here because my family and I get on each others' nerves. Mainly, to work on a thesis about Gilbert Hazlitt, the writer, who used to summer here—maybe you knew him. And incidentally, to help my major adviser, Dr. Dahlberg, with research for a book about narrow-gauge railroads. Not that I know anything about the subject—my help will be clerical and secretarial. He plans to get a lot of stuff here about a defunct old line called the Granger, Glory Cloud & Western. Ever hear of it? I guess there was a lot of dirt connected with it way back when, and if there's any dirt to be excavated, Axel Dahlberg is just the guy to do the digging."

The silence was breathless, as if everyone were waiting for someone else to speak first, and my attempt at the light touch couldn't have fallen flatter. I sensed strong undercurrents of hostility and I began to smolder. Ridiculously, my resentment was directed both ways: toward this bunch of characters who acted as if Dahlberg were some sort of outcast and toward Axel himself, who had apparently created a situation here and sent me blundering into it, all innocent and unwarned.

The quiet was becoming uncomfortable when Sarah Walker spoke harshly from the dining room door.

"Come and get it or I'll throw it out!"

Milton Evans jumped up with an admiring laugh. "You'd do it too, wouldn't you, Sarah?"

Jeff Calhoun was lounging behind Sarah as we went in, but my greeting was absent-minded. I was disturbed by the reaction to Dahlberg's name and was relieved when Luella Greenfield insisted I sit by her. She seemed as nearly normal as anybody and was much interested in my thesis about Gilbert Hazlitt. Of course she would be. Culture, you know.

Also it developed that she had charge of the Hazlitt cabin, Glory Cloud's sole sight-seeing attraction if you didn't count the scenery. The job had no pay except honor, but the hours were easy: the cabin was open to the public only weekends and Wednesday afternoons during the summer.

I told her about my inspiration of advertising in the *Saturday Review* for hitherto unpublished letters and papers of Hazlitt and she thought that a wonderful idea. She was so friendly and encouraging that I seized a moment when everyone was talking at once and asked quietly:

"What is all this about Axel Dahlberg anyway? Why is everybody so sore at him?"

She glanced around and shook her head warningly. "Later."

Such taciturnity from Luella Greenfield further fired my curiosity.

Nor did I get a chance to question her further that evening. After dinner, which was as good as Amanda had promised, Fay St.

Vincent wanted to play bridge and commandeered Mrs. Green-
field and the two men. This would have been a fine chance for
Jeff Calhoun and me to do a little getting-acquainted, but Sarah
Walker kept him tied up in the kitchen.

In fact, I got the impression that everyone was working at being too busy for conversation. The bridge game was grimly silent
except for an occasional disgusted exclamation by Milton Evans
or an attempt at chatter by Luella Greenfield, quickly squelched. I
drifted about the room, staring at faded photographs on the walls
of gay picnic parties in Glory Cloud back in horse-and-buggy
days. In one corner there was an old glass-fronted bookcase, but
the selection of reading material left much to be desired. *Ma-
dame X* and *Chip of the Flying U* were the cream of the crop.

Growing bored and sleepy, I found my coat and prepared
to slip out without disturbing the game. I didn't quite get away
with it—somebody looked up and there was a brief babble of
apologies for neglecting me, but they were involved in an exciting rubber and cheerfully turned back to it when I insisted I was
awfully tired and didn't mind walking home alone.

When I stepped out onto the front porch, two things hit me.
First, the darkness. It was as if I had suddenly dropped from
a sunlit noon into a deep hole. Never had I experienced such
utter blackness. Not a streetlight, not a lighted house. There
must have been stars too many million light-years away to matter
and there should have been a quarter moon, but it had already
disappeared behind the wall of mountains to the west. And then
the cold bit into me. It had been far from warm all day, but this
cold was an aggressive, bitter thing that made my teeth chatter
despite my sweater and heavy coat.

I was just realizing I could never find my way to the Barlow
cabin in this inky night when there was a light touch on my arm
and a quiet voice said, "Gail. It's okay. It's Jeff."

I didn't jump much.

"I didn't want to scare you," the deep, slow-talking voice said
in my ear. "Here—take this flashlight."

"What a wonderful thought," I said. "How can it be so dark?"

"I know. It takes a little getting used to. I had hoped to walk you home but Sarah's dreamed up a hundred things for me to do."

"Better luck next time," I murmured.

"Yeah, I hope so. Anyway, listen Gail, there's nothing to be afraid of up here. It's plenty dark, sure, but you're safer in Glory Cloud than you'd be in Denver. There may be more coyotes here, but not nearly so many wolves." He laughed briefly. "So take it easy now. See you tomorrow."

He gripped my shoulder in a buck-up-old-man gesture, then was gone.

It was a fine flashlight with a big powerful beam, and as I went down the steps and started up the road I resolved to get one just like it. I'd as soon he'd left that out about coyotes. But they never bothered people. Did they? Not people with a good flashlight.

At first I stopped every so often and swung the light in a circle. But I didn't see any coyotes or wolves—nothing but the blank hostile faces of boarded-up houses. Presumably they were occupied now by ghosts—this was a ghost town, wasn't it? A very unfunny thought, and I stopped the peering-around routine and walked faster.

Instead of dwelling on ghosts and coyotes, I would speculate on people. A good interesting subject. I was curious about everyone I'd met in Glory Cloud. How about this triangle of Fay St. Vincent, Greenfield and Tuckerman? Fay was quite proprietary and fond with the old doctor and he was obviously mad about her—what was stopping them? It was equally apparent that Fay was not fond of Milton Evans, but that posed no problem. He was a type I disliked and distrusted on sight: too slick, too smooth and much too filled with his own importance, and with a nose grown long and sharp from sticking it into other people's affairs. At dinner I'd gathered he owned a place in Glory Cloud and had known the others a long time, but that this was his first summer here for many years. Most vacations he and his wife visited her family in Iowa. I wondered what had brought him back this particular summer. He was temporarily staying at the inn till his long-unused cabin was made habitable.

And I asked how anyone could cook like such an angel and have such a foul disposition as Sarah Walker obviously had. The questions about Jeff Calhoun were numerous and personal, but then I started wondering again why Axel Dahlberg's name was such a bomb shell, and that sixty-four-dollar question took me clear home.

I hadn't lied about being tired and sleepy. I'd been told the change of altitude would make me drowsy all the time till I got used to it. I could scarcely keep awake while I locked up, dug out all the blankets I could find and crawled under them.

I was too dopey to notice the hour and I must have dropped off right away. So I had no way of knowing how much time had passed when I was roused by loud, insistent rapping at the door. I turned the flashlight on my watch. Twelve-thirty. I turned the light off and waited, thinking whoever it was might call my name and I'd recognize the voice.

But there was only silence for several seconds, then the rapping again, this time louder and more insistent. I slipped out of bed and felt for my coat, wrapping it around me against the Arctic chill. Silently and in the dark I went into the bath between the bedroom and kitchen. The knocking was coming from the kitchen door. The bathroom window was on the same side of the house as the kitchen door, and it was open a cautious few inches. I called out the window: "Who's there?"

No answer. After a few seconds the rapping was renewed. It was a pounding by this time.

I shivered. Of course, that was because I was barefoot.

"Who's there?"

Silence. I waited, but the knocking didn't come again. At last I started back into the bedroom only to be brought up short by a perfect torrent of blows at the door. They were loud and somehow insolent enough to make me angry, and with the courage of anger I marched straight to the door and unlocked it. Snapping on the kitchen light and gripping my flashlight in one hand I threw open the door.

Nobody. Not a soul. Still sore, I swung the light around the yard, across the road, over the inscrutable face of the vacant house across the way and I called,

"Well, who is it? What do you want?"

The utter silence of the mountain night answered me. And suddenly I knew that somewhere in that blackness just outside my flashlight beam eyes were watching me. Hostile eyes. Not coyotes. I could feel and smell and almost taste the human hostility flowing from the darkness, and abruptly I was no longer angry, but very frightened. I slammed the door shut and bolted it and snapped off the lights.

In a perfect panic I did what I hadn't done for twenty years. I scrambled into bed and pulled all the blankets up over my head. And, while I lay there shaking with cold and terror, the knocking started again.

II

"I just don't get it," I repeated. "Why should anybody want to scare me out of a year's growth?"

Jeff Calhoun took a drag of his cigarette, shook his head.

It was the afternoon after my unsettled night, and we were headed for the Bar Circle T ranch where Jeff had to pick up fryers and eggs for the inn. He had stopped by that morning to ask me to go along and had found me struggling with the stove. Bleary-eyed and still jumpy even in the sunlight of 10:00 A.M., I hadn't said anything then about my experience.

This afternoon hiking at that altitude soon winded me and we'd paused for a breather. Following a steep, rocky trail that led from the road, we'd emerged after fifty feet on a small, shelflike clearing where one had a panoramic view of the toy village and crowding green woods below and the whole backbone of the continent beyond. There was a bronze tablet bolted to a tall, flat-topped stone and on the tablet was etched the rugged outline of the Continental Divide with the names of the various peaks. You could pick out a certain mountain in the vast chain, find the same outline on the marker and see whether it was Mt. Evans or Long's Peak. Just beyond the marker the ground dropped away, at a forty-five-degree angle for some feet, then apparently straight down to the floor of a gulch too far below to be seen. A few tenacious shrubs and some straggling grass clung to the steep slope where the ground fell away from the edge, but beyond it was a sheer wall of rock.

Nervously retreating, I sat down on a boulder several feet back. After lighting up, I told Jeff about the knocking on my door last night.

"How could I have any enemies here?" I demanded. "I came only yesterday. And I'm a friendly, harmless type. I love everyone."

"Everyone?"

"Well, I'm not exactly smitten with Milton Evans. And Sarah Walker's a bit of a pill. I was making a broad generalization about my sweet nature."

Jeff carefully ground out his cigarette on a flat stone, abstractedly shook another from the pack in his shirt pocket.

"The only thing I can figure," he said slowly, "is that you're allied with Axel Dahlberg, although what harm it does *him* to throw *you* into a nervous breakdown, I don't see."

"Well, what *is* all this about Dahlberg?" I asked. "I know he's sharp with people at times, but basically he's an awfully good egg and he's terrifically brilliant, you know."

"I'm not acquainted with the gentleman," Jeff said dryly. "I'll have to take your word for it. He was here last summer, but I wasn't. This is the first summer I've been in Glory Cloud since I was a kid."

I opened my mouth to ask a question, then closed it. He spoke slowly always, with a definite pause between phrases and even words.

"However," he continued, "it didn't take any mental giant to see what a monkey-wrench you threw last night when you started talking about Dahlberg and his book."

"I didn't think you were there."

"Oh, I was hovering back-stage. And what you perhaps didn't realize is that about everybody present was hooked up, one way or another, with that old scandal about the Granger, Glory Cloud & Western to which you so blithely referred."

I stared. "But that was years and years ago."

"Sure. 1921. The year I was born. My dad lost ten thousand himself. Earlier, of course."

"But if people all lost money," I insisted, "and there was dirty work afoot, I should think they'd be glad to have it dragged out into the open. Mr. Dahlberg told me it was one of the most flagrant examples of graft and corruption he'd come across to date."

Jeff unmistakably looked sour this time. "He did? Well, he was right. But did he add that Herman Tuckerman's father was president of the line and the main promoter and organizer? And that he shot himself when it all blew up? And that Fay St. Vincent's father was vice-president and there was talk of a murder charge in connection with old Tuckerman's death?"

I know my jaw was hanging open by this time, but Jeff Calhoun was just gathering momentum.

"Did that great, good, wise man, Professor Dahlberg, mention that Milton Evans—"

A sudden blast from a car horn cut him short, and we looked toward the road to see Amanda Plumb leaning from her Ford, smirking.

"Ah youth! Ah springtime!" she bellowed in a voice that must have reached Granger.

We scrambled down the path to the road. Amanda shook her head.

"Sarah'd have kittens if she'd see you mooning around doing nothing that way."

"We weren't mooning," I said. "We were admiring the view."

"All Sarah asks," Jeff said, "is twenty-four hours a day of hard labor and your life-blood. Plus burning up your own shoe leather instead of her gas and oil. How about giving us a lift to the Bar Circle T turn-off?"

"Climb in."

The old car was reluctant to continue up the steep grade, but Amanda coaxed it into action. This was the Alpine road; Amanda drove up to Glory Cloud via Coyote Canyon and went down via Alpine. The only other road leading out of Glory Cloud was a seldom-used wagon trail wandering off southwest of town through the pines and eventually reaching a hamlet known as Pinto.

What astonished me about this Alpine route was that on leaving town it went up. Going from Glory Cloud's elevation of approximately ten thousand to Granger's five thousand, you would imagine the only way to go would be down. But the Alpine road climbed with dizzy suddenness right out of Glory Cloud and, for some miles, ran along a narrow ledge high above a deep valley before starting to descend.

At the top of the climb I noticed an overgrown trail to our right, marked by a weathered sign: Glory Cloud Mine. Nothing was visible, and I wondered where the mine was.

"It's not far back there," Jeff told me. "But there's darned little to see. Just a couple of beat-up shacks and an old shaft. We'll go over some day and throw in stones—you'd be surprised how long it is before you hear them splash."

"You kids want to be careful clambering around over these hills," Amanda said grimly. "They're honeycombed with those old shafts and anybody who'd fall in would be in an awful fix."

Jeff smiled, told me:

"That hole in the ground back there is where the St. Vincent fortune started. Fay's father, old Julius St. Vincent, struck the first gold in these parts there, and he made plenty before the veins pinched off."

"That reminds me," I said, "you know what you were saying—ouch!"

Jeff Calhoun had done what no gentleman would have: kicked a lady. Right in the ankle too. He was frowning at me.

"What's the matter?" Amanda asked.

"That last bump kind of jarred me," I said weakly.

"You need more padding," Amanda said. "Bumps don't bother me none."

When Amanda let us out at the lane leading into the Bar Circle T and drove away I glared at Jeff.

"What was that for?"

"I didn't want you to start again on that railroad business in front of Amanda."

"Why not?"

"Amanda's husband was killed in the wreck. He was the brakeman on the runaway car."

"Look," I said, "will you take a couple of days off some time and fill me in on this background? I didn't even know there'd been a wreck."

"Well, there sure was, honey. But your hero can tell you all about everything. He's so hot on disseminating information and knowledge. When will the great man arrive, anyway?"

"If you mean Mr. Dahlberg," I said coolly, "within the next week."

The coolness might have developed into a full-fledged row if we hadn't reached the ranch-house just then. We collected the chickens and eggs and were starting the long hike back when an old fellow puttering around at one of the stock fences hailed Jeff and waved. Jeff waved back.

"Hi ya, Charlie. How you doing?"

It was Amanda's toothless friend, and as we continued down the driveway I asked, "Does he work here?"

Jeff laughed. "Old Charlie doesn't work anywhere enough to hurt him. Sometimes when a ranch needs a handyman to get things in shape for summer, he'll work a couple of days."

"Amanda told me he used to have a lot of money. You know all about everyone—what do you know about him?"

"I don't think there's much to know. Just another of the old prospectors these hills are full of. Plays a mean guitar. During the season he'll come down and entertain the guests at the inn about one evening a week for a free dinner. How are you at square-dancing?"

"Square-dancing! You don't look like the square-dancing type to me."

"You'd be surprised what type I am."

"A leading remark, if I ever heard one. What type are you?"

"I'm the type who doesn't know when he's well off," Jeff said in his deliberate way. "Out of all the guys who were graduated with me from Princeton I'm the nut who didn't want to sell bonds or insurance or start at the next rung below the top in

the advertising game. Or go into my dad's firm as junior part-
ner. I'm the screwball who wanted to knock around the world
and see what it's all about. I've tried a lot of things—deck-hand
on a freighter, roughneck in the oilfields, bouncer in a Mexican
gambling dive, fruit-picker in the Napa Valley. Not to mention a
stretch in the service of our esteemed uncle."

"Gosh, that sounds wonderful."

"If you mean the stretch in the service, it wasn't."

"No, the rest of it, I mean. But why Glory Cloud?"

"I just wanted to get away from it all," Jeff grinned Then
he sobered, added, "That's about the size of it, though. I'll be
twenty-nine this fall. It's time to stop horsing around and decide
where I'm heading. When I was a kid we came to Glory Cloud in
the summers, and I thought it would be a quiet, peaceful place to
collect my forces and take stock. Besides I wanted to meet you."

"But you didn't even know—" I broke off, flushing. "What a
coincidence!" I exclaimed. "I came here because I wanted to meet
you, Mr. Calhoun."

"Don't try to kid me, sister," Jeff said darkly. "You came to be
near your hero. Say, is that bird Dahlberg married? And how old
is he, anyway?"

"He's a broken-down old guy of at least forty and he's married." But my revolting passion for accuracy compelled me to
add, "He's getting a divorce."

"Aha!" Jeff's eyebrows were eloquent.

"What do you mean 'aha!'?"

"*Why* is he getting a divorce?"

"Because he doesn't like his wife, I suppose. Or vice versa.
How do I know why he's getting a divorce? People do it every
day, I've heard."

"You know what I think?" Jeff demanded. "I think he's tired
of that poor, good woman who's given him the best years of her
life, and he's looking around for some fresh, young girl. A pretty,
bright young thing with an interest in academic matters, who
can help him in his work, as well as solace his declining years.
What does he care—"

"Oh, stop," I said, laughing. "You're perfectly ridiculous and you know it."

We had paused in front of the inn and now Sarah Walker came out on the porch, observing our merriment with disapproval.

"I'll take those eggs," she said. "They've probably hatched by this time." Today she had shed the wire curlers and her salt-and-pepper hair formed an unlikely halo of tiny curls. Giving me a hard look, she added:

"Fay St. Vincent's been looking for you."

Despite Sarah's remark, I was startled to find Fay in the dusky living room of my cabin. I thought I had locked the place up tight. Fay was slimly elegant and serene in an English tweed skirt and cashmere cardigan.

"You don't mind my coming in to wait for you, dearie? We're all friends and neighbors here in Glory Cloud—nobody ever locks his door."

"That's ducky," I said, snapping on the table lamp. "But, as it happens—"

I had started to tell her about my scare of the night before, but I stopped.

"What were you saying, sweetie?"

"I just wondered how you got in," I said lightly. "Because I could have sworn that I *did* lock up."

"Oh, you locked up," she said. "Dr. Tuckerman let me in. Herman stays in Glory Cloud all winter, and most of us leave a key with him so that he can keep an eye on things."

I didn't much like the idea of spare keys to my cabin floating around, but certainly Dr. Tuckerman was a harmless old soul.

Fay probably sensed my curiosity about her visit. Her air of faint, romantic tragedy was intensified and her face colored girlishly as she said:

"I came to talk with you about your thesis, dearie. I suppose you know that Gilbert Hazlitt and I were engaged to be married?"

"No, I didn't know. So far I have very little data on his personal life."

I did know that Hazlitt had been unmarried at the time of his death, an unseasonable thirty-two, and I wondered what had happened, but consideration for Fay's feelings restrained my tongue.

"It was a great tragedy," she said sadly. "So poignant. Now, after all these years, I can bear to speak of it, but my life has been quite empty since I lost dear Gilbert. We were to have been married in June and then there was all that horrid business about the railroad and everything was so upset we postponed the wedding till fall. And that summer poor Gilbert died. I could never quite forgive Mother for insisting on the postponement."

I murmured sympathetically.

"But it makes me so happy, dearie, to know that you're doing a paper on Gilbert. It's a further sign of his growing recognition by the literary world. He never achieved the fame he deserved during his life, but I always maintained it would come some day. He was a really great writer, of course."

Once more, consideration for Fay kept me silent except for a murmur that could have meant anything. Although I hoped to get my M.A. by writing about him, I entertained no illusions about Gilbert Hazlitt's having been a great writer. He had done rather stylized short stories, obviously influenced by Stephen Crane. Some lyric poetry and one short novel, highly impressionistic, about mining in the west. Nothing that could be termed a *magnum opus*. However, it was true that literary posterity had been viewing Hazlitt's work with growing respect till he was important enough to be the subject of a thesis. By literary posterity I mean the *cognescenti*, not the wide reading public.

"So you see I want to give you all the help I can, darling," Fay was continuing. "I always had faith in Gilbert's genius and that's why I gave his cabin to the State Historical Society. Everything has been kept just the way he left it so that future generations may visit it as a shrine."

Jeepers, I thought. A real screwball!

"Did he leave you the cabin?" I asked.

Fay looked surprised. "Why, it was mine all the time, dearie. That is, Papa owned it and I inherited it with the rest of Papa's property. Dear Gilbert was awfully poor, you know, but so proud. When he quit his job in Denver and came here for the summer, he wouldn't stand for Papa's letting him use the cabin for nothing. Even though he was my fiancé and he had to have some place to live and do his writing, and what difference did it make—Papa had lots of property. But Gilbert was too independent; Papa had to pull strings and get him the job as summer postmaster before he felt right about it."

"Maybe I should be taking notes," I said. I found my notebook and fountain pen. Lighting a cigarette, I remembered my manners and offered Fay the pack.

"No thank you," she said graciously. "Gilbert never approved of ladies smoking." Then she added, "But I didn't mean you shouldn't, darling. It's different for you."

"Thanks," I said. I was reflecting that her parents had known what they were about when they named her Fay. Only it should have been spelled Fey. But I liked her. Under all that flutter and froth she had a sharp, quick mind and a sort of gentle sweetness. And I marveled at her ability to call everyone dearie without sounding like a shopgirl and to wear as many superfluous bracelets and bangles as she did without looking cheap. I suppose it was because basically she was such a lady. An outdated term, but the only one for Fay St. Vincent.

For the next hour I listened and made occasional notes while Fay told me about her great romance. She had met Hazlitt when he was a reporter on a Denver newspaper, sent to interview her father. For Fay, at least, it had been love at first sight.

"When was this?" I asked.

"March sixteenth, 1920. I can see him now as he looked in Papa's office that day. So dark and handsome and intense-looking. When we were introduced he just looked at me from under those heavy black eyebrows and it was so poignant." She sighed.

Stripped of the frills, there was nothing too remarkable about Fay's story. Hazlitt had started courting her that spring and the affair had progressed rather slowly through the summer while

Fay was in Glory Cloud with her parents and Hazlitt could come up only occasionally. When the St. Vincents returned to town in the fall the pace had quickened, and at Christmas their engagement was formally announced. A large and flossy wedding was planned for June, but then came that horrid narrow-gauge business, which Fay hurried over lightly, and her mother urged postponement till fall. Hazlitt had died that summer and Fay had never married. I wondered where Dr. Herman Tuckerman fitted into the picture, but I didn't ask. Instead I said, as gently as possible,

"What happened? I mean, was he sick?"

Tears filled Fay's lovely eyes. "He fell into one of those awful old mine shafts," she said, "and it killed him. He used to go out and take long walks at night, thinking over what he was writing, you know. I begged him to be careful, but he just laughed. He was a reckless boy at heart."

She produced a lacy handkerchief and daintily blew her aristocratic nose. Then she came out with one of her *non sequiturs* that left me trailing far behind.

"When is Professor Dahlberg coming?"

"Why, I don't know exactly," I replied, surprised. "In a few days, I think."

"And just what is this book he's planning?"

"It's a history of narrow-gauge railroads in the west. I thought I'd mentioned that. He's going to call it *Narrow Gauge to Gold*."

"And he's going to put in everything about the Granger, Glory Cloud & Western? Why?"

She certainly could get to the point fast enough when she wanted to.

I smiled. "If you knew Axel Dahlberg as well as I do, you wouldn't need to ask. He's a wild-eyed reformer in some ways, and he just loves a nice, juicy exposure."

Fay retrieved a little silver comb that had slipped from her upsweep and glanced at the diamond-encrusted watch on her slim wrist.

"Gracious, I had no idea it was so late." She rose. "I'll have to hurry."

"Don't rush away," I said tritely. Things were moving too fast for me.

At the door she paused and said off-handedly, "When Professor Dahlberg comes I wish you'd tell him that dear Papa had nothing to do with the Granger, Glory Cloud & Western when all that horrid business happened. He was out of it years before, you know."

"Why don't you tell him?" I asked.

"Oh, he might misunderstand if I said anything. Now, don't hesitate to ask me again any time you want more help with your thesis, darling. I'm simply delighted to do what I can. *Au revoir*, dearie."

"So long," I said, closing the door, and I had abstractedly walked back to pick up my notebook before her line hit me. Where did she get that stuff, ask her *again?* I hadn't asked her anything in the first place.

III

When I wakened Saturday morning and consulted my watch, I thought it must be raining. Nine o'clock and the bedroom was still dimly gray. But I didn't hear rain and when I looked out the window I didn't see rain. I didn't see anything.

Glory Cloud was wrapped in impenetrable fog, the air grayly opaque and damply cool. I learned to dread and hate these mountain fogs, but this first morning I was enthralled.

After breakfast I pulled on my hooded raincoat. This was the day I intended to get my teeth into my research. Dahlberg would be arriving any time and I knew how demanding he was. Axel was a high-energy person himself and would expect me to spend every moment helping him, meanwhile magically producing a top-notch thesis of my own, written with my left hand.

As I reached the road a dark shape soundlessly emerged from the pearly dimness and became old Charlie. He was certainly ubiquitous. He greeted me with his cheerful, toothless grin, and was swallowed up again in about three feet.

I was picking my way toward Luella Greenfield's, and just when I was sure I must have missed her place I heard voices. Peering intently, I made out the picket fence around Luella's cabin and, as I watched, the gate opened and Luella and Dr. Tuckerman swam into view. She was flirting with him, of course, and he was looking uneasy.

"Mrs. Greenfield," I said, "I'd like to settle down to work today. Could we open the Hazlitt cabin now?"

"Why, of course we can, child. I've been intending to go there to dust and tidy up before the tourist season. Isn't it lucky Herman's with us? He can go along and help."

Dr. Tuckerman tried to crawl out of it, but he didn't have a chance.

"Oh Herman," Mrs. Greenfield protested, "you know how I hate to go into a closed-up house alone the first time. Why, there might even be spiders!"

I got a bang out of Luella's technique. You could imagine this wiry, decisive little woman beaning a housebreaker with a broom-handle and no monkey-business about it, but she always used a helpless, fluttering approach on Dr. Tuckerman. And the amazing thing was that it worked. At least he went with us.

We walked back past my place and the post office, following the road which ran slightly uphill westward into the pines. After about a block the road stopped, and I could barely make out dim outlines of tall trees. A narrow path led to our left and we walked along it to the Hazlitt cabin, invisible from the road today, although it wasn't set back far.

It was a small, unpretentious place of gray shingle, and we had trouble getting in. The screen doors had been secured from outside by large blocks of wood high on the frame which pivoted crosswise to hold the screens shut against the prying fingers of children. It seemed an unnecessary precaution, and I'm sure Dr. Tuckerman agreed with me. The block wedging the front screen was recalcitrant from disuse, and he got a splinter in his finger before succeeding in forcing the block to swing vertically so that the screen could be opened.

Luella unlocked the door and officiously preceded us inside. A combination living room and study, a small bedroom and a kitchen. The modern conveniences must be out back. Near the front door stood a small wooden table and an old rocker. Luella proudly explained this was her post of duty when the cabin was open to the public. Dr. Tuckerman, having unshuttered the windows, started a fire in the fireplace. What drew my eye was an old roll-top desk with a shabby, comfortable chair. That would be a swell place to work.

"Is it all right for me just to poke around and see what's here?" I asked.

"Yes, but be careful to put everything right back where you find it," Luella said primly. "I don't allow sightseers to touch things at all, but it's different with you. You're a scholar."

Much flattered, I pulled out the deep filing drawer of the old desk. It was crammed with Manila filing folders, slugged: Plot Ideas, Character Notes, Backgrounds, Clippings. I smiled, noting a fat one: Rejection Slips. This drawer would be a gold mine.

I snapped on the old-fashioned reading lamp. In the middle of the blotter stood an antiquated Oliver typewriter with a half-finished sheet of manuscript in it. Skimming the typing, I recognized a passage from Gilbert Hazlitt's one novel.

"This effect of incompleted work in the typewriter isn't completely authentic, is it?"

"Well, no," Luella said reluctantly. "We just thought it made a nice touch. But that's Gilbert's machine, right enough. It was Fay's idea to have a sheet of work in it, and when Fay gets her head set she's awfully stubborn in that sweet way."

At this point Dr. Tuckerman announced he had to be going, and no amount of blandishment from Luella could stop him. When the door closed, she remarked tartly:

"I suppose Herman's miffed because of what I said about Fay. No fool like an old fool, I always say."

"They must have been friends a long time."

"They've known each other all their lives," Luella said. "Why, I remember when Herman came home after interning in Chicago—1913, that was, the year my Nellie had summer flu so bad and we were so worried about her. Usually I helped Jeb—that was my husband—with his work right along, but I was taking care of Nellie night and day that summer. Anyway, when Herman saw Fay again for the first time in several years, he went right off the deep end. Jeb said he felt sorry for Herman Tuckerman because his mother would never let him get married if she could help it."

"And wouldn't she?"

"I don't know about that summer," Luella said. "Fay was only seventeen, and Herman was going abroad to study. I guess he thought he'd give her time to grow up. Then, you see, he was still over there when the World War started and he got in the medical corps and what with one thing and another he didn't get home again till the end of 1919."

Luella paused, poking the fire. "But land, child, you're not interested in all this. You have work to do and here I sit gabbing!"

"Don't stop now! Surely by then Fay was old enough to be married."

"She was as grown up as she was ever going to be," Luella said. "And Herman started to court her in earnest. But it was that spring—just a few months later—she met Gilbert Hazlitt and poor Herman's goose was cooked proper. Just shows you what a flighty, romantic piece Fay always was—passing up a solid, faithful man like Herman Tuckerman for that scamp, Hazlitt. Oh, I know he was an artist and very cultured, and here in Glory Cloud we're mighty proud of his work, but just between you and me, child, I always considered Gilbert Hazlitt a little—fast!"

"Well you know how these writers are," I agreed soberly.

I had been following Luella, but I had also been rummaging further in the filing drawer. Now, at the very back, I came on a bulky folder slugged, GRANGER, GLORY CLOUD & WESTERN.

I hauled the folder out and riffled the contents: mainly clippings, letters and typed notes. A few pix. At the front was a sheet with the scrawled notation: "Rich possibilities. Ballad? Short story? Maybe even a novel."

Dahlberg should give me a gold star for unearthing this, although of course there might not be any material in it he didn't already have. I called to Mrs. Greenfield who was now sweeping the kitchen.

"Look, I found a whole folder about the narrow-gauge railroad."

Luella hurried in, took the folder. "Well, of all things! Why do you suppose he collected all that stuff?"

She frowned. "I never have gone through all those drawers to sort things out and classify them properly. Fay has always been so silly about wanting everything left just the way it was and she made that a condition when she gave the cabin to the Historical Society."

"When Mr. Dahlberg comes, may I lend him this folder?"

Luella hesitated, said decisively, "I don't see why not. Fay doesn't have to know everything." She donned her official, self-important look, adding, "But I'll have to look it over first. After all, I'm responsible to the Historical Society for this place and everything in it."

She was getting into her coat and wrapping the folder in a newspaper to protect it from the fog.

"I'm going down to start lunch," she announced. "After another half-hour why don't you come have a bite with me? Be sure the screen's tight in front of the fire and lock the door when you leave."

Agreeing to the injunctions, I returned to my work. It was snug by the crackling aromatic fire and the insulating silence of the fog was absolute. Absorbed in reading and note-taking, I ran only fifteen minutes over the allotted half-hour. Meticulously, I replaced everything in the desk, checked the fire-screen, put on my coat. Turning off the lamp, I opened the door and pushed at the screen.

The screen door seemed to be jammed. It wouldn't swing outward very easily. In fact, it wouldn't swing outward at all. Impatiently, I shoved it hard, but it remained stuck. The dampness had made it swell. Disgusted, I went to the kitchen door, unbolted it, shoved that screen. Same deal.

This time the frame gave slightly toward the bottom, but stayed firm at the top. And I realized with sudden clarity that these screen doors weren't merely being difficult with the perversity of inanimate objects. Somebody had swung the wedges back into place from outside to keep the screen doors from opening. Surely Luella wouldn't have done such a thing when she left. Then who?

And why? It was so silly. There were several unscreened windows large enough to climb out and I unlatched one in the living room, pushed it open.

Fog rolled into the room, and outside it seemed denser than ever. With one foot across the sill, I paused. How did I know who or what was waiting out there in the murky day? Someone could be standing close enough to touch me, listening. And it would almost have to be the someone who had secured the doors. Almost certainly the same someone who had hammered at my door night before last. Someone whose attitude could only be described as unfriendly.

I yanked my foot back inside, slammed and locked the window, pulled the shade. Then I ran to both doors, locking them from inside. Two could play at that game. I scurried around like a frightened chipmunk, and then I began to do a slow burn.

This business of being scared witless for no good reason was getting old. I hadn't done anybody in Glory Cloud dirt, nor did I intend to. What was behind all this? Whoever was responsible was showing poor judgment all along the line. I might be frightened by these inexplicable incidents, but they were also making me fighting mad.

My belligerence coked me up almost to the point of climbing out the window after all. Almost, but not quite. I was standing there, wavering, when I heard voices. One was Luella Greenfield's and the other sounded incredibly familiar. Incredibly because I didn't see how it could be the person it sounded like.

There was urgent knocking on the door and Luella's call:

"Gail! Are you in there? Are you all right?"

Then the male voice joined in. And I wasn't crazy—it was Axel Dahlberg. He sounded both amused and annoyed.

"Gail! Open the door! What the hell are you up to anyhow?"

The flood of relief washed away all my trumped-up courage, leaving only the jitters. I threw open the door and fell on Dahlberg's neck, ignoring Luella's elevated eyebrows.

"Somebody's after me!" I chattered.

Occasionally I yearned to slug Axel Dahlberg, even if he was, as Jeff Calhoun had jeered, my hero. Now he was tremendously amused; his sharp eyes danced impishly behind the horn-rimmed glasses; a mocking grin appeared on his clever, homely face.

"Ho!" he said. "Listen to the girl brag! I know plenty of guys are after you, but you're being true to me, aren't you?"

"Don't be so funny!" I snapped. "When I tried to leave for lunch, the screen doors were both fastened from outside."

"In that case," Dahlberg said, conveying strong doubt, "why didn't you crawl out the window?"

"Why wouldn't *you*," I retorted, "if you thought some un-friendly character had locked you in and was waiting out in that pea-soup to see what you'd do?"

Luella had been standing by, looking faintly shocked at my disrespectful attitude and at Dahlberg's departure from her orthodox conception of a college professor. She was also, I learned later, drawing faulty conclusions from Dahlberg's genial hug when I fell on him. Now she spoke crisply.

"Well, the screens certainly weren't fastened from the outside when we got here. And if we're going to eat lunch today, we'd best be about it."

At the gate Dahlberg said, "You gals wait here a second." He faded back into the fog toward the cabin. Luella cocked her head.

"I hadn't remembered Professor Dahlberg as such a handsome man," she fished.

I chuckled at this far-fetched gambit. Whether you loved him or hated him, handsome was not the word for Axel Dahlberg. Medium-tall and slender, with a nervous, high-tension wiriness, he had a face one remembered, all right, but not for its beauty. It was a long face with a sharp jaw and a dark, almost leathery skin. His shrewd, alert eyes were brown, and they could be dis-concertingly penetrating. His nose was long and straight and he had a wide, mobile mouth, capable of a great range of expression. The most frequent of these was a sardonically amused, almost Voltairean grin. His students adored him and trembled before his tongue, which was hung in the middle and forked at both ends. His intense intellectual excitement and curiosity gave his face a singularly dynamic character and colored his whole personality, and the quality made him an exceptionally stimulating teacher. I was not the only Dahlberg fan on campus.

Now he reappeared, looking thoughtful. He took my elbow and squeezed it, grinning at Luella Greenfield.

"What are we waiting for? Let's eat. I'm starving by inches—nothing for breakfast but coffee and one of those godawful sweet rolls at the station in Denver."

On the way to Mrs. Greenfield's cabin and in her toasty kitchen, Dahlberg furnished some of the answers I wanted. Yes, he'd arrived in Denver on the same early-morning train that had brought me, and he had come to Granger by bus. He'd got through at school a few days sooner than expected. He'd tried to find me as soon as he got to Glory Cloud. Someone had seen me heading for Luella Greenfield's that morning, so he'd had his cab-driver take him there. When I didn't turn up for lunch he and Luella decided to walk up and surprise me. She had invited him to eat with us. Any more questions?

"You came up from Granger in a cab?" I said. "Gee, Mr. Gotrocks, huh?"

That was an unfortunate crack. Axel Dahlberg was sensitive about money since his wife was trying to soak him for an alimony settlement out of all reason.

"How did you get here?" he demanded. "Walk? Or did you take the streetcar?"

"I rode with Amanda Plumb."

"Oh, oh." His features relaxed into that mischievous grin. "Well, Mrs. Amanda Plumb informed me it was against regulations to carry passengers. Not even for five dollars would Amanda consider fracturing the regulations."

Luella Greenfield's comment was a gentle snort.

"Amanda," Dahlberg added, "is not one of my admirers."

Luella was one of those cooks who love to see people eat, especially a pair like us who, in her opinion, needed fattening up. After apple cobbler with heavy cream Dahlberg stood up, lighted a cigarette and started giving directions.

"Now look, Gail. I'm going down to my place and get straightened around. I just dumped my bags and came right on up to find you. You help Mrs. Greenfield with the dishes and then you go back to the Hazlitt cabin and work another couple of hours.

And no nonsense this time about being locked in because I want you to report at my place around four. We'll go over what you've done, if anything, and get our working schedule organized. I'll stop on the way and tell Sarah Walker, the old witch, to expect us for dinner. That way we can work right up to six and then go over to the inn."

He was as bossy as ever. Telling me to help with the dishes!

I said meekly, "Yes, Professor Dahlberg. Where is your cabin, please, Professor Dahlberg?"

I knew he didn't like to be addressed as either Professor or Doctor Dahlberg; his students were trained to call him simply Mister. But he merely gave me a reproachful look and said his cabin was the small log one across from the inn, half a block east.

"Thanks, Mrs. Greenfield," he said casually. "Swell food." And he was off.

Luella sniffed. "I don't think your professor has very good manners. I'll wager he doesn't eat a lunch like that every day."

"I'm sure he doesn't," I soothed. "It was out of this world, Mrs. Greenfield."

To mollify her further, I followed instructions and helped with the dishes. But when I left her place I staged a revolt. The fog was still reducing visibility to about three feet, and I wasn't in the mood to go right back to the Hazlitt cabin. Despite Dahlberg's skepticism, I knew I hadn't dreamed up that business about the doors.

So when I made out the row of mailboxes indicating I had reached the crossroads, I turned toward my own cabin. As I entered the yard I heard a car approaching from the south, and I paused.

Amanda Plumb's Ford chugged to a stop in front of the mailboxes and, climbing out, she started distributing mail.

"Hi," I said. "Anything for me?"

Amanda didn't look unduly friendly.

"Yeah. Here."

I glanced at the envelopes, postmarked New York, Chicago and San Antonio. They must be more replies to my ad in the *Saturday Review*. Stuffing them in my pocket, I tried to sweeten up Amanda.

"I don't see how you manage those roads in this fog," I said admiringly. "Isn't it difficult?"

"I'm used to it."

"It certainly hangs on, doesn't it? I thought the sun might come out by noon."

Amanda got back into the car, shifted gears.

"Spells like this last about three days," she said grimly, "and you never do see the sun. It's not really fog at all—it's just big clouds sitting down on top of the mountains."

Starting to turn around, she paused, leaned out the window.

"When you see your friend, Professor Dahlberg," she said, "you can tell him I'm a public servant and not to be bribed. Understand?"

She tramped the gas and the old car leaped off into the gray blanket.

I smiled, but I was disturbed too. It was a shame Axel had such genius for rubbing people the wrong way. And the worst of it was, he didn't care. He took sardonic delight in needling people—stirring up the animals, he called it.

Inside the cabin, I opened my mail. From Chicago an old lady who had known Gilbert Hazlitt's parents wrote about his precocity as a lad. The San Antonio writer sent several of Hazlitt's poems clipped from periodicals, items available in any anthology. The third, from a New York newspaper editor, was the most amusing of the lot, but again nothing I could use. In a wry covering note, he described the enclosed as a valuable piece of Hazlittana: an IOU for twenty-five dollars which Hazlitt had given him in a poker game back in their reporting days.

I was tempted to stay by the fire and nap. But when Jeff came to the door shortly before four o'clock, I was glad I had freshened up and put on my blue jersey. He was looking grouchy.

"This is not a social call," he said. "I was sent."

"By whom?"

"Who do you suppose? Dear old Dr. Dahlberg, in person. Seems your paranoia's been troubling you again and he wanted to be sure you arrived at this important conference safe and sound. You weren't at the Hazlitt cabin, so I came here."

Dahlberg must have been more impressed by my tale of being locked in than he had revealed. It made me feel good to think he was concerned, but Jeff's attitude infuriated me, especially that paranoia crack.

"You didn't have to come, if it's such a hardship," I said coldly.

"No. But now that the great man has arrived I probably won't get to see you unless I snatch these crumbs he tosses me."

He looked like a sulky, overgrown kid, standing there kicking his boot toe against the stove leg; my annoyance vanished and I laughed. "Cheer up. It's not as bad as all that."

"It's worse," Jeff replied stubbornly. "He's already insulted Milton Evans, thrown Fay St. Vincent into a crying fit and told Sarah Walker he'd be over for dinner when he was damned good and ready—that she's running a hotel, not an exclusive club. Sarah's fit to be tied."

We started out through the fog which seemed even denser in the oncoming darkness of late afternoon. Jeff caught my arm, pulling me over to walk closer beside him.

"I'm sorry, Gail. But we've had fun together and were going to have more, and then that over-bearing character has to come along and spoil everything."

"Look," I said, "Axel Dahlberg is just a guy I'm going to work for. If you'll stop behaving like a spoiled child, there's no reason why his being here should make any difference."

"Not much," Jeff muttered.

The cabin Dahlberg had rented the summer before and again this summer was by no means so deluxe as the Barlows'. It stood at the junction of the Alpine and Coyote Canyon roads with Glory Cloud's main street. No inside plumbing, and water had to be carried from the well in back. At some stage in the shack's past, a summer resident had started to rejuvenate it, and the main room had the inevitable knotty pine and a lot of book-shelves. The sporting touch was added by an old gun mounted over the front door. But the furniture was the dreadful assortment of cast-offs found in too many mountain cabins. Axel Dahlberg wouldn't care. If he had a roof over his head and a place to work, he wouldn't demand an artistic décor.

When we knocked, Dahlberg shouted, "Door's unlocked.
Walk in." He was slumped in a big chair, nose in a book. He
finished his paragraph before looking up. Then he glanced at his
watch.

"What did you kids do—come by way of Pinto?"

Quickly to forestall Jeff's explosion, I said, "You can't make
much time in a fog like this."

Axel's grin was only slightly malicious and I'm sure he meant
his sly grimace at Jeff to be comradely.

"If you can't make time in a fog with a pretty girl, when can
you?"

The implied slight on his prowess was all Jeff needed.

"Listen, you stuck-up, disagreeable bastard," he shouted,
"don't think you can get away with needling me all the time the
way you do these local yokels. You don't impress me one little
bit, Dr. Axel Dahlberg, Ph.D. Any time you want trouble, you've
come to the right place."

Dahlberg looked mildly startled by the violence of Jeff's outburst, but he only narrowed his eyes and continued smiling that
maddening, superior smile.

"Simmer down, boy," he said.

That was the wrong advice. In his knocking around, Jeff Calhoun had picked up a rich descriptive vocabulary, which he now
drew on to make his opinion of Axel Dahlberg crystal-clear. The
fact that Axel merely sat back and took it quietly, wearing his
sly, amused grin, had the effect of fighting a mountain brush-fire
with gasoline. Once, while Jeff was drawing breath, I thought I
heard a step on the narrow porch, but I was too fascinated by the
pyrotechnics to give it thought.

I suppose eventually he would have run down; Dahlberg seldom lost his temper when others did and trying to fight him
was as unsatisfactory as chewing Jello. But midway through one
of Jeff's more lurid passages a knock sounded. He strode to the
door and yanked it open, barking, "Well, what do you want?",
even before he saw who it was.

Old Charlie Armstrong stood there, blinking plaintively.

"Don't shoot, pardner," he said. "I ain't armed."

Jeff relaxed and laughed. Charlie stuck his head in the door, asked Dahlberg:

"Where do you want this here firewood put, perfessor?"

Axel rose, walked to the door.

"Oh, anywhere, Charlie. Just dump it at the end of the porch." He went out to supervise.

Jeff came over and looked down at me soberly, shamefaced. "I'm sorry, Gail. Are you sore at me?"

"No," I said carefully. "Why should I be sore? But I hope I'm not around if you ever lose your temper."

He was pale and still shaking a little.

"I'll shove off," he said. "See you tonight?"

"Sure," I agreed.

He left as Dahlberg came in from paying Charlie for the wood. Glancing at my expression, Axel sighed and sank back into his deep chair.

"Don't look so upset, girl. The male is always marked by excessive belligerence during the mating season."

I was not amused. With a start like this, I foresaw a complicated summer. I was sorry it had happened. And I was sorry old Charlie Armstrong had eavesdropped, for I was sure it was his step I had heard on the porch.

IV

By the time we left Dahlberg's cabin at six-thirty, I was primed with information about the Granger, Glory Cloud & Western narrow gauge till facts were running out my ears.

After Jeff Calhoun left, Dahlberg had set about cheering me up. He had got a fire going and brewed coffee, plunging into a discussion of the summer's work. The contagion of his enthusiasm soon caught me, and the old admiration for his facile mind.

"Before we go into the technicalities," I interrupted, "I need a quick briefing on the Granger, Glory Cloud & Western. I didn't know a thing about it when you asked me to do this job, but since I've been in Glory Cloud I've learned it's loaded with dynamite."

"That's an apter figure than you realize," Dahlberg remarked.

"Why, every time I open my face about it people go into a tailspin. Did you know Fay St. Vincent's father was involved and Dr. Tuckerman's, and that Milton Evans is hooked up in some way I haven't heard yet, and Amanda Plumb's husband—"

"Sure," Axel said. "Do you want to hear about it or do you want to tell me how much you know?"

"I want to hear about it."

It was the kind of set-up Dahlberg doted on. He was a good listener when he had to be or when it suited his purposes, but he did love to talk and he especially loved to hold forth on a subject where he could impart knowledge, preferably a little spicy. Now he slumped deeper into the big chair and stared at the fire.

"In the first place, you know *something* about the history of Glory Cloud, don't you?"

"Only what Amanda Plumb told me on the way up. That it was a gold boom town around the turn of the century. And Jeff told me it was Fay St. Vincent's father who first discovered gold here at the Glory Cloud mine."

"That's right," Dahlberg nodded. "And he named the town Glory Cloud after the mine and he did everything he could to help the town grow and prosper. I imagine that's how he got mixed up with old B. J. Tuckerman, who was a different breed altogether. There's no telling what may come to light, but so far as I can tell now Julius St. Vincent was strictly on the up and up. My guess is that he got on to B. J. and got out before the crash, because everything I've found yet indicates that he severed all connection with the railroad years before."

"That's what Fay told me. She said dear Papa wasn't involved."

Dahlberg straightened. "She did? Now why do you suppose she did that? Maybe I'd better dig deeper into old Julius—see whether he was so upright, after all."

"What a nasty, suspicious mind!"

Axel grinned. "That's how I find out things, girl. Anyway, here's your story. The Glory Cloud deposit was struck and the mine opened in 1891. Other strikes in the area followed and by 1895, when B. J. Tuckerman came along, the town was roaring. Full of opportunity. B. J. was a lawyer from somewhere back in Ohio and, though I haven't yet checked this, I'd be willing to lay a quiet wager that he was in something shady there that made it expedient for him to come west. That's the kind of guy he seems to have been. The big promoter type with a finger in all the pies and every pie a bit on the rank side.

"So he looked over Glory Cloud and saw easier ways to get gold than by digging it out of the ground. His most ambitious project was organizing the Granger, Glory Cloud & Western narrow-gauge railroad. That was in 1899 and work on the road was completed in the summer of 1902. It would have been a good business proposition even if he'd kept it clean. There was a great deal of passenger travel between Glory Cloud and Granger, and the railroad was faster than horse and wagon. There was freight to be hauled, both here and to the tungsten town of Bitter Creek, where a spur ran. Another spur ran on to Pinto. And there was the summer tourist angle. During the season they ran scenic excursion trains up in the morning and back at night."

"Hold on a minute," I said. "What did you mean: 'even if he'd kept it clean'?"

"Why, girl," Dahlberg said impatiently, "you know how the robber barons, big and little, operated. B. J. may have been a junior edition, but he had all the craft and greedy instincts of the species. He followed the classic pattern. He sold stock in the venture, both in Colorado and to eastern investors, to the amount of two million dollars. Then he formed a construction company, owned by the officers of the railroad, and hired the company to do the building. Haven't you heard this song before? Don't you know how much waste and graft there was in the set-up, how soundly the stockholders were fleeced right from the beginning, how warm and cozy were those pockets full of profits for the inner circle?"

"Well, I don't see why Julius St. Vincent gets a clean bill of health in a deal like that."

"Oh, he hasn't yet," said Dahlberg quickly. "Old Julius will bear looking into. But all the evidence so far points to his having been the unwitting pawn of B. J. Tuckerman. St. Vincent was well thought of here and in Granger, as well as in Denver business circles. Honest as the day is long, his word as good as his bond, and all that. My theory is that he was just the sort of fall-guy B. J. was looking for, that, from the first, B. J. deliberately cultivated St. Vincent to cash in on the other man's reputation. After striking it rich with the Glory Cloud, St. Vincent had become involved in a wide variety of enterprises, and he left the details of the narrow gauge to Tuckerman. Julius was vice-president and his name lent prestige to the undertaking. He was in favor of the railroad because he thought it a good thing for his baby, Glory Cloud."

"Then if he wasn't actually crooked," I said, "I think Julius was a dope."

"No," Dahlberg said, "he was no dope. For one thing he was smart enough to hang on to his money and property, which was more than most of those old guys that hit the jackpot did. Smart enough to snowball his assets till he was an important financial figure in the state. And for another thing, he was smart enough to get out of the railroad racket before the real stink.

"Besides watered stock," Dahlberg went on, "the road had a heavy bonded indebtedness. Almost from the first it lost money, and in 1908 it went into receivership. All the original stockholders were washed out. Now B. J. had a railroad all his own to play with. It was reorganized with the same management, but this time Julius St. Vincent wanted no part of it. The records prove that he was out in 1921, but I'm not sure just when he got out, because B. J. tried to give the impression St. Vincent was still involved after the reorganization. St. Vincent was apparently a quiet little guy who minded his own business, not the kind to go blowing around if he found a former associate had been rooking everybody. But I'll bet you the price of a dinner at the inn that Julius bowed out when the reorganization took place. That's one of the points we have to check."

"Okay," I said. "So the railroad was fraudulent. What is there for everyone to be so steamed up about?"

"That's right," Dahlberg agreed. "Just a piece of run-of-the-mill crookedness. Virtually standard business procedure. You've learned the facts of life young, girl. People don't get steamed up over a mere matter of principle—nobody but screwballs like Dahlberg. Their emotions have to be involved before they give a damn."

I was inured to his outbursts of righteous indignation, and I refused to be diverted.

"Let's get on to the emotions. That sounds promising."

Axel gave me an irked look and retaliated by making me wait while he dug around in a bag for his favorite pipe.

"I like to smoke a pipe," he said benignly. "Makes me look like a college professor, don't you think?"

"Very much so," I agreed. "Don't feel hurried, Professor. It's only a quarter to six."

"As soon as the heckling ceases, I'll continue."

After a few moments of complete silence, he grinned and went on.

"After the reorganization the road went along, barely breaking even, till the World War. World War I, of course. Then that spur running over to Bitter Creek became very important and started producing heavy revenue. Tungsten, you see. War material. For a few years the narrow gauge really made money and most of it went into B. J. Tuckerman's pockets. He didn't put any of it back into the road even in flush times. With increasing use, the equipment was becoming defective and in poor repair. After the wreck there was testimony that Tuckerman had been warned the road was becoming hazardous because of the run-down state of the rolling stock, but B. J. was milking the line for every possible penny of profits and ignored all warnings."

Axel bit down hard on his pipe stem and scowled.

"As too frequently happens, the punishment meted out to the guilty fell also and more heavily on the innocent. One fine June morning in 1921 the daily excursion train left Granger, loaded with passengers. Mainly tourists and mainly women and children. In general, the line followed the Coyote Canyon road: out of Granger via Granger Canyon, then branching off up Coyote through Quartz. Not too far below Quartz was a tunnel through the rocky hill. This particular morning a freight train was switching off a car at Quartz. It was a car loaded with dynamite for the tungsten mines, and was being switched of onto the Bitter Creek spur. Somehow, in the operation, the freight car with the dynamite broke loose and started down the main line toward Granger, a runaway. There was a trainman on the car who undoubtedly tried to stop it, but the weak, faulty brakes must have given out altogether."

Dahlberg paused to relight the pipe and I stared at him.

"You came up Coyote Canyon," he continued. "Imagine the momentum a freight car of dynamite would pick up plunging down that grade. Then imagine that runaway car entering the tunnel from above at the same moment the excursion train enters it from below."

I could only gasp.

"Precisely," he said. "They heard the blast in Granger that morning and they heard it in Glory Cloud. The trainmen working at Quartz got down as fast as they could, but there was nothing to do when they got there but start dragging the bodies out from under chunks of the mountainside. The explosion dislodged parts of the rock roof and walls of the tunnel, of course."

Dahlberg was silent a moment, then said slowly, "I wonder whether in the next few days B. J. Tuckerman ever heard the screams of little kids lying crushed under boulders?"

"Stop it," I said. I felt sick. Then I remembered what Jeff had said and I asked, "So Tuckerman shot himself, right?"

"He shot himself, apparently," Axel said, "but I don't imagine remorse had much to do with it. He probably just didn't see any way to beat the rap. The newspapers played the wreck up big and it made a stink from Cheyenne to Albuquerque. It was brought out in print that Tuckerman had been warned of the dangerous state of disrepair in the equipment and, specifically, that most of the cars had faulty brakes. Now that the damage was done, the press was loud and brave about shouting corruption and malfeasance. Public indignation reached such a white heat there was talk of lynching. In Granger they held a mass memorial service for the victims and that didn't cool people off any. The D.A. started the machinery to prosecute B. J. for criminal negligence."

Questions kept popping into my mind, but before I could voice them there was a quick knock. Jeff stood there, looking doghousey. He spoke to Dahlberg.

"I want to apologize for losing my temper, sir."

Dahlberg grinned. "That's all right, boy. I was young myself once."

"And I wanted to tell you," Jeff went on, "that maybe you ought to come on over. Sarah is tearing up the floor because her dinner's being ruined."

"Okay," Axel said. "We'll humor the old witch. Wait a minute and we'll walk back with you."

"No," Jeff said, "nobody knows I came over. I'll dash back and you come along."

Five minutes later Dahlberg and I stepped out into a night blacker than the inside of a mine hole. I was feeling good in spite of Axel's hair-raising story because it looked as if he and Jeff might be friends, after all. And I was giving Jeff credit for having the courage to say he was sorry. Later I wished he had done it at dinner, right in front of everybody.

Looking around the big, family-style table that evening my eye rested on Milt Evans' eager-beaver countenance and I wondered where he fitted into the lurid yarn. Axel hadn't got to that. I had already learned that Evans was a hot-shot insurance man who had high-pressured himself right to the verge of a nervous breakdown. His doctor had advised him to go some place quiet and take it easy before he went clear to pieces, so he'd thought of his long-unused cabin in Glory Cloud. At least, that was his story. And I wondered what in the world Axel had said to insult him, as Jeff reported. I had Milt Evans figured as the guy who could be insulted only by throwing him out the second-story window.

Toward the end of the table I noticed Charlie Armstrong, coping as best he could with the crusty fried chicken. He was a cheerful old soul, and his cackling laughter helped dispel the gloom cast by Sarah's wrath at us for being late, and by the currents of animosity converging on Dahlberg. After dinner when we drifted in to cluster around the roaring fireplace, Charlie picked up his guitar and began softly strumming "Oh, Susanna."

After a while Dr. Tuckerman said:

"Give us the full ensemble, Charlie. I haven't heard you play that mouth organ for a blue moon."

Charlie beamed and shuffled over to his mackinaw, taking out something he unfolded to form a fearful and wonderful contraption, which went around his neck and held a mouth organ in front of his face so that he could play it and the guitar simultaneously. The combination produced an amazing amount of music and we started harmonizing on "Home on the Range." Axel muttered something about getting a drink and went to the kitchen.

That chicken had been salty. I wished I'd asked him to bring me a drink. I rose to get one myself, not thinking it probably looked as if I couldn't let him out of my sight. As I neared the swinging door to the kitchen the racket from the group around the fireplace retreated and I heard quarrelsome voices in the kitchen. Were Axel and Jeff at it again?

No, it was Sarah and Axel. I hesitated long enough to hear Axel, angry himself this time, saying: "Good lord, Sarah, why not? You know that's the way it was."

And Sarah's acid retort: "Because I don't choose to, that's why not. I don't owe you any favors, Axel Dahlberg."

Flabbergasted at the idea of Dahlberg's asking favors from anyone, much less Sarah Walker, I turned away from the door and almost bumped into Luella Greenfield. She was clutching a flat, newspaper-wrapped package.

"It's all right to let Professor Dahlberg borrow this," she whispered furtively. "But don't let Fay know we took it out of the cabin or she'll be cross."

I deduced that the package must be the filing folder of material about the narrow gauge, and I was amused by Luella's twittery state about Fay's reaction. Fay didn't impress me as such a fire-eater. But Luella managed to act terribly solemn about the whole thing.

"And tell Professor Dahlberg," she added nervously, "that I'd like to talk something over with him after he reads it. He'll understand."

At this point, I was much more interested in what was going on in the kitchen than in the Granger, Glory Cloud & Western. I murmured assent and casually tucked the package under my coat which lay across a bench.

As Luella and I rejoined the others, the front door opened and Jeff came in with firewood. After disposing of it he sauntered over and sat on the arm of my chair, joining his deep voice to the chorus. I noticed Fay St. Vincent and Luella eying us and exchanging a fatuous glance.

Dahlberg soon came back from the kitchen and sat down near old Charlie, but he acted restless. After another half-hour he stood up.

"I know how sad this will make all of you," he announced abruptly, "but I'm tired and I'm going home to bed."

Only Charlie protested. Axel grinned mockingly as he waved his hand and stepped outside. I suddenly remembered the folder and grabbed it up along with my coat.

"Excuse me a minute, I'll be right back."

If eyebrows were lifted and if Jeff Calhoun flushed, I ignored it. I caught Dahlberg at the foot of the steps and gave him the folder, explaining what it was. I didn't think it necessary to re-peat all Luella's injunctions about keeping this dark deed from Fay St. Vincent. Then I said:

"Not that it's any of my business, but that sounded like a good rousing brawl you and Sarah were having."

What with the darkness and the fog I couldn't see his face, but his voice sounded cross.

"No, it's none of your business, girl." Then he sighed and added, "Not that it's any great secret. I just don't feel up to going into it now. I'll tell you tomorrow."

"Okay chief," I said. "Pleasant dreams."

I couldn't say about his dreams, but mine that night were delightful. When Jeff walked me home after the jam-session finally broke up, we didn't discuss narrow-gauge railroads or other people's business or theses or projects of any kind. Nor did we evaluate the future of the United Nations. And if Dahlberg thought Jeff Calhoun couldn't make time in a fog or under any other climatic conditions, even he could be wrong.

V

Amanda Plumb had been right: these mountain fogs lasted three days. And the novelty soon wore off. Even by the second day, Sunday, I found myself depressed.

I tried to ignore the weather by spending most of the day at work in the Hazlitt cabin. Everything was so peaceful I began to think perhaps I *had* imagined the hocus-pocus of the day before. Late in the morning Axel Dahlberg popped in on the first of a day-long series of brief visits.

I had decided not to ask again about the argument with Sarah Walker, but Dahlberg brought up the subject himself. I knew, of course, that his wife was getting a divorce—and demanding an alimony so sizable it would reduce Axel to living in a tent. Nedra Dahlberg was a flighty baby-doll, and I was not surprised when he said she'd been playing around off the reservation. Axel looked weary and older than his years, talking about it.

"I don't want to make a row in court," he said. "But I damned well know that when we were here last summer Nedra used to meet some guy at the inn. Sarah Walker knows it too. I wanted her to make a sworn statement of the fact. It would be handy to whittle down Nedra's big ideas."

"And Sarah refused? But why?"

"Because she's just damned ornery. Because she has a lot of sex antagonism. Because it's against her principles to be cooperative about anything."

"I'm sorry. About the whole mess, I mean."

Dahlberg shrugged. "Smarter people than you and I have been crossed up by that old biological urge. There's more to marriage than you might think on a moonlight night. Or a foggy one. Incidentally, where's Jeff today?"

I could feel myself blushing, and the naiveté of it made me furious.

"How do I know where he is? I'm not riding herd on him."

"Well," Dahlberg said mildly, "it might be fun to have a steak fry some night soon—maybe tomorrow if the fog lifts—and I thought we could ask Jeff to go along." He grinned. "I'm getting too old to chop wood and build fires."

"What about food? The trading post isn't open."

"I brought up staples yesterday," he said, "including plenty of beer. Why don't you try to catch Amanda Plumb today—she comes up to deliver Sunday papers—and proposition her about bringing along steaks and buns tomorrow? Turn on your girlish charm, and just be sure to skip any mention of that horrid man, Dahlberg."

"Okay," I agreed. "Where are you heading now?"

He was putting on his coat.

"I have to see a guy."

"About a railroad?"

"Maybe. Be good."

I sighed and returned to the salt mines.

A little later, en route home for a quick lunch, I managed to see Amanda and file my request. I kept Axel's name out of it and Amanda was almost affable.

After lunch I returned to the Hazlitt cabin and my research. Late in the afternoon I shoved papers and notebook away and wearily rubbed my eyes, wondering how everybody else had been spending this long, dreary Sunday. As nearly as I could gather, Dahlberg had been engaged in making a series of social calls, for reasons known only to himself. He'd stopped in a couple of times since our morning visit, but he never stayed long and was incommunicative about his activities.

The person I really wondered about, of course, was Jeff Calhoun. We hadn't made any date; there was no sound reason for feeling piqued because I hadn't seen or heard from him all day.

But I did feel slightly piqued, and when I heard someone at the door of the Hazlitt cabin my spirits lifted, but it was only Axel. He breezily informed me he'd been invited to dine with Fay St. Vincent that evening.

I said: "I shouldn't have imagined Fay could boil an egg. But I suppose she has help."

"Not here," Axel said. "Glory Cloud is her retreat to the simple life."

I must have looked skeptical at the idea of Fay's spoiling her manicure with household routine, for Axel went on to outline the life Fay led away from Glory Cloud, pointing out how such an existence might make a servantless summer in the mountains a refreshing change. He mentioned the plush apartment in Denver, the beach-house in La Jolla, the compartments on swank trains, the theater seasons in New York, the luxury-liners abroad. Everything super de luxe with all the service her little heart desired. Julius had left plenty of what it takes, and Fay had been shrewd enough to keep it.

"But our Fay has a romantic streak a mile wide." Axel grinned. "It appeals to her imagination to come here and get away from it all and commune with her soul. And I believe old Charlie takes care of anything heavy like window-washing. I don't suppose she does enough actual work to hurt anybody."

I nodded. "Of course, she takes most of her meals at the inn."

"Sure. Except when it strikes her fancy to entertain. Like tonight. I would have rung you in on it, girl—given you a chance to see her lay-out. But I want a tête-à-tête with Fay."

I said gloomily, "That's all right. Nobody cares about me."

Dahlberg chortled. "Self-pity is the lowest form of human emotion. Say, what was that again about Fay's telling you dear Papa had nothing to do with the narrow gauge?"

"That's all. She dropped in late the other afternoon, ostensibly to discuss her great romance with Gilbert Hazlitt." I repeated what Fay had told me about herself and Hazlitt, adding: "But I'm not sure that was her real reason for coming. She tried to sound casual about dear Papa, but she came to the point a lot faster than usual."

"Hm-m-m," Axel said. "Very interesting." Then he asked: "How are you coming with your thesis research? Have you had any replies to that ad in the *Saturday Review?*"

"A few." I handed him a large envelope containing the lot. "Nothing that amounts to anything."

He scanned them hastily, making a wry face.

"Wouldn't you think people who read the *Saturday Review* would be brighter?" I demanded. "What do I care what a cute little boy Hazlitt was?"

"Patience, girl, patience. Why should I care whether or not Herman Tuckerman loved his father? You must know that in any job of research you have to dig through a mountain of irrelevant debris to find a few nuggets of significant fact."

"I don't follow you. How did Herman Tuckerman get into this conversation?"

"Just an illustration. I had a nice long chat with the good doctor this afternoon."

"And insulted him, no doubt?"

It was meant as a crack, not a compliment, but Axel's dark face looked pleased and he wore an air of excitement.

"No doubt," he agreed cheerfully. "Close up your shop here and I'll walk down with you."

We locked the cabin and started down the road.

"I thought you were going to Fay's," I said. "Isn't her place up in this direction?"

"It's off in the woods beyond the end of the road. But first I have other fish to fry."

He left me at the Barlow cabin and went on his way, the clammy fog and the dusk swallowing him in about three steps. I resisted the impulse to tag along as far as the inn. Anybody who wanted to see me knew where I lived.

But apparently nobody wanted to. I dined on canned soup and spent the evening answering letters, making the one to Jan Polenski especially cordial.

It was mid-afternoon Monday before the fog lifted. I was working again in the Hazlitt cabin when, coming out of my absorption, I observed a shaft of brilliant sunlight across the floor, making the light from my lamp feeble and washed out. I jumped up to throw open the door on a Glory Cloud magically released from gray bondage. The sun was dazzling in a blue, blue sky, and a strong wind whistled down from the high range, hurrying the clouds on their way. All the greens and blues and golds of the landscape seemed sharpened in their emergence from obscurity, and the cold, thin air had a Martini-like quality.

I abandoned work right now. I felt like going places and doing things, and I refused to be thwarted by Glory Cloud's limited opportunities. I would celebrate by walking down to the inn and telling Jeff about our steak fry. My mood of yesterday, I realized now, had been sheer petulance, aggravated by the depressing weather; why should he check in with me every twenty-four hours?

I found Jeff behind the inn, stacking firewood. He was all for the fry.

"I suppose Sarah will raise the roof," he said, "but that's mere routine. How would it be if we'd take off a little after seven from Dahlberg's cabin? Now that it's cleared off, it will stay light longer, so I could stick around here till dinner's under way."

"Suits me."

"I'm hungry right now," Jeff announced. "Let's duck in the kitchen for coffee. Sarah baked this afternoon, too."

The big old-fashioned kitchen was warm and empty. Mouth-watering smells floated from kettles simmering on the cook-stove, coffee steamed in a big enamel pot, and fresh cookies cooled on a rack on the table. Opening a dish cupboard to get cups, I noticed a half-empty bottle of Old Sunny Brook in the back corner. An odd place to keep whisky, but Sarah Walker was an odd character.

Jeff said she was upstairs, getting rooms ready for occupancy.

"Tomorrow's Decoration Day. That's supposed to open the tourist season, although we haven't any reservations for a couple of weeks yet."

I suspected Sarah wouldn't be overjoyed if she came down and found us devouring her cookies. And since I felt in too fine a mood to row with anybody, I didn't linger over my coffee.

Outside the inn, a voice hailed me, and I saw Axel coming up the Coyote Canyon road. While I waited, my glance roved across a second-story window of the inn. Sarah Walker was glaring out, arms characteristically akimbo. I chuckled, reflecting she would probably go right down to the kitchen and count those cookies.

Axel was huffing and puffing. "I smoke too much," he said. "This altitude gets me."

"You shouldn't do all this chasing around. Where have you been now?"

"To see old Charlie. Charlie's an interesting conversationalist. Very interesting."

"They're all conversationalists in these parts," I said. "I never heard such an outfit of big talkers."

Then I told him I'd seen Jeff and that we were all set for the fry.

Axel groaned. "What ever gave me that brainstorm? Okay, I started it and I'll go through with it. One more little jaunt before I go home to recuperate. Come along with me, girl. I may need a strong young shoulder to lean on."

"Where are we going?" We had passed his cabin and started up the steep rise of the Alpine road.

"This way," Dahlberg said, deserting the road and scrambling up an embankment to our right. He strode rapidly along a narrow, twisting path so overgrown it was barely discernible, and I had to hurry to keep up. The tall pines met overhead, shutting out the sunlight and blue sky; the air was cool and moist with a smell of last year's needles and cones drifting up from the ground.

Before I could ask more questions, we came to a tumbled-down shack stripped of its roof by savage winter winds. Once it had stood in a small clearing, but now scrubby timber had closed in. The sagging stoop sheltered a drift of snow.

"Brrr!" I exclaimed. "Whose cozy little hideaway is this?"

"I don't know," Dahlberg said shortly. "Some old prospector's probably." He walked once around the shack, frowning, then said: "Let's go."

We turned back, and I was choosing among various caustic comments on his idea of recreation when I noticed what appeared to be a boarded-up well right beside the path. I thought it would have been handier nearer the house, but the place was no dream of convenience at best.

As we re-emerged onto the Alpine road, Dahlberg said abruptly: "You know Milt Evans owns several pieces of property up here. His dad was in real estate in Granger and did a lot of swapping around."

"Is that one of his properties we just inspected?" I asked gravely.

Axel shook his head. "Not that I know of."

"Look, professor," I said sympathetically, "you're all tired and confused. Why don't you go take a nice nap now and we'll see you later."

"I know," Axel grinned, pausing in front of his cabin. "You think I'm nuts. Did you ever hear the expression 'crazy like a fox'?"

"Hear it? I made it up."

But as I went on toward the Barlow cabin, I wondered whether he was touched by the altitude. If he didn't know whose shack that was, why in the world had he wanted to look it over?

That evening Dahlberg kept grumbling about the steak fry as if it had been somebody else's idea. He said it was too early in the season and too cold, which it was, and that the spot we headed for was too far after a tiring day, which was also true. But at the same time he vetoed any suggestion to call it off or stop any place nearer.

We left his cabin at seven-fifteen and hiked up the Alpine road. When we reached the trail to the view of the Divide, the spot where Jeff and I had rested that first day, Dahlberg paused, winded. He put down his share of the picnic load, and momentarily alarmed me by patting his chest in the region of his left breast-pocket. Had he been overdoing? But he only grinned and said:

"Guess I'll check up to see whether Mt. Evans is still on the job. You kids have probably looked at the marker before this— I'll be right back."

I was bushed myself and glad to collapse by the side of the road. He was back in five minutes; he couldn't have spent much time admiring the range.

"Well," Jeff said, "are all the mountains still in their proper places and behaving?"

Dahlberg nodded cheerfully. "Everything's right where it should be. Excelsior!"

At the summit we took the path back past the Glory Cloud mine and kept going for what seemed miles. It was almost dark when we reached a high, rocky clearing with a circle of blackened stones in the center.

Depositing our supplies on a flat-topped boulder, Jeff and I shagged around collecting firewood. But when we were all set to start cooking, nothing would do but that we must climb farther and see the view. Axel had been resting while we labored and was raring to go again.

I did my share of grumbling then, but when we achieved the highest rocky promontory and looked out across the plains in the deepening dusk I subsided. It was worth it. To the east you could see the great plains of America stretching away into infinite distance, to the west the towering peaks of the high range, its snows pale blue and lavender in the failing light. Off to the southeast a twinkling cluster of lights steadily increased in number and brilliance as darkness closed down.

"That's Denver," Jeff told me.

"Denver! What kind of sucker do you take me for? Denver must be seventy miles from here."

But Dahlberg backed him up. I said:

"Why can't we see the lights of Granger? It's a lot closer."

"It's too close," Jeff said. "It's right below us."

"Can I see them if I lean out and stretch my neck?" I took a step nearer the edge.

Jeff and Axel each grabbed one of my arms. "Good Lord, girl! That's five thousand feet and it's mostly straight down."

Jeff merely drawled, "Tired of living, honey? Let's go eat."

Inside my cocoon of heavy clothes and wool gloves, I was as cold as a Birdseye chicken. Hot food helped and the thermos of coffee, but everybody shuddered in unison at the thought of cold beer. Now that he'd eaten, Dahlberg was better-humored.

"We were balmy to lug along beer on a night like this," he said. "We'll have a nightcap when we get back."

"I should have appropriated that bottle from the dish cupboard at the inn," I said.

"What bottle?" Dahlberg asked.

I told him, adding, "I only noticed because it was a screwy place to file it and because I've never seen Sarah Walker take a drink when the rest do."

"Don't get so excited about one bottle, baby," Jeff said dryly. "You should see the barrelful of empties in the woodshed."

Axel chuckled. "A barrelful, hey? I like that."

And I said to Jeff, "What do you mean?"

"He means Sarah prefers to do her drinking in private," Dahlberg said.

I had barely grasped his meaning when an inspiration hit me.

"How about this?" I exclaimed. "You could threaten to publicize her secret vice if she won't play ball. You know what I mean."

Axel's lazy amusement mocked me. "Why, girl, you amaze me. That's nothing more nor less than blackmail you're suggesting. In the first place, it's immoral and in the second place, it isn't practical. Everybody knows that Sarah is a quote secret unquote drinker."

"Well, it was just an idea."

Jeff looked curious, but remained silent, puffing on his after-dinner cigarette and shying pebbles at the empty olive jar. "Gee, I'm good. Did you see me hit that right on the label? Ever do any target-shooting, Dahlberg?"

"Only when I go to a carnival."

"It's a lot of fun," Jeff said. "And out here is a safe place to do it. Hey, how about that gun hanging in your cabin? We could take it out and shoot beer cans."

The reference to his wife-trouble had made Axel cross again and I could have kicked myself.

"Nothing doing. That old gun is too valuable for you kids to play with. Besides, that kind of thing is more dangerous than you realize. Leave it alone, you hear me?"

"Okay," Jeff grumbled. He pointed to the ground just beyond our makeshift table. "But I bet if the bear that left those tracks came along, you'd be sorry we didn't have a gun."

I jumped up and hurried to look where he pointed. "You're kidding," I said. But there certainly were big tracks of some kind where the ground was still damp from slow-melting snow.

I glanced toward the dark woods and started gathering up the debris from our meal. Jeff got to his feet and helped me while Dahlberg watched us, whistling softly.

Now a cold white moon, almost full tonight, appeared above the treetops. Its frosty light would help in finding our way back. Axel stopped whistling, said:

"I may have to go to Granger tomorrow. I wonder whether I can hitch a ride."

"Why are you going to Granger so soon?" I demanded. "I thought you were going to hole in for the summer and do research."

"This is research," he said quietly. And I remembered the main offices of the Granger, Glory Cloud & Western had been in Granger.

Using our flashlights to supplement the moonlight, we found our way to the road and headed back toward Glory Cloud. The air was getting more Arctic by the second, and when Dahlberg repeated his invitation to stop in for a nightcap, Jeff and I leaped at it.

As we climbed the steps to the dark porch we heard a sound that halted me in my tracks. My blood seemed to coagulate and I clutched the nearest masculine arm.

"What's that?"

Both men laughed, and Axel said: "Bears!" But the voice attached to the arm I'd grabbed said in Jeff's deep tones: "It's okay, honey. Nothing but coyotes howling at the moon."

We listened and it came again. Not too far away, either. The most mournful, eerie, unnatural sound I'd ever heard. Not a long drawn-out musical howl as I'd always imagined, but a shrill, high-pitched babble of yapping from dozens of throats at once, like a pack of dogs gone berserk.

"Let's get inside," I said.

After Axel turned on the lamp and lighted a fire, I tried to be casual again.

"My girlish illusions are being shattered right and left," I said. "I always thought the howling of coyotes was supposed to be such a romantic sound."

"It is romantic," Dahlberg said. "At least the coyotes think so. Don't you recognize Love's Old Sweet Song when you hear it?"

"I'm no coyote."

And when Axel said we needed more wood and Jeff offered to help get it, I said, "Oh no, you don't. You're not both going to tramp out there and leave me alone. I want protection."

Dahlberg was still amused, but his underlying gentleness and his fondness for me showed briefly in his sardonic brown eyes.

"So the girl wants to be protected! Well, it's a tried and true approach. Okay, you protect her, Jeff, and after you've done that long enough, you might look in the kitchen for some glasses and the bourbon."

I grew steadily braver with Jeff's arms around me. Time passed, as time does at the pleasant business of being protected, but finally my social conscience asserted itself. Pulling away, I said:

"Sorry to be such a dope. You can go help the poor guy carry in wood now."

I hadn't consciously taken a leaf from Luella Greenfield's book in my helpless femininity, but Jeff had really gone for it. Before he would leave he insisted on turning on the kitchen light and generally bracing me up.

By now it seemed that Axel Dahlberg had been a long time just getting wood. Maybe he was being tactful. About leaving the kids alone for a while. And of course there was the matter of outside plumbing. But just the same it had been quite a while, and I urged Jeff to get going.

Finally he stepped outside. I carried glasses and the bottle in by the fire. And then he didn't come back as soon as I thought he should. What a worry-wart I was getting to be!

I was starting toward the door to shout at them and ask what they were up to when it opened and Jeff came back in. Alone. His blue eyes looked almost black under the heavy brows.

"Sit down, Gail," he said gently. "And take it easy. Something has happened to Mr. Dahlberg."

"Happened? What? Did he fall?"

Jeff didn't answer.

"What happened?" I repeated. "Did he break a leg? Let's get out there and help him."

Jeff shook his head. "No, he didn't break a leg, Gail. He died. And somebody did help him."

VI

I stared at Jeff Calhoun and I didn't believe him. It was a trick they'd cooked up to get me excited. How could Axel be dead? It hadn't been ten minutes since I'd seen him, very much alive, go for wood. Or had it been a half-hour?

Axel Dahlberg was too vital a person to be dead, too dynamic, too warm with the pulse of living. I would fall for this gag and do some silly thing and the two of them would knock themselves out laughing. With stubborn skepticism, my mind kept trying to ward off the shock of acceptance.

Jeff was silent, watchful eyes on my face. I made myself shrug and I said, "Well, that's too bad. I wonder what we should do about it."

"Gail—"

I walked toward the door. "I don't think it's very nice to leave him out there on such a cold night, dead or alive. I think we ought to bring him in by the fire."

With one of his Indian-swift and Indian-silent movements, Jeff stood between me and the door. "Don't go out there, Gail," he said. "Not while you're thinking the way you are."

I searched his solemn face and stared into his shadowed eyes, and I knew it was no gag. The dam of disbelief crumbled and the icy waters of grief and loss and outrage swept me along like a flash flood down a mountain canyon.

Jeff's arms were around me again and one big, gentle hand soothed my shoulders while the other hand pulled a handkerchief from his hip pocket, and his deep voice was sad, but somehow relieved, as he kept saying: "There, there, baby. That's better, honey, you cry."

The sheriff's name was Dan Sawyer and he was a big, slow-moving blond young man. Not more than thirty, and this surprised me till I learned he was a veteran and that there was a big G.I. vote in Granger County. His hair and lashes were so fair they could be called tow-colored; his eyes were light blue; and he was almost handsome in a large-boned, stolid way.

At first, I thought Dan Sawyer was stupid. For quite a while I thought so. He was so deliberate and so phlegmatic that it seemed unlikely any thought processes were functioning behind that sluggish exterior. He had a slowness in speech quite different from Jeff Calhoun's drawl. With Sawyer it was that for long periods he just didn't speak at all. He would listen and then, without comment or visible reaction, stare at you till you were convinced he didn't know what you'd said. And when you asked a question, he would stare, unblinking, for a matter of minutes, as if it hadn't registered, while he weighed his answer.

Not than anybody other than Sawyer himself was allowed to do much questioning that first night. When I had pulled myself together after the first shock of accepting Axel's death, Jeff outlined a plan of action.

"One of us ought to stay with—him," Jeff had said, "and the other go notify the authorities. Would you be afraid to walk over to the inn alone and use the phone?"

It was in another life I had been capable of tremors at the sound of coyotes howling. "No," I said dully. "I'm not afraid."

"After you call, maybe you'd better get Dr. Tuckerman to come over. Just as a matter of routine. You know his place? That big, white-frame house across from the inn and a short way west."

As I started down the road, I didn't look back. But I knew Jeff watched me from that black patch of shadow on the ground just beyond the west end of the front porch. I knew he leaned against the uprights supporting the porch, quietly smoking, and that the same shadow which concealed him from the moonlight also concealed the huddled figure on the ground at his feet. Reluctantly, when I insisted, he'd told me Axel Dahlberg had been stabbed in the back.

I moved in a coma, still unable to grasp it. The sense of bereavement would come again and, later, the anger, but now I felt only dull emptiness.

The front door of the inn was unlocked, the big lounge cold and empty. I'd seen the phone in a corner of the dining room. Using my flashlight, I located the chain that hung from the central light fixture in that room.

The operator was ringing the sheriff's office when the door to the kitchen opened and Sarah Walker appeared, holding a half-wiped glass and a tea towel.

"Well!" she said. "What do you think you're up to, sneaking around here at this hour, my fine young lady?"

There was a voice at the other end of the wire and I motioned for Sarah to be quiet. But I watched her face while I talked. After the first surprise, an expression of malicious satisfaction crossed her face and I was suddenly so furious my hand shook, holding the receiver.

And I realized how many people in Glory Cloud were going to be more relieved than grief-stricken at the news of Axel's death, and I hated every one of them.

The deputy who answered the phone said that he would notify Sawyer and they would be up at once. As I hung up, Sarah Walker said:

"That's a toll call to Granger. Costs twenty-five cents every time you call down."

Honestly! I pulled my coin purse out of my jeans pocket and with silent contempt tossed a quarter on the table. Picking up my flashlight, I said quietly:

"If the sheriff wants to know how people reacted to the news, I won't forget your cat-that-swallowed-the-canary expression. Where were you this evening, Mrs. Walker?"

She sniffed and tossed her head, the ubiquitous wire curlers jangling. "Right here in my own kitchen doing up the dishes that lazy Calhoun boy ran out on. And I'd just as soon tell the sheriff or anybody else that Axel Dahlberg deserved anything he got. Persecuting his poor wife!"

I remembered I was supposed to get Dr. Tuckerman, not to stand here wrangling with Sarah Walker. Without answering, I turned and walked to the door, but she hadn't finished her condolences.

"Maybe this will teach certain young ladies not to chase around after married men!"

I wondered why somebody hadn't murdered *her* long ago.

The lower floor of Dr. Tuckerman's house was dark, but a light showed in an upstairs room. It was the only home in Glory Cloud that had a second story; I suppose it had been the town's show-place: a foursquare, white-frame structure with neat green shutters and heavy lace curtains.

After knocking I waited several minutes before the porch light flashed on and Dr. Tuckerman, sporting a gaudy silk robe, opened the door. His white hair was disheveled and his bushy white brows curious.

"Why, Miss Rawson, come in. Is somebody ill? I was just getting to bed."

Briefly, I told him the news. If he was either pleased or relieved, he didn't show it. He seemed terribly upset, and his blue-veined old hands shook as he took off his glasses and slowly polished them.

"Oh dear!" he said. "I can't believe it. Murdered, you say? Are you sure? Maybe it was an accident."

"Maybe," I said. "The sheriff will know about that."

"The sheriff! Oh dear me! I suppose he'll be coming, won't he?"

"He's on his way now. That's customary in a murder case, I believe."

"Oh, I know, I know," Herman Tuckerman said hastily. "I'm just so bewildered I can't seem to think straight." He sighed. "I'll go put my clothes on, Miss Rawson. You wait here a minute—I'll be right back."

Waiting, I looked around the over-furnished living room. No, it would have been a parlor, I decided. All the bric-a-brac and antimacassars and heavily ornate furniture of the 'nineties was there, creating an atmosphere that made it hard to realize yourself in a broken-down mining village high in the Rockies. Apparently Herman Tuckerman's mother had been of the dressing-for-dinner-in-the-jungle school.

Dr. Tuckerman was down in five minutes, carrying a worn physician's bag. He still seemed unnerved, but I reflected that he was after all an elderly man and this was an unnerving business.

I didn't want to stay while Tuckerman went through his routine, but neither did I care to return to the inn. I started to go inside Dahlberg's cabin, then paused on the porch, observing someone coming along the road in the moonlight.

It was Milt Evans, and just then the subdued murmur of voices from the ground below rose to an angry shout.

"Oh no you don't, you old fox," Jeff yelled. "Give me that."

Then Tuckerman's voice, raised too, protesting. I ran to the end of the porch and looked down. Jeff was struggling with the old doctor who kept sputtering, but soon gave up. I heard him say wearily, "All right, young man. I hope you know what you're doing."

And he handed Jeff something which Jeff promptly pocketed.

Milt Evans had witnessed the fracas and now he said in his officious way: "What's going on here? As soon as I heard what had happened I knew I'd better get over and take charge. You probably don't know—"

"I probably don't know how you got wind so fast that anything *had* happened," Jeff retorted. "Gail didn't mention seeing you, Evans."

"If you're trying to insinuate something," Evans said coldly, "it's uncalled for. Sarah Walker told me about the—uh—unfortunate circumstances. You ought to be ashamed, Calhoun, jumping on an old man like Tuckerman."

"He ought to be ashamed," Jeff snapped, "trying to conceal evidence."

"What evidence?"

"Never mind, what evidence. It's in my pocket now and that's where it's staying till the sheriff comes."

Even in the moonlight I could see Evans draw himself up importantly.

"I'm not so easy to fool, Calhoun. You may not realize that I know something about police procedure, myself. And I insist you show what's in your pocket now, in front of witnesses."

"Why should I?"

Milt Evans' voice was pompously patient.

"If you don't exhibit your so-called evidence at this time, how are we to know you turn the same thing over to the sheriff? How do we know Dr. Tuckerman didn't find an item incriminating to you, yourself, Calhoun, and that you won't make a switch?"

Jeff was silent while I wondered what stone this know-it-all Evans had been lurking under when I was at the inn. I hadn't seen or heard anything of him. Then I heard Jeff say grumpily, "Okay, you can see it. But I'm hanging on to it myself, understand?"

I looked down. At first I couldn't make out what lay in Jeff's open palm, but then he turned his flashlight full on the object and it glittered.

It was one of the little silver-mounted combs Fay St. Vincent used to secure her upswept coiffure.

It had been almost ten-thirty when I called the sheriff's office, and, by the time he arrived with the coroner and two deputies, it was eleven-thirty. The deputies routed everybody out to wait in miserable, sleepy silence around the lounge of the inn, and it was after midnight before the sheriff was ready for us. He had given the scene a preliminary going-over and the coroner had finished examining the body.

Examining the body! That was Axel Dahlberg, Ph.D. A body. But what of the brilliant mind and the dynamic personality? Never again would youthful brains be stimulated by the contagion of his intellectual curiosity; never again would a difficult problem become lucid as his incisive mind stripped away superfluities; no more would one be determined to do one's very best on a job because of Dahlberg's confident belief in one's best.

And someone in this big room with its barn-like chill had been responsible. Must have been. Who else? I glanced around me and I thought, Was it you, Luella Greenfield? Mrs. J. Reed

Greenfield, sitting there properly shocked, but with your sharp little eyes glittering with excitement? Was it you, Dr. Herman Tuckerman, so distressed because the sheriff was en route, so ready to conceal the comb belonging to your one true love? How about you, Fay St. Vincent, looking coolly aloof and perfectly turned-out at this hour and under these circumstances? What sweet and airy explanation will you have when the sheriff produces that comb?

Jeff leaned over to whisper in my ear, caught the baleful eye of the deputy posted in front of the kitchen door and refrained. I continued my inventory. Was it you, Sarah Walker, with your once-pretty face ravaged by ill-temper and secret drinking, with your spite and your sex antagonism and your assertion that you were washing dishes all evening? Or was it Milt Evans, closeted now in the kitchen with the sheriff, undoubtedly telling the sheriff how to go about the business of crime detection? Mr. Know-it-all Evans with his unctuous self-importance, his alleged near-nervous-breakdown and his return to Glory Cloud after so many years.

The sheriff had questioned me first, getting a brief report of the evening's activities. Then Jeff. And he'd said that he would want to talk to us again when he was through with everybody else.

Now the big front door opened and old Charlie appeared. He looked around in surprise at the silent group, then cackled:

"Well, who's having a party this time of night? I seen a car go by, a while ago, hellbent for election, and then I heard a lot of voices gabbling up here. Thought I'd just come see what's going on."

I thought the deputy, Henderson, a tall, lean man in his late forties, with a dark, weathered face, was unnecessarily curt with old Charlie. In the fewest possible words he told him what had happened, adding, "Since you're here, you'd better stay. Sawyer will want to talk to you too."

Looking dazed, Charlie sank into the nearest empty chair. "Well, I'll be doggoned," he muttered. "Why, that pore old perfessor. He was a right nice feller, too. I liked him."

My heart warmed to old Charlie. He was the first person who had troubled to say anything good about Axel Dahlberg or to appear saddened. The deputy, however, was not touched. He was quite cross because when he was rounding up the residents nobody had thought to tell him about Charlie, and he was openly skeptical of Charlie's ability to hear voices so far away. I thought it possible: Charlie's shack was a fair distance down the Coyote Canyon road from Dahlberg's cabin at the turn, but the men in the sheriff's car hadn't been particularly quiet and sounds carried unbelievably through that thin, clear air.

The big room was uneasily silent again, and through the dining room from the kitchen came the murmur of voices. And out of nowhere a thought hit me.

Nedra Dahlberg! Who would be happier than Nedra to see Axel dead? She could have stolen, unseen, into Glory Cloud, killed Axel, stolen out again. Right now she might be speeding east, high above the plains in an airliner.

Fantastic? Maybe. But although Axel hadn't been liked in Glory Cloud, who had hated him violently enough for murder? Or feared him, as Nedra must have?

I was so preoccupied that I lost track of the coming and going to the kitchen; now the deputy beckoned me again. "You too, Calhoun," he said.

Sawyer had taken over the big work-table in the middle of the kitchen and was solidly planted in a chair behind it. It was 2:00 A.M. by now and the coroner, a chunky middle-aged man named Dr. Bailey, slumped in a chair by the stove, his feet on another chair. He yawned repeatedly. The second deputy, a younger chap called Murphy, was staying with Dahlberg's body.

Dan Sawyer didn't look sleepy nor did he look alert. He looked stolid and patient and immovable, as if time meant no more to him than fatigue or human emotion. His pale blue eyes were expressionless as he nodded toward chairs and sat looking at us in silence. Then he spoke in a calm, unhurried voice.

"What was your quarrel with Axel Dahlberg, Mr. Calhoun?"

"Quarrel?" Jeff looked surprised. "We weren't quarreling. I told you what a fine time we all had together on the steak fry and how we stopped in for a nightcap at his invitation. Does that sound as if we were quarreling?"

Jeff and Dan Sawyer must have been very nearly the same age, but the contrast between Jeff's volatile charm and Sawyer's ponderous soberness made it seem there was ten years' difference.

"You are known to have quarreled violently with Dr. Dahlberg the day he arrived," Sawyer said flatly.

Jeff looked shamefaced and slightly flushed. "Well, yes, I lost my temper, I guess. But it was nothing serious. I apologized to him afterwards."

"When?"

"That same evening. Not more than an hour later."

"Who heard you make this apology?"

"Why, Gail here was present. Don't you believe me?"

Sawyer looked at him quietly, as if he hadn't heard. At last he said, slowly:

"Nobody else heard you make any apology. Nobody else in Glory Cloud remembers noticing you and Dahlberg having anything to do with each other till tonight when you claim you found him dead."

"That's ridiculous!" I broke in. "Axel Dahlberg didn't take Jeff's blow-up seriously. He was just amused because Jeff was jealous and it was so silly. As for seeing them together, it was still daylight when we all left Dahlberg's cabin this evening. Last evening now. Somebody surely saw us then."

"Nobody did."

"So what?" Jeff demanded. "If my word isn't enough, how about Miss Rawson's? I don't see why you're taking this attitude with us, anyway—we were the only two friends Dahlberg had in Glory Cloud."

"Miss Rawson's testimony is not altogether objective," Sawyer said. "I am given to understand that you two have been almost constantly in each other's company. And I am given to understand that Miss Rawson was fonder of Dr. Dahlberg than a girl her age should be of a married man. At least, until she met you."

I gasped. Jeff jumped to his feet.

I thought he was going to swing on Sawyer. But the sheriff sat in placid silence, watching. I jumped up too, catching Jeff's arm.

"Don't be a sap," I said. "Where will that get you?"

With visible effort, Jeff controlled himself and tried looking amused. "What kind of hooey have they been feeding you in here?" he demanded. "How do you see this picture? Gail and Dahlberg having a clandestine affair and then my coming along to make it a triangle? And he wouldn't let her go or she wanted to have us both or some damnfool thing so I bopped him? You ought to keep away from those comic books, Sawyer."

That way Sawyer had of staring at you without speaking was disconcerting. I don't think it was cultivated—I think it was innate slowness and carefulness of both speech and thought, but it couldn't have been better contrived to make people talk too much. You got jittery under that silent stare and started saying whatever came into your head.

"Say," Jeff exclaimed, "didn't you tell me Amanda Plumb brought up the steaks and buns? She could back us up that we were all planning a steak fry together."

"That's right," I agreed. But I remembered how Axel had warned me not to mention his name to Amanda Plumb or she'd find the errand against regulations.

No comment from the sheriff, but I saw him quietly set down the name, Amanda Plumb, on his note pad. When he spoke to Jeff again, he went back to what he'd apparently ignored earlier.

"Why do you say 'bopped' Dahlberg? He was killed by a knife wound."

"Sure," Jeff agreed, "but any fool could plainly see he'd been hit on the head first. In fact, there was a stray piece of firewood lying just beyond him that probably did the bopping."

Now Sawyer seemed off on another tack altogether.

"Last week, Calhoun, when you thought you were catching cold, did Dr. Tuckerman give you the name of an antihistamine he considered effective?"

Jeff looked as baffled as I felt, but he said:

"Yes, he did."

"Did he write the name down for you on one of his prescription blanks?"

"That's right."

"And did you get the antihistamine he recommended?"

"No," Jeff shrugged. "I threw off the cold with aspirin and then I mislaid the slip."

"When would you say you mislaid it?"

"If I could say when I mislaid it," Jeff pointed out, "I could probably say where. What difference does it make?"

Dan Sawyer stretched out a big hand holding a pale blue slip of paper, scrawled in a doctor's indecipherable writing.

"Is this it?"

"Looks like it." Jeff reached for the slip, but Sawyer slowly put it back in his pocket.

"Where did it turn up?" Jeff asked. "And again, what difference does it make? I didn't knife Axel Dahlberg and neither did I give him an overdose of antihistamine."

The sheriff didn't smile. He said slowly:

"You were right in your theory. If it *was* a theory. That stray piece of firewood has strands of hair caught on it and traces of blood. It's pitch pine and just about heavy enough to kill a man by itself if it was swung hard."

He paused while the silence in the kitchen grew ominous. "And under that piece of pitch pine, Calhoun, my deputy picked up this little slip of paper."

VII

There were no Decoration Day picnics in Glory Cloud that Tuesday. Dan Sawyer let us go home at daylight and I suppose everybody felt the way I did: punchdrunk with fatigue and emotion.

Monday night after our first amazement, Jeff and I had burst forth with explanations for the prescription slip's turning up where it had. Jeff pointed out that, since he had lost it, anybody might have picked it up and placed it where it was found. And, fond as I was of old Dr. Tuckerman, I couldn't help mentioning that he could have written a duplicate and planted it when he was examining the body. I had also expounded my ideas about Nedra Dahlberg. Following the usual pause, Sawyer said soberly:

"Mrs. Dahlberg has been notified and asked to come to Granger for her husband's body. She was at her home in Illinois when my office telephoned at one o'clock this morning."

Then he added: "You feel very bitter toward Axel Dahlberg's wife, don't you, Miss Rawson?"

So all I had accomplished was to deepen his distrust of my affection for Axel.

Sawyer had dismissed us abruptly.

"There will be an inquest in the schoolhouse Wednesday morning at ten. I expect you to be present." And he added:

"You are naturally not to leave Glory Cloud till further notice, not even as far as the Bar Circle T ranch. Special surveillance will not be necessary. Everybody in town will be watching you two."

The reporter from the *Granger Record*, who came up just before noon on Tuesday, was not much interested in the case. Axel Dahlberg had not been a regular resident of either Glory Cloud or Granger; he hadn't even been a Coloradoan. The fishing season had just opened, and I noticed a rod and reel protruding from the back seat of the reporter's jeepster parked in front of the inn. No doubt he intended to wind this up fast and stop along a mountain stream en route back.

There was also the angle, I learned later, of playing down anything that would be poor publicity for the mountain resorts. The summer tourist trade was one of Granger's principal sources of income; the local merchants didn't want potential customers scared away by lurid tales of death in the hills.

Of course, murder was still news, and the Denver papers picked up the story from the wire services. It must have hit the home-town paper Wednesday afternoon because it was that evening I had the long-distance call from Mother, urging me to come home at once.

But late Tuesday morning, as I moved groggily about the kitchen of my cabin, making motions toward breakfast, I wasn't thinking about reporters or about the reaction of my family. I was looking for the breadknife and not finding it. I knew I had used it late yesterday afternoon to split and butter the buns. Where could it have gone?

Then it hit me where it could have gone. And I no longer felt hungry.

A sickening vision presented itself. A vision of that ordinary breadknife being plunged into Axel Dahlberg's prostrate body. And close behind the picture came the question: where would it turn up? I didn't doubt that whoever had borrowed my knife would arrange to have it discovered where it would do me or Jeff the least good.

I jerked open the implement drawer and rummaged frantically. It still wasn't there, and then I missed something else. That super-duper carving knife was gone too—the one with the long, stainless steel blade and the monogrammed silver handle and the transparent plastic sheath protecting the cutting edge. It was a knife I'd pushed to the extreme rear of the drawer and not used at all in my half-hearted cooking efforts; it was a knife worthy at the least of a roast turkey or prime ribs of beef.

For some crazy reason I felt better about two knives being absent. And, remembering something, I went into the living room. The hunting knife in a leather case, which had hung over the fireplace below the snowshoes, was also missing. It was hard to understand why having them all gone seemed so much less sinister.

It was sinister enough, as I soon found out. I had barely swallowed my too-strong coffee when a deputy appeared at the door. It was Henderson, the same one who had chaperoned all of us last night. He said the sheriff wanted to see me.

At the corner by the schoolhouse we met Luella Greenfield scurrying along, a worried frown on her rosy face. She stopped, saying, "Gail, I want to ask you—"

But Henderson's frown matched hers. "No talking till she's seen the sheriff. Sawyer's orders."

At the inn, Henderson guided me to a small, infrequently-used back sitting room on the first floor. Jeff told me later that Sarah raised so much hell about having her kitchen cluttered up that even the sheriff's granite imperturbability had yielded.

Sawyer nodded when we entered and continued his silent contemplation of an extraordinary display of hardware spread out on the old-fashioned library table. An array of knives, from well-worn bone handles to Woolworth's pride, gay with bright enamel. There must have been twenty-five or thirty of them, neatly arranged in little groups, each group tagged to indicate in whose possession it had been found.

Sawyer's tacit philosophy that too many words are wasted in this world had a certain soundness. I got the point at once. My eyes found the implements grouped under my name. And an involuntary sigh of relief escaped me as I saw the missing breadknife. Also the hunting knife, and a saw-toothed old item I'd forgotten all about. But then my muscles tightened again. The super-duper number with its beautifully lethal blade was not there.

I could feel Sawyer's intent blue gaze and I wondered how to dodge what was coming. Did I dare lie to him?

"All there, Miss Rawson?"

I took the plunge. "I guess so. All but the paring knife."

"It would be wise not to guess," Sawyer said. "It would be wise to know."

"It's not my cabin. I've been in it only a few days and I haven't taken a complete inventory."

I could see he wasn't going for that, and I hurried on, sparring for time. "What I wonder is when and how you got hold of all these presumptive weapons."

I should have known he was stringing me along when he answered in a mere matter of seconds. "That wasn't difficult, Miss Rawson. After they came for Dr. Dahlberg's body last night, my other deputy, Murphy, went around to everybody's place while you were all detained here. Dr. Tuckerman helped him."

I thought I'd try beating the sheriff at his own game. I could keep still as long as he could. But I couldn't. I had to come out with what a suspicious circumstance it was that Tuckerman carried keys to everybody's cabin. Sawyer ignored that as he apparently ignored so much of what he heard.

"It would be wiser not to lie, Miss Rawson. You can get in enough trouble by telling the truth."

"Meaning what?"

"Meaning that you're not the first person to look over these knives. Mrs. Greenfield, a friend of the Barlows, has often observed Mr. Barlow carving with an unusually handsome knife. A long, sharp knife with a silver handle. Too handsome a knife for a mountain cabin, in Mrs. Greenfield's opinion. She missed it at once."

My silence now was no game. What was there to say? And I mentally damned Luella Greenfield's gossipy tongue. When we had met her on the way here she must have wanted to ask the question Sawyer now put to me.

"Where have you hidden it, Miss Rawson?"

Patient submissiveness has never been my long suit, and my having tried to deceive him gave me an uneasy conscience that added to my wrath. I exclaimed:

"Talk about injustice! These old-timers probably know down to the last pin what belongs in the Barlow cabin. But what can I, a comparative stranger, come back with? There could be an Indian scalping knife missing from Fay St. Vincent's menage and I wouldn't know it. Or a cute little surgical instrument from Tuckerman's!"

It was no answer and Sawyer didn't accept it as one. He waited.

"You're hunting a particular pine cone in the woods, anyway," I argued. "Why, look at all these abandoned places! Lots of them are just the way they were when their owners walked out—furniture and everything. Anybody could have found a knife in one of those kitchens, used it, put it back and who would ever know the difference? It's a cinch you wouldn't."

Berating Dan Sawyer was like throwing pebbles at Long's Peak. He did blink, however, and then he beckoned to the waiting deputy. I couldn't hear what was said, but I saw Henderson shake his head apologetically.

The sheriff got to his feet in a movement almost swift.

"Let's walk over to Axel Dahlberg's cabin, Miss Rawson."

"What for?"

But he obviously didn't have to inform me what for and he didn't.

It was a golden day with air so crisp and clear it seemed impossible the past three days of fog had ever been. The sky was that uniquely intense blue seen only in the Colorado Mountains, and bits of its color had been caught by the wings of a flock of bluebirds swooping across our path.

But inside Dahlberg's cabin, it was dark and chill and it was somehow shocking to see the bottle of bourbon and three glasses still standing on the little table near the cold fireplace. The sheriff led the way to the kitchen.

Pulling on the overhead light, he loomed ponderous in the cramped little cubicle, looking around in silence. Whoever had

done the re-decorating in the living room hadn't got to the kitch-
en, and it was pretty dismal.

Sawyer spoke softly.

"You're a bright girl, Miss Rawson. Working for your M.A.,
I understand. What would you pick as a likely place to conceal a
missing knife? A place so obvious it might easily be overlooked
till you had time to retrieve it?"

I stared back at him, and I knew with devastating certainty
what was about to happen. There was no use stalling for time.

Hypnotized by the inevitable, I started slowly opening drawers. The third I pulled out was the right one. It was the drawer
containing the eggbeater, the potato masher, the pancake turner,
the measuring spoons. It was the drawer containing, under the
jumble of other implements, a long, sharp carving knife with
a monogrammed silver handle. The protective plastic sheath
was missing, but there was something else on the knife. A faint
brownish stain on the blade, as if it had been used to carve a
deliciously rare beef roast and a careless cook had neglected to
wash it afterward.

I couldn't allow myself the luxury of feeling faint

"Can't you see somebody else must have left that here?" I
said desperately. "You just said I was a bright girl. Would that be
smart of me to use a knife from my own kitchen on Dahlberg and
then leave it virtually in plain sight?"

"It was smart, Miss Rawson," Sawyer said, his voice grimmer
than I'd heard it yet. "We almost missed it. Your mentioning the
kitchens of deserted houses was what reminded me to question
whether this place had been checked."

I don't know why I started to pick up the thing. Sawyer didn't
seem to move fast, but he caught my wrist several inches from
the drawer. His eyes were hard.

"Don't try that again. If there are prints on that handle, I'd
prefer to know they weren't put there just now."

"I only hope there *are* prints," I said.

"Do you?" The sheriff hadn't released my wrist, and his big
fingers were painfully firm, turning my hand over and back,

scrutinizing it carefully. While I stood there bewildered, he dropped my right hand and took my left, to give it the same careful inspection.

"What are you looking for?" I said. "Lady Macbeth to the contrary, one *can* wash blood stains off one's hands, you know."

"Very funny," he said quietly. And he asked: "Don't you ever wear nail polish, Miss Rawson?"

My perplexity must have showed. "Sometimes," I said. "Why?"

"When, for instance?"

"Oh, when I have a heavy date or am going to a big dance or something that seems worth the trouble. When I want to be glamorous."

"And did you want to be glamorous last night? For Axel Dahlberg or for Jeff Calhoun or for both?"

I shook my head wearily. "Mata Hari couldn't have looked glamorous bundled up the way I was. Anyway, it was so cold I wore wool gloves even while we were eating."

Something flickered behind his blank gaze and I realized it had been a mistake to mention gloves. I said:

"Can't we go in the other room and sit down?"

He nodded assent. I felt bleakly empty, but I hadn't quit trying. I ignored the pang when he seated himself in Axel's favorite chair, and I made my voice calmly reasonable.

"Mr. Sawyer," I said carefully, "this thing just doesn't hang together. You've been led to believe that I was in love with Axel Dahlberg. That's not true. I thought a very great deal of Dr. Dahlberg, but it was nothing like love. He was my teacher, my adviser, my friend. Call it a schoolgirl crush on someone I admired tremendously, if you like, but don't call it a love affair. I could name more than one student on our campus who will feel as I do about his death—that we've lost a friend and a leader who won't be easily replaced."

Sawyer's fair-skinned, big face was smoothly expressionless, and he went on listening.

"However," I said, "whether you think I was in love with him or whether you believe the truth, is it logical that I would have been the one to kill him?"

No answer.

"And then there's this attempt to drag Jeff Calhoun into it. You've been told that Jeff and I are in love. That's something it's a little early to say about. Certainly we enjoy each other's company, but that hasn't been made a crime yet, has it? And if I were in love with Jeff, why should he be jealous enough of Axel Dahlberg to kill him? Again, it just isn't logical."

To which Sawyer replied deliberately:

"Crimes of passion aren't usually marked by logic, Miss Rawson. You've made your speech. Now I'll make mine. You cite logic. Let me ask you this. According to your own story, you and Jeff Calhoun were the only two people in this cabin last night—aside from Axel Dahlberg himself—until some time after Dahlberg was killed. You went to the inn to call my office, but Calhoun stayed here. He waited outside on the ground at the west end of the front porch, where he could have observed anybody attempting to enter the cabin either by the front or the back door. After you returned with Dr. Tuckerman, you were all together. Milton Evans was here too. Then I arrived and the place was closely watched from then on."

He paused briefly, continued in even tones.

"Just what would be your logical explanation of how and when any person other than you or Calhoun could have entered that kitchen and placed the murder weapon where we just found it?"

For a wild second I thought, "But maybe it wasn't the murder weapon, at all." Then I remembered the evil discoloration on the blade and I had no answer.

The inquest Wednesday morning was held in the little schoolhouse on the corner. Despite a fire in the pot-bellied stove, a dusty, schoolroom smell still pervaded the dank, long-closed building. I had half expected to go away from there in handcuffs. I could see the headlines: BEAUTIFUL GRADUATE STUDENT KILLS FACULTY PARAMOUR IN MOUNTAIN LOVE NEST.

But before the inquest, something had happened to temper Sawyer's certainty. And he must have passed the word to the coroner. Except for close questioning about the circumstances of Monday evening and the discovery of Dahlberg's body, Jeff and I were treated like everybody else.

The sheriff had rounded up enough Granger County residents from Pinto and Quartz to form a jury, and they were outside the circle of old friendships and old animosities of Glory Cloud. Whatever Sawyer and the coroner may have ascertained from the procedure, all I learned was that nobody could account to the last minute for his time Monday night.

After dinner at the inn there'd been the usual bridge game till shortly before nine. When it broke up, Dr. Tuckerman had walked home with Fay St. Vincent, but had left her at the door. Luella Greenfield had walked with them as far as the corner above her place, the corner where the Barlow cabin stood, and then turned down the half-block to her own house. Sarah Walker insisted she had washed dishes all evening. Milton Evans had thought a moonlight stroll before bedtime would relax his nerves. (Here we had a digression of five minutes while Milt instructed the jury on the beneficial effects of relaxation.) He had returned to the inn just after I had been there to call the sheriff. The main direction of his walk had been along the seldom-used road to Pinto.

I was surprised to see Amanda Plumb at the inquest, but of course she was in Glory Cloud daily and knew everybody. My respect for Sawyer's thoroughness increased, although I thought he was wasting it on Amanda. According to her story, she had driven to Denver late Monday afternoon to shop, had eaten dinner there alone and attended a movie, returning to Granger around midnight.

Jeff and I knew that Dahlberg had been killed between nine and ten Monday evening. The coroner corroborated this. So it boiled down to the fact that nobody had much of an alibi for that time. Jeff and I came the closest to having one, but I knew the sheriff wasn't taking our word about each other.

The coroner even questioned old Charlie, which was ridiculous on the face of it, and found that Monday evening a man from the state old age pension department had called on Charlie from eight o'clock to a little after ten. So I guess Charlie had the only real alibi in the lot, but who cared?

Both Fay St. Vincent's silver comb and the prescription slip Tuckerman had given Jeff were introduced as evidence, but there wasn't enough to go with either to make it conclusive. Jeff testified that he'd mislaid the slip, and Fay said sweetly that those little combs were always slipping loose, that they were apt to turn up anywhere. You could tell from the jurors' faces that the St. Vincent name still carried prestige in these parts.

No mention was made of the silver-handled carving knife. I wondered about that. I wondered whether there had been fingerprints, whether that was why Dan Sawyer had eased off Jeff and me, whether he knew something he was holding back till he found more to substantiate it. The afternoon before, an expert had driven up from Granger to get everyone's prints.

It took the jury less than ten minutes to decide that Axel Dahlberg had been murdered, and that they didn't know who had done it.

Following the adjournment, I felt a hand on my elbow, and turning, I saw Luella Greenfield.

"I must talk to you, Gail," she said in a low voice, and she drew me into the far corner.

I thought, "You're the one who blabbed to the sheriff about the Barlows' knife."

But she was too wrapped up in her problem, whatever it was, to sense my antagonism. "Listen, Gail, did you give Dr. Dahlberg that folder about the narrow gauge? You know, the one I said he could borrow but not to tell Fay?"

It required prodigious effort to remember what she was talking about. That had been so many years ago. And it seemed so unimportant now.

"Why yes," I said. "I gave it to him Saturday night right after you gave it to me."

Luella's frown deepened. "Have you mentioned it to the sheriff?"

Luella really took to heart her cultural responsibilities as caretaker for the Hazlitt cabin. But I saw a chance to give her a dig. "No," I said, "I haven't. I'm not like some people who tell him everything that comes into their heads."

Luella flushed and was starting to expostulate when Henderson approached. I saw then that everyone else had gone except Sawyer and Jeff.

"The meeting's over, Mrs. Greenfield," Henderson said. "And the sheriff wants to talk with Miss Rawson."

Luella clamped her mouth into an offended little knot and scuttled out. The deputy closed the door behind her, and the sheriff motioned for Jeff and me to sit down again at desks in the front row.

Sawyer stared at us somberly, and for the first time I identified the difference I had sensed in him this morning. There was actually human emotion flickering behind that pale blue gaze. He had been impassive during the inquest, but now I saw he was quietly smoldering.

"Somebody," he said slowly, "is trying to make a horse's neck out of me. If I thought it was you two, I'd—"

The sheriff's suppressed wrath gave him the look of a lumbering mountain bear trapped in a dead-end ravine; it was a dangerous look.

I was dying to ask a question. Finally, timidly, I came out with it. "Were there any fingerprints on that knife handle, Mr. Sawyer?"

That seemed an innocent inquiry, but his look of outrage intensified.

"No, there were no fingerprints. The handle had been wiped clean. The blade itself lacked a full inch of being long enough to inflict the wound, even if it had been thrust in as far as possible. Dr. Bailey swears to that."

"Then it wasn't the murder weapon at all! But—"

"Exactly, Miss Rawson. But! But you saw blood stains on the blade. As I did. Now who around here thinks I'm so dumb I wouldn't have that blood checked?"

"Wrong type, huh?" Jeff put in. The heavy, bear-like gaze swung to him.

"Calhoun," the sheriff said, "it wasn't even human blood! That's what burns me up. To think anybody would rate my intelligence and my efficiency so low they'd expect me to swallow a plant like that."

In his wounded pride Dan Sawyer looked dangerous, but he also looked younger. I even found it possible to pity him for this insult to his acuteness.

"That smart-aleck trick, whoever did it," he said, "gives you two a stay of execution, so to speak. I don't say you're in the clear because you're not. But it's the first real indication that somebody is trying to plant evidence on you. It was a stupid try, but a murderer usually does something stupid before he's through."

I couldn't see why the sheriff wanted Jeff and me to go with him that evening, up to the spot where we'd picnicked Monday night. But we didn't argue. We went.

Shortly after dinner, he loaded us into his station wagon, along with Henderson, and chugged slowly up the Alpine road to the Glory Cloud mine turn-off. I shouldn't have cared to drive my car over that rough trail back to the fire-site, but his belonged to the county.

When we reached the circle of blackened stones, Sawyer ordered us out, the deputy remaining with the car. It was very nearly the hour we'd been there Monday evening, and it was hard to take the memory of Axel Dahlberg lounging by the fire, making his lightly caustic comments on life and people. Off in the woods a whip-poor-will called, and all the wild night noises of the hills were beginning to murmur.

The sheriff made us go over in detail just what we'd done, where we'd sat and stood, even what we'd had to eat. But there's little to distinguish one steak-fry in the mountains from another; I don't know what he hoped to learn.

Then we had to walk up to the lookout point from which we'd viewed the plains. Everybody who picnicked at this spot also looked at the view, so that hardly seemed significant.

Jeff mentioned that if either of us had wanted Dahlberg out of the way, a shove from that eminence would have been ideally simple. Sawyer's reply was a noncommittal grunt, but on our flashlighted way back to the car he said:

"Don't crowd your luck, Calhoun. There's nothing humorous about murder."

When the station wagon stopped in front of the inn, Sarah Walker peered out the door.

"Long distance has been trying to get you, Miss Rawson. You're to call Operator Seven in Denver."

It was Mother, of course, and she was wild. Sarah had simply told her the sheriff had taken me some place, and had let her draw her own conclusions. After I'd assured her I was really all right and not in jail at all, she seemed to feel better. But it took a lot of soothing noises on my part, and I sighed wearily as I finally hung up.

"You're tired and why not?" Jeff said. "I'll take you home so you can get some sleep."

Sawyer looked at us, and he didn't say we could leave, and he didn't say we couldn't, so we went out into the before-moonrise darkness. At the door of my cabin Jeff said:

"I'll see that you're in all right and then be on my way."

He reached in, snapped the switch beside the door. Then he took a quick step inside, giving a sharp exclamation. I pushed him aside to enter myself.

The place was a shambles. Every drawer, cupboard, closet, nook and cranny had been ransacked, but good. And I seethed at my first thought that the sheriff had taken us on that fool's errand while his second deputy, Murphy, made such a mess out of my cabin.

But this was none of Dan Sawyer's work.

VIII

Jeff and I goggled at the wreckage. Then we moved slowly through the rest of the cabin, confirming that every room was as storm-struck as the kitchen. Not till Jeff bent to look under the beds on the porch did I realize he was also making sure the intruder had left. When he rose, he walked to the unused door at the end of the porch.

"The lock's been forced," he said.

I had been assuming the sheriff's deputy had borrowed a key from Dr. Tuckerman, and I had been planning to give Sawyer a piece of my mind about his methods. It outraged me to think of a stranger pawing through my belongings, even dragging bottles out of the medicine cabinet. But if it hadn't been Murphy, who had it been? I was abruptly less annoyed and more frightened.

"Maybe you should take a room at the inn for tonight," Jeff said. I was weighing that possibility when a sharp, imperious little knock fell on the kitchen door.

"I'll go," Jeff said quickly, striding toward the door with an air of being ready for anything.

But it was only Luella Greenfield, smiling, her bright old eyes widening with amazement.

"Why, I never!"

She marched in, her inquisitive glance sweeping everything.

"What in the world—?"

"Somebody must have been looking for more evidence to plant," I said, forgetting the sheriff's injunction not to talk about the phony knife business. Then I remembered and added weakly, "Unless it was that other deputy—Murphy—and Sawyer sent him."

But Luella shook her head. "Oh, no. You mean that young one with the glasses who's been staying around Dr. Dahlberg's cabin? No, he couldn't have done it because he went to Granger tonight. His wife is having a baby and her brother came up and got him so he could be at the hospital. Right after you children left with Mr. Sawyer."

I wondered how Luella kept track of everyone's goings and comings, and I wondered who else had known when Murphy left.

"Well, you just come home and stay with me tonight, you poor child," Luella said. "I've been wanting to talk to you anyway and I wouldn't rest easy for one minute to think of you here all by yourself and that robber maybe coming back. Goodness! I don't know what it's coming to when people go around breaking down doors and messing into your private belongings and killing each other." She shuddered. "Poor Dr. Dahlberg. Who do you think could have killed him?"

Obviously a rhetorical question. She added slyly, "Dear me, I suppose that now Dr. Dahlberg is dead you won't be staying the summer out, after all. I mean, it was his idea for you to come here, wasn't it? I mean you were such good friends and all—that is—"

She floundered around in the implications she didn't quite dare voice.

"Why shouldn't I stay? I'm barely started on my thesis research. Furthermore, I intend to take over Mr. Dahlberg's material and finish the book as a tribute to him."

Jeff and Luella looked startled. I felt startled myself. Such an idea had been furthest from my mind when I started talking; I had only wanted to cut her off short. But as soon as I'd voiced it, the thought took hold of my imagination. Why not? I knew Axel had most of the research finished, had the book outlined by chapters and some of the writing done. I couldn't do the job that Axel would have, but at least all his work wouldn't be wasted.

"Oh my!" Luella twittered, "wait till certain people hear that!" She looked half of a mind to rush out right now and start spreading the word. And she added staunchly, "Not that *I* have any objection, child. I think it's a very sweet thought."

What Jeff thought of my brainstorm he didn't say, but he did suggest that I accept Luella's invitation.

"I'll go tell Sawyer what's happened here," he said.

I'd already been worn to a nub before this latest shock. Now I felt paralyzed, and I welcomed Luella's suggestion of coffee. I sat limply by her kitchen table while she bustled around, measuring water, getting date bars out of a canister.

"Maybe we can talk now without one of those old deputies interrupting," she said. Her sharp little face looked solemn and worried, as it had after the inquest.

"It's about that folder," she went on. "You're sure you gave it to Dr. Dahlberg Saturday night?"

Here we go again, I thought drearily. I nodded.

"And have you seen it since? Do you know what he did with it?"

"I haven't seen it. I suppose he put it with the rest of his background material. Why?"

Luella didn't answer my question. She said peevishly, "I went down there this afternoon to see if I could find it, but the deputy wouldn't let me in. Said it was sheriff's orders."

I thought she was making a lot out of a very little. I said: "What difference does it make? What's so important about it, anyway?"

"That's just it," she fretted. "I don't *know* whether it's important. I want to see it again and decide. Besides, it belongs in the Hazlitt cabin and Fay wouldn't like its being gone and I'm responsible to the State Historical Society." She poured coffee. "I wish I'd had more time to talk to Dr. Dahlberg."

"Didn't you have a chance to see him Sunday or Monday?" I asked. "It looked to me as if he was talking to everyone in town."

"Well," she said carefully, "I talked with him just a little bit early Sunday afternoon, but I couldn't tell him what he wanted to know. He said he'd see me again after he'd done more research. He said not to tell anybody what I'd asked him till he got more information."

I decided Luella was badly confused. In the same breath she said Dahlberg had asked her something and that she'd been questioning him.

"Then," she went on, "Monday morning I thought of something, and I went over to Milton Evans' place to see whether I could catch Dr. Dahlberg there—he had said he was going over to talk to Milt. But he had just left, and Milt was busy bossing old Charlie, and just as good as told me to run along and tend to my knitting." She sniffed indignantly.

"For my money," I said, "Evans is a pain in the neck anyway."

Luella sniffed again. "He's just a common crook!"

"How do you mean?"

"I mean just what I say." Luella pushed back her cup, picked up her eternal embroidery. "A common crook. Oh, Julius let him off easy because he was only a boy, but Fay knows, of course, and that's why she's never had any use for Milt Evans, for all his smart-aleck airs and his pretending to know everything about everything."

"I don't know what you're talking about," I said. "You mean Julius St. Vincent?"

"Well, of course. It was Julius who gave him his start, and Milt could probably have been managing the St. Vincent interests today if he'd minded his p's and q's. Her father left Fay all that money, you know," she added resentfully. "Fay can afford a mountain place with three bathrooms, even if the pipes do freeze up every winter."

"You mean Fay's father gave Evans his start in the insurance business?"

"Oh, no, child, that was later, when Milt had to get out and shift for himself. Julius thought a lot of that boy and he was awfully disappointed the way things turned out."

"Why don't you start at the beginning? I don't know all these people as well as you do, and it's hard for me to keep things straight."

"Well, let me see." Luella put down her fancywork and closed her eyes, concentrating. "Milt is about the same age as my Nellie, and she was forty-seven this spring—born in 1903. And Milt must have been sixteen when he managed to attract Julius St. Vincent's notice. So that would make it around 1919, wouldn't it? He was always a fresh-acting young sprig, and I used to tell Jeb I didn't see how Julius could stand having him around. Why, when Milt was just a squirt he used to call Julius by his first name all the time—thought it was smart. I'd have boxed his ears!"

"That's our boy," I murmured.

"But I guess Milt was bright," she said reluctantly. "Never any brighter than he thought he was, but he skipped grades and that sort of thing, and he used to help in his dad's office before Julius got interested in him. Milt's father was a real estate man in Granger, and he handled mountain property and rentals too, so they were up here a lot and they owned a cabin where they stayed most of the time during the summers. Milt must have had a sharp head for business or Julius St. Vincent wouldn't have taken to him."

"But he did take to him?"

"That's right. Julius took Milt under his wing—made a business protégé out of him. Julius didn't have any son to fuss over, and even after Fay got engaged to Gilbert Hazlitt you could tell Hazlitt would never be any help to Julius—he was an artist and probably couldn't even balance his own check book. I suppose Julius was looking for a sharp young fellow he could train to help him in all the businesses he was mixed up in by then. Jeb always said he thought Mr. St. Vincent was grooming Milt to be his personal assistant. He gave him summer jobs at first and used him as an errand boy, but all the time he kept pushing Milt and giving him a little more responsibility. For a while Milton Evans was just like one of the St. Vincent family—and if you think that didn't go to his head! I remember one Decoration Day—it was in 1921—when we all had a picnic and went over to the Tuckermans' afterward—that was just a week or so before poor B. J. shot himself—and Milton acted so cocky all evening—just a high school kid, you know—that B. J. finally had to squelch him since Julius wouldn't. Milt sulked around, but several of us were glad to see him get his come-uppance for once."

"Did Milton go to college then? And did St. Vincent help him?"

"Oh, not financially. Milt's father could afford to send him, though of course the money Milt made working for Julius helped. But Mr. St. Vincent advised him what to take—business courses, and so on—and kept an eye on him. I guess Milt was in several scrapes, but he always wriggled out, and when he finished college he started to work full-time in Julius' Denver office."

"That would have been—?"

"The summer of '25 when he started. But that fall our smart young man just plain outsmarted himself. He'd always been too big for his britches, and it was just like him to think he could put something over on Julius St. Vincent."

"What did he do?"

"I don't know that I can just rightly explain it. Jeb understood it and he tried to make it clear to me, but I never was too good at understanding business. Jeb said it was something that would have been within the law, if it worked, but if it didn't work, it would have looked mighty bad for Julius St. Vincent. He was always awfully proud of his reputation for fair-dealing, you know, and he couldn't stand for that sort of thing."

My let-down after the build-up was terrific. I said quizzically: "But you're sure it was something crooked?"

"Oh, it was crooked right enough!" Luella was firm. "You know how those things are in business—if you get away with something, it's just smart business, but if you don't get away with it, it's crooked. Jeb said all that was wrong was Milt's timing."

It sounded to me as if Jeb hadn't disapproved quite as wholeheartedly as Luella, but it was getting late and in my opinion her yarn had fizzled out. I stood up, yawning, and stretched.

"And this is the night I was going to turn in early." My arms were still raised in a luxurious stretch when the scream came, shrill and high-pitched, a woman's voice crying out in anguish. I froze, arms rigid above my head. The cry came again.

Luella wasn't frightened. But she didn't laugh at me. "I know," she said, "doesn't it sound awful? Just a mountain lion, my dear, but you would think some poor woman was being murdered. Oh dear, I shouldn't have said that—I mean—"

"A mountain lion! But aren't they dangerous?"

"Oh, no, mountain lions aren't dangerous unless they're cornered. They're awful cowards. Coyotes are cowardly too, but even they are bolder than a cougar."

I thought there was just too damned much wildlife in these hills.

"Those coyotes have more nerve than you'd think sometimes," Luella was saying. "I keep a few old hens out here in back so I can have fresh eggs during the summer. When I leave I sell them to Sarah for stewing. And the other day—Monday afternoon I guess it was—one of those little rascals came right up to the shed and killed a nice fat hen. One of my best layers. He was bold, you see, because of the fog."

"Did you catch him at it?"

"They're too sly for that. I hurried out as soon as I heard the squawking, but I was too late. He dropped what was left behind the shed, but all I saw of Mr. Coyote was just his tracks."

I said slowly, "Axel Dahlberg used to say that all life was a struggle for survival in one way or another. He always said man was the most predatory of all the animals and the most ruthless."

And the question that I had been brooding over floated like an evil underwater growth to the surface of my consciousness again. What crafty animal of the human species had lain in wait for Axel Monday night, using the dark shadows for concealment as Luella's Mr. Coyote had used the fog?

It took most of the day Thursday to get my cabin back into livable order. Sawyer had been as loquacious as usual when he surveyed the chaos, but he made me wait till the fingerprint man came up again Thursday morning before he okayed my dealing with the mess. He also asked me to check whether anything was missing, but nothing was. Nothing that I knew of.

I kept getting mad again as I worked. My typewriter out of its case, my notes rummaged through, all my clean underwear in a heap on the floor, pillow slips torn off pillows—it had been a thorough search and a fast one.

Late afternoon found the place in a semblance of order and
me the mess. I was trying to choose which to have first—a Coke
or a bath—when Jeff appeared.

"I came to make you a proposition." He grinned.

"Why, Mr. Calhoun—please!"

"I know how strong your convictions about square-dancing
are," he said, "but the mad social whirl of Glory Cloud doesn't
offer much to choose from. Old Charlie's playing for a dance
tonight at the Bar Circle T, and I think a change of scene is just
what the doctor ordered."

"Never mind the doctor's orders," I said. "What about the
sheriff's?"

"I asked him," Jeff replied, "and he gave me a snap decision.
After pondering only fifteen minutes he said okay."

I fished a couple of Cokes out of the refrigerator. "Sounds
like a big night," I said. "Jumping around like a jackrabbit—
making a fool of myself right in front of God and everybody."

"It's not that bad," Jeff said.

"That's a long hike over there."

"Ah, but wait till you hear. I wheedled Sarah into letting us
use the station wagon."

"It's a conspiracy," I said. "I'm trapped."

But I wasn't as reluctant as I pretended, and when Jeff left,
I started rummaging in my closet. I was hunting that red plaid
gingham I'd bought in a moment of madness. Not my style at
all—too demure and ruffly—but just the ticket for this evening's
function.

I was pleasantly surprised when I climbed into the gingham
number after my shower. I adjusted a flounce and revolved in
front of the mirror, the full skirt whirling. Pretty darned girlish,
but rather fetching. I found a narrow red ribbon for my hair and,
watching my hands in the mirror, I remembered Sawyer's questions about nail polish.

Feeling in some obscure way that I'd show him, I went to
the medicine cabinet and dug out a bottle of polish to match
the ribbon. In the melee last night it had been spilled, but there
was enough left for one quick coat. Applying it, I returned to

brooding over Axel's death and the sheriff's suspicions. And I wondered again why Luella was so upset about that filing folder. I wondered whether the folder had any bearing on last night's devastating search of my cabin. My anger came back and this time I got mad enough to take action.

When Jeff knocked at the door I opened it with fire in my eye, waving my hands to dry the polish. He was sporting a gaudy flannel shirt and a silver-buckled Western belt over tight blue jeans. When he saw me he whistled wolfishly.

"Gosh, you look cute, baby."

"Never mind the guff," I said. "I have a proposition for you this time."

"I accept."

"Wait till you hear what it is. Are they still watching Dahlberg's cabin?"

"No. That young deputy is still down in Granger at the hospital and Sawyer and Henderson drove to Pinto an hour ago."

"Okay," I said, "sit down while I tell you something. There's no rush about this brawl at the Bar Circle T, is there?"

"Well, Charlie said he wouldn't be there himself till about eight-thirty. But I thought since we had a car for once we might want to stop somewhere and admire the view."

He leered.

"Business before pleasure," I said, and I gave him my ideas on the subject of the filing folder Luella was so exercised about. I told him how I'd come across it, how reluctant she had been to have it leave the cabin and how insistent that Fay St. Vincent shouldn't know, how Luella had quizzed me about it repeatedly.

"And look," I added, "maybe it *is* important. Don't ask me why or how. Maybe the person who ransacked this place last night thought I still had that folder."

"What was in it, anyhow?" he asked. "Did you read the stuff?"

"I told you what was in it. Papers about the Granger, Glory Cloud & Western. Clippings. A few pix. No, I didn't actually read it—just riffled through fast. I didn't notice anything to get in such a stew over."

"And your proposition?"

"On the way to the ranch," I said, "let's stop at Dahlberg's cabin and see what this is all about. I'm sure he would have kept it with his other research material—maybe we could lift it temporarily, look it over at our leisure. Sawyer doesn't know anything about it, according to Luella."

"The woman tempted me." He shook his head. "I have an awful feeling it isn't smart, but I'll string along. But I don't think we should snitch it. We had better just give it a fast once-over there and get out."

I agreed and we went out to the car. The sharp night air smelled of pine-wood fires and the breeze carried the scent of living pines. The moon hadn't yet risen, and we drove the short distance to Dahlberg's cabin through Glory Cloud's Stygian darkness. The headlights cut the blackness like giant flashlights, but beyond their range everything was shrouded and still. Reaching Dahlberg's cabin, Jeff swung the station wagon around in back, although there wasn't a real road there—only a couple of worn-down ruts.

"Just as well to have the car out of sight," he murmured, switching off the lights.

We sat there in the cold and the dark for a long silent moment and my enthusiasm left me.

"I never thought about how we'd get in," I said. "The place is probably locked up tighter than the Denver mint."

But, once started, Jeff was not one to back down. "I've noticed that back door," he said quietly. "Any skeleton key will do it, and it just so happens I have one." He handed me a small flashlight, remarking it would be better if we each carried one.

Still aware of an odd reluctance, I followed him as quietly as possible over the uneven, rocky ground. As Jeff had predicted, the back door creaked open at the first try. If anything was amiss in the dismal little kitchen, we didn't stop to notice. The filing folder would probably be on Axel's desk in the living room; we groped our way on in there.

Jeff was ahead of me and as he swung his light around the room I heard him swear softly.

"We're too late," he said. "Somebody else knew the place wasn't guarded tonight."

Axel Dahlberg's vacant cabin had been subjected to as complete and devastating search as had mine And I shivered as an
inexplicable but urgent impression came to me: that whoever
had done it had been there a very short time before.

"Let's get out of here." I clutched Jeff's arm. "It'll be gone
now, anyway."

But he had to get stubborn. "We might as well make sure."

The quickest way to move him would be to prove that the
filing folder was missing. I walked to the table Axel had used as
a desk and started pawing through the heaped disarray of papers
and notebooks. I swept one corner clear, and as I finished looking over each handful of notes I placed it on the rejected pile. My
hands felt moist and faintly trembling. Having to hold the light
in one hand and work with the other didn't help.

Jeff was examining the bookshelves beside the fireplace. We
worked doggedly for some time before he muttered something.

"What is it?" I asked.

He flicked his light over the shelves. "Whoever was here
didn't get through. See how jumbled everything is on the shelves
this side of the fireplace? But on the other side the shelves are
still neat and orderly."

So I had been right in feeling we had all but surprised the
intruder. I was aware of a choking sensation, but I continued the
search. Time passed—perhaps twenty minutes, perhaps forty. I
had been so sure the folder concerning the Granger, Glory Cloud
& Western would be missing that when it turned up I stared at it
stupidly, incredulous. Then I whispered, "Jeff! I found it."

He was beside me in a swift motion. "Well, look inside, baby.
See whether there's anything that's worth all this."

As I flipped it open a stealthy sound caught my ear. I stood
rigid, listening. Jeff heard it too—a heavy foot trying to walk
lightly on the squeaky front porch. Jeff's light was out in an
instant and I doused mine. I could feel my heart pounding, and
Jeff's big hands hurt my shoulders as he thrust me behind him.

That was all we had time for. The front door yielded to a key,
swung open. There was the snap of a light switch, and we stood

blinking in the sudden overhead glare, like rabbits caught in a car's headlights.

All I felt at first was relief. The panic came later.

Dan Sawyer stood in the open door, the stolidity of his big face hardening to anger.

"How will you two talk yourselves out of this one?" he asked.

IX

Sawyer advanced deliberately, one big hand casual on his holstered gun. A curt nod directed Jeff to Axel's big chair and me to the one by the desk. Standing with legs apart, he looked us over. His cold gaze circled the disheveled room; a muscle tightened in his jaw.

"I *thought* that dance gag was a stall," he said. "I figured if I gave you a little rope, you might tie yourselves up with it."

"Now look, Sawyer—" Jeff began, but the sheriff growled: "Shut up! You talk too much!"

I could see Jeff's temper rising, but he shut up. Sawyer had that baited grizzly look again. He intended to dope this out for himself, in his own good time, and he wasn't going to be heckled in the process. He added slowly:

"And I don't like liars. Gail Rawson should have told you that, Calhoun."

"I wasn't lying. We *are* going over to the Bar Circle T."

Sawyer's glance ran over Jeff's gaudy shirt, my flouncy frock.

"You mean you *were* going—maybe. Now you're not going anywhere except to my office at the inn. Possibly down to Granger."

I pleaded, "Honestly, Mr. Sawyer, we didn't make all this mess. It was this way when we came."

He looked at me, and I knew he was remembering how I'd tried to fool him before. "Honestly, Miss Rawson," he mimicked, "and I suppose you didn't make all that mess in your own cabin last night to set the stage for this."

I gasped. "I certainly did not. What do you think—?"

"I think it's very strange that my fingerprint man found no distinguishable prints in that cabin except yours and Calhoun's. And I think, if you wanted to make a good story of it, you would have been smarter to claim something was missing."

"Speaking of stories," I said, "would you care for an explanation of what we're doing here?"

Sawyer's expression said he had his own ideas, but that he would listen.

I told him about the filing folder, including my discovery of it in the Hazlitt cabin, Luella Greenfield's reluctance to have it lent Dahlberg, her recent perturbation over its whereabouts, my conclusion that it must contain something significant, my resolve to discover what that could be.

"And I think," I added, "that's what the person who ransacked my cabin was looking for. He or she couldn't get in here to search and there was an outside chance Dahlberg might have given it back to me."

Face skeptical, the sheriff heard me out, then shook his big blond head.

"You're reaching, Miss Rawson," he said flatly. "You're reaching too far. I've heard of the Granger, Glory Cloud & Western, of course, although it was before my time and I don't know much about it. But why would anybody choose right now—thirty years later—to get steamed up and start ransacking cabins because of a filing folder that has been available all the time? A folder containing only what was common knowledge anyway?"

Put that way, it sounded thin.

One big paw picked up the folder from the desk. Then he grunted and bent to retrieve something from the floor under the table. He glanced briefly at what he'd picked up and shoved it into his pocket.

He shook his head again. "It doesn't wash. You claim this place was worked over before you arrived, that the same person went through your stuff last night, that whoever did it was after this folder. Then why is it still here?"

"Because it hadn't yet been found," Jeff said. "Because we came along and interrupted." He pointed out how the fireplace marked the division line where the search had abruptly stopped.

"Yes," Sawyer said, "there was an interruption. I was it." As yielding as a granite boulder. He added: "When you were caught Miss Rawson noticed this folder and she dreamed up the first thing she could. Very ingenious. Very improbable."

He motioned us to the door.

At least it was warmer in Sawyer's back-parlor office at the inn than in Dahlberg's closed-up cabin. Milton Evans was sitting by the big fireplace, and we could hear Sarah Walker moving around the kitchen. But Sawyer and Henderson herded us along as if we might make a sudden break for freedom. The deputy closed and locked the door.

Sawyer sat down heavily behind the table, staring at my hands. When he looked up, our eyes met. It was the first time he'd smiled tonight, and I'd rather he hadn't. It was a smug smile, and his voice was gentle, almost purring.

"Being glamorous tonight, I see. Very pretty, isn't it, Calhoun? How could you say nail polish is too much trouble when the effect is so charming, Miss Rawson?"

His manner had a craftiness that made me think, not of a lumbering bear, but of the smooth ripple of powerful muscles under the skin of a mountain cat.

"It *is* a lot of trouble," I said slowly, "to get it on evenly. And it's hard to keep it looking decent."

"How is that?"

"It chips. It cracks and peels and then it looks awful."

Sawyer nodded gravely. "It flakes off, doesn't it? And when it starts that, you're apt to scrape at it with the nails of your other hand, the way a kid will worry a skinned knee."

"No. I can't stand tacky-looking nail polish. When it starts to chip I take it all off with polish remover."

"But if you were absent-minded and nervous, you might pick at it without thinking."

"I suppose so."

"Now you claim you weren't wearing nail polish Monday night?"

Unreasonable panic constricted my breathing.

"You saw enough of me Monday night. Do you remember nail polish, chipped or otherwise, on my hands?"

"I don't remember. I wasn't interested then."

"Why are you so interested now, if I may ask?"

"You may," he said with heavy satisfaction. "And I'll tell you. I've become interested since we discovered tiny flecks of a bright red, enamel-like substance caught in the rough wool of Axel Dahlberg's lumberjack. Need I tell you where on the jacket those traces were found, Miss Rawson? Right where it was slashed by a knife-thrust."

I don't know what protests or denials I might have made if a knock hadn't sounded. Scowling with annoyance, Sawyer gestured for Henderson to open the door.

Milt Evans stood there, his smile a nice blend of the ingratiating and the patronizing, his voice oily.

"I just thought, sheriff, that you might like some assistance. I'm an older man than you are and I've been around. If these youngsters are giving you any trouble, I've had considerable experience—"

Sawyer's wordless scrutiny would have warned anyone less insulated by his own conceit. Under the fair skin, color rose in the sheriff's face, and when he spoke his voice was ominously gentle.

"When you have a leaky pipe in your kitchen do you call a plumber, Evans, or do you fix it yourself?"

Evans looked nonplussed. "Why, I call a plumber. I—"

"And when he gets there, do you stand around telling him how to do his work?"

"Well, sure. I know quite a bit—" He broke off, flushing as he met the sheriff's lifted brows. Sawyer nodded toward the door.

"When I want your help, Evans, I'll ask for it."

Milt Evans slid out, muttering.

Sawyer picked up where he'd left off. But we'd had a breather in which to rally, and now we argued.

Jeff mentioned opportunity and reminded the sheriff that nobody in Glory Cloud could account for the time during which Dahlberg was killed, that if we'd had lethal intentions, our golden opportunity was earlier.

"Why wouldn't we have done away with him right there at the steak fry," Jeff demanded, "leaving his body hidden in the woods?"

And I bore down on motive, pointing out that, although he insisted on regarding the murder as a crime of passion, his analysis of the motive was foggy. "Hatred can be passionate, too," I said, "and fear. You've made so much of Jeff's little row with Dahlberg—don't you know Axel had been rowing with everybody in town?"

"Nice guy," Sawyer murmured and I bit my lip.

We talked ourselves hoarse. The knife from my cabin had been a plant—he had admitted that. The prescription slip had been a plant. We were being framed. His eyes said he had heard that one before. How about Fay St. Vincent's comb? How about Tuckerman's trying to conceal it? How about whatever Sawyer had picked up from the floor of Dahlberg's cabin tonight?

At the last question Sawyer pulled a card from his pocket, tossed it on the desk. We both bent to look: a Texaco credit card made out to Amanda Plumb, the expiration date May 31.

"You've both been in Amanda Plumb's car with her," Sawyer said. "You rode up from Granger with her, Miss Rawson, and the next day she gave you both a lift to the Bar Circle T."

I said disgustedly, "And we were planning our crime of passion several days ahead, so we just snitched Amanda's credit card in case it might come in handy."

"In all this chatter," Sawyer said, "I haven't heard any explanation of those flecks of nail polish."

"I wasn't wearing nail polish Monday night and that's that," I said. "Why don't you ask other people whether I was wearing it?"

"You didn't eat at the inn. And between the time Dahlberg was killed and everybody saw you over here, you had more than enough time to use polish remover."

"Doing that would mean I was aware of its wisdom," I retorted. "Wouldn't it have been simpler to whip out a clothes brush and brush off Dahlberg's lumberjack?"

Another knock sounded on the door. I pitied Milt Evans if he'd come to offer more gratuitous advice. It was Milt, but he was coldly dignified.

"Granger wants you on the phone, Mr. Sawyer. It's urgent."

The sheriff went toward the dining room, leaving us under Henderson's wary eye. In five minutes he was back, looking gloomy. He picked up a pigskin briefcase, shoved papers inside. Pausing, he glanced at the deputy.

"Bates Mercantile was broken into and robbed this evening."

Henderson whistled.

"Yeah," Sawyer said. "When it's the mayor's store, you go."

My heart sank as I saw the filing folder disappear into the briefcase. The sheriff closed the case, sat looking at Jeff and me. I knew he was pondering whether to take us along, and I believed I knew the answer. I was so sure that I thought I must be hearing wrong when he finally said to Henderson:

"Can you keep these two on ice till I get back?"

Henderson rubbed his jaw and reckoned he could manage. I hardly noticed Sawyer's instructions about what we were and were not to do. I felt the way I had Monday afternoon when the three-day fog lifted and I'd seen blue sky again.

I couldn't understand why he'd done it. Put us on ice, I mean, instead of in the can. I had to see a lot more of Dan Sawyer and know him a lot better before I understood what kept us out of jail that night. It was the stubborn, basic slowness with which he accepted ideas. It was that deliberation with which his mind walked around a problem, looking it over from all angles, weighing, discarding, insisting on proving to its own satisfaction the verity of the obvious. When Sawyer appeared to leap to a conclusion, it was only an appearance.

I knew that night he felt virtually certain of our guilt. But virtually wasn't good enough. He was holding out for absolutely. I think, too, he wanted to see justice done, but I don't think that was the prime factor; I think Sawyer himself was helpless against the way his mind inexorably worked. But once he achieved absolute certainty, heaven help you. It was like the mills of the gods.

But all I felt immediately was that the cavalry had galloped up in the nick of time. And after my first relief I was annoyed. Sawyer had pounded away at us while the person who killed Dahlberg no doubt sat back chuckling. And now Sawyer left the whole thing hanging fire to run look after the affairs of the mayor's store. Politics!

I knew I was being choosey about the teeth of a gift horse. But just the same it griped me and I said as much to Jeff when we were alone.

That wasn't right away. Henderson had tagged along on our silent walk to my place. At the door I invited Jeff in for a bedtime snack. The deputy started to protest, then shrugged, pulling a pipe from his pocket.

Cheese and milk were in the refrigerator, crackers on a shelf. I slammed the cupboard door and I said, "How about that! Sawyer charges off to take care of the mayor's store while a murderer goes merrily on his way!"

"We're lucky, Gail," Jeff said soberly.

"Oh, I know that. But it still isn't right. What if we were actually guilty?"

"It's an old feud between the hills and the towns in this county," Jeff said. "The mountain communities think that Granger and other sizable towns in the county get a disproportionate share for their tax dollars because the towns have the concentration of population. Population equals voters."

He cut a slice of cheese. "But that's not our worry, Gail. Sawyer isn't through with us just because he's gone. He'll be back soon."

"But what can we do? I know I didn't kill Axel Dahlberg and I'm reasonably sure you didn't. Can innocent people be railroaded this way?"

"You'd be surprised," Jeff said. "Baby, there's only one thing left to do. Try to find out who did kill him."

I looked at Jeff Calhoun and I couldn't say I cared much for his idea.

"I know we'll be sticking our necks out," he went on. "I know it isn't smart to mess into murder—getting caught the way we did tonight shows that. And what if it had been somebody else who caught us? Somebody worse than Sawyer?"

I'd thought of that too.

"But we've got to do something," Jeff said. "We can't sit around waiting for Man Mountain Dean to wrap us up and haul us away."

I kept turning his suggestion over in my mind, and I began to like it better right along. To take action, even the wrong action, would be preferable to this spineless waiting, this docile acceptance of the role of stooges for the murderer.

Sure, it would be risky. But, the way things had been going, it would be riskier just to drift.

"Okay," I said, "I'll buy it. Where do we start?"

"Not tonight." He stood up. "It's too late and we're too tired. I'll be around in the morning."

He told me not to worry, but if he meant it, he should have omitted his injunction not to answer the door for anybody—not even Henderson.

After he'd gone I lay awake, assailed again by misgivings. And I knew I'd bolted the door after him, but I wondered. I heard footsteps and voices and saw faces at windows. I was working myself into a fine state when I recalled something I myself had said not too long ago. I had used an expression that stuck in my mind, and when I wondered why it stuck whole new vistas opened up.

I jumped up to get my robe, my notebook and pen. Climbing back into bed for warmth, I scribbled furiously, getting it all down while it was fresh, and I completely forgot to worry over whether the door was really locked.

X

"It's as plain as the nose on Milt Evans' face, once you think about it."

Jeff laughed. "That's pretty plain, but I still don't follow you."

He had come over early, reporting that Sarah had driven to Granger on a marketing expedition. "She was sore because I couldn't do it," he said, "but Sawyer's deputy said uh-uh."

"Aren't you supposed to stay and chop wood or something?"

"Sure. But I thought our project was more important. Have you had any bright ideas?"

"I think so," I answered slowly. "Look. What one item ties everything together? It isn't Axel's trouble with his wife—she's out, and besides that was strictly his own affair. It isn't that Axel riled people—they don't murder a guy because they don't like his attitude. There's only one thing it can be. The thing that throws everybody whenever it's mentioned, that's had Luella running in circles, the thing Sawyer shrugged off so lightly. Remember what I said last night about being railroaded? There's your key word."

"The narrow-gauge railroad? A good try, but I'm inclined to agree with the sheriff—what's to it after all this time?"

"I don't know what. But there has to be something. And the sheriff didn't say what's to it? He said *why?* Dahlberg is why. He's the—what's that word?—the catalyst in the situation."

"Yeah. I see what you mean. Everything is going along smoothly in the happy little village of Glory Cloud. Maybe there was disaster and scandal thirty years ago concerning a narrow-gauge railroad, but that's all ancient history. Even the people involved have pretty well put their memories up in the attic with the rest of the trash. Then along comes this snoopy professor, planning to drag everything out and publish it."

"Exactly!" I said. "Doesn't that answer Sawyer's question?"

"It does and it doesn't. As I get it, there was nothing secret about the scandal. Didn't the newspapers play it big?"

"Yes—from what Axel told me. But suppose something vital never got into the papers? Something that Axel Dahlberg, with his sharp nose for dirt, turned up in the course of research."

"Such as?"

"It would have to be something pretty important to make anybody resort to murder to keep it quiet, wouldn't it?"

"Seems so to me," Jeff said.

"Look at it from the murderer's angle. What would be a strong motive for murder? Why would you, for instance, do somebody in?"

Jeff hesitated, said: "To save my own skin. The same reason we're straining our brains now."

"But what could Axel have learned that would endanger anybody's skin at this late date?"

"There's no statute of limitations on murder," Jeff said.

I shook my head. "The narrow-gauge wreck was mass murder. And the person mainly responsible—B. J. Tuckerman—is already dead. He killed himself."

Our eyes met. I could see it strike him at the same instant it did me. I gulped. "Maybe he didn't, though. Maybe—"

"Yeah," Jeff said in his careful drawl. "Yeah. If I'd killed the old scoundrel thirty years ago, I wouldn't be keen either about having the past catch up with me."

I remembered something Jeff had told me a week ago today. "What was that line of yours about Fay St. Vincent's father being under suspicion?"

"It was only suspicion, based on B. J. Tuckerman's being shot with St. Vincent's gun."

"But good heavens—"

"I don't know the details, but St. Vincent apparently never had any trouble clearing himself. And they never even considered anybody else."

"Well!" I said. "Just wait till we see friend Sawyer!"

Jeff smiled.

"Contain yourself, honey. We haven't quite solved his case yet."

"No, but don't you see how it fits? Remember how Monday night Axel said he might go to Granger next day? And that it was research? Somebody knew the time was getting short."

"The thing that bothers me," Jeff said slowly, "is how did the murderer know what Dahlberg was up to?"

"Who knows? However it happened, the murderer *did* find out Dahlberg was on his trail. Because he did kill him. And then he went around looking for whatever it was that Dahlberg had on him in order to destroy it."

"You keep saying 'he,'" Jeff pointed out. "But if Sawyer is right about that nail polish business, it must be a woman "

"Not necessarily. And I'll show you why."

I went to the kitchen, found the pancake turner I'd used that morning for my easy-over egg. It had a yellow enameled handle, but the enamel had started to crack and peel. Holding it, I sat down beside Jeff and pulled off a flake of yellow enamel, crumbling it.

"Look," I said. "Suppose this were red."

He took the fragments from my cupped hand and pulverized them further, frowning. "Yeah."

"Particles of red enamel don't have to be nail polish," I said. "Enamel is enamel. It could be off a cigarette case or a lighter or a pillbox or a knife with a red handle. It could be off a cookie in or a kid's metal toy or old furniture that's been refinished."

Jeff stood, brushed his hands over the fireplace. "I'll buy it. But will Sawyer?"

"At least he'll have to think it over."

"Leaving that for a moment," Jeff said, "where are we? We've decided that everything is tied up with the narrow gauge, going back to the death of B. J. Tuckerman, which was probably murder, and that Dahlberg found something so incriminating that the murderer killed again to keep it quiet. So what did Dahlberg find and where is it now? And what can we do about it?"

I didn't have any answer. "Of course," Jeff added, "this is all theory. It will have to be more concrete to impress Sawyer."

"Why don't we work it from the other end? Go back to the heart of the problem: find out as much as we can about B. J. Tuckerman's death."

He thought it worth a try. I went to the desk for a notebook and pen. Jeff said:

"This theory certainly eliminates Dr. Tuckerman. He wouldn't have killed his own father."

But I remembered a comment of Dahlberg's about Herman Tuckerman's relations with his father, and I remembered sly intimations in some of Luella Greenfield's remarks.

"No. I mean no, I don't think we should eliminate him—yet. I'll go into reasons later."

"Then what now? A list of suspects?"

"Yes." I started writing. "And with two questions under each name. One, what was his or her connection with the narrow gauge and with B. J. Tuckerman? Two, where was he or she the night that Tuckerman allegedly shot himself?"

"Basic," Jeff agreed.

"So far I've got Milton Evans, Herman Tuckerman, Fay St. Vincent, Luella Greenfield, Sarah Walker. Anyone else?"

Jeff grinned. "And lo! Milt Evans' name led all the rest!"

"That's right," I agreed cheerfully. "I'd love to hang something on that nosey-know-it-all. It's a toss-up which is my first choice—Milt Evans or Sarah Walker."

"But Sarah's one of the few who doesn't seem to have been connected at all with the narrow gauge."

"So far as we know now. But we'll sure as hell look into it. I'm not giving up Sarah as a suspect that easily."

He hesitated, asked: "Shouldn't Amanda Plumb's name be on the list?"

I started to pooh-pooh him, then remembered Amanda's brakeman husband. Also Amanda's credit card. I added her name.

Jeff was counting on his fingers. "Six, I make it. You concentrate on Tuckerman, St. Vincent and Greenfield, and I'll take the rest."

"But that gives you both my pet suspects. And besides, I'm fed up with Luella's carrying on about that filing folder. That was what got us into this mess. I'll trade you Greenfield for Evans."

"It's a deal," Jeff said. "You can have Evans and God bless him."

Then he sobered. "Has it occurred to you, Gail, that Luella has probably circulated all over town with the story of your intention to finish Dahlberg's book? And that if there's anything in our theory, that makes you a potentially dangerous person to somebody? I'm not sure I like this."

Remembering how someone had tried twice already to throw a scare into me, I didn't like it either, but I said:

"It was your idea we should do something before Dan Sawyer lowers the boom, and so far as he's concerned the picture hasn't changed. We're in a situation where it's damned if you do and damned if you don't."

The sooner the quicker, so we decided to go our separate ways and meet later for consultation. Jeff reported that Murphy's wife had finally had her baby and that he was now back on the job, so each of us could expect a deputy at our heels.

As we stepped outside my cabin, Jeff lowered his voice and gripped my arm briefly. "Watch yourself, Gail."

"You too," I said.

Nodding, he headed toward the inn and I struck off up the road leading west. The two deputies, lounging against the wood shed, conferred hurriedly. Then Henderson took off after Jeff, and Murphy followed me.

Where the road met the pines I started along the path toward Fay's place. Murphy hurried to catch up.

"Hey, you're not supposed to leave town."

"I'm not leaving town. I'm going to call on Miss St. Vincent. There's nothing in this direction anyway except more trees and eventually the Continental Divide. What do you think I am—an antelope?"

He grumbled, but fell back. Chipmunks scurried through patches of sunlight across the shaded path and stopped, sitting up to regard us. A mountain jay scolded from a low branch, and there was a flirt of heels and tail as a rabbit took off across the ground cover of fallen needles. The air was filled with the sweet smell of pines. It would have been very delightful with a different companion and under other circumstances.

I came to a barbed-wire fence and signs about this being private property, no trespassing. But I decided that didn't mean me; I found the gate and went in, Murphy following at a careful distance. The house wasn't visible for several minutes; when it was I caught my breath.

The lodge stood in a clearing on the edge of a deep ravine which fell away precipitously from a low stone wall protecting a terrace. Across the ravine the pine-covered hills rose again, and beyond, towering in white majesty, the high range loomed. A magnificent view, but not one I should have cared to live with. I preferred something cosier.

Nor could you describe the house as cozy. At first, by comparison with the outsize backdrop, it seemed just another mountain cabin, rather more attractive than most, but when I adjusted my perspective I saw it was as large as the inn. The peeled log exterior and wide porches and rambling informality of the architecture gave an impression of casual comfort and even luxury. And I wondered if Fay St. Vincent never felt lonely out here in this house that could have accommodated several families. Perhaps that was why she spent so much time at the inn. I remembered Luella's crack about Fay's liking privacy—sometimes.

Continuing around the near end of the house I came out on the sunny terrace overlooking the ravine. Two people were there, bright canvas chairs close together, one talking rapidly in low tones. Coughing seemed a bit obvious. I stopped with my eyes fixed on the distant view and exclaimed as if I had just now become aware of it.

Dr. Herman Tuckerman visibly jumped, and, smothering his half-finished sentence, turned to see who had intruded. What was the emotion that flickered in the genial blue eyes? Annoyance, antagonism, fear, worry? Almost at once his kindly smile beamed forth and he started talking again, leaping up with amazing agility to place a third chair, remarking on the fine June morning.

With an indulgent smile, Fay watched the old doctor fussing around. She hadn't stirred her elegant tailored self from a gracefully lounging position, but she extended a slim, well-kept hand.

"How divine to see you, dearie. And how sweet you look today. Not a bit distressed over this dreadful business with sheriffs and such people." She sighed wistfully. "Ah, it's lovely to be young, isn't it, Herman?"

I looked at her narrowly. After beating my brains most of the night and holding a council of war with Jeff early this morning, I looked a hag and I knew it. And I realized that it was a bum break to have encountered Dr. Tuckerman here. The kind of confidential information I was after would more likely emerge in a tête-à-tête. (Yes, Mr. Evans, that is French. I know.)

I sat down and lighted a cigarette, considering whether there was any point in lingering. Then, while I was mentally sorting possible openings, Fay plunged in with a direct offensive.

"Tell me, dearie," she said sweetly, "is what we've heard true? That you're going to finish poor Dr. Dahlberg's book?" Looking pensive, she added, "That is, if the sheriff will let you."

I thought Fay's claws were showing this morning; some instinct warned me against a categorical answer. I shrugged.

"I've thought about it. But I haven't decided. What would you advise?"

Dr. Tuckerman's white mustache bristled. "I'd advise you to let sleeping dogs lie, young woman."

Fay shook her head sympathetically. "I know how you feel, Herman, and my heart aches for you, darling. But you and I have nothing to be ashamed of, have we? With all this modern psychology nowadays, everyone knows how unjust it is for the father's sins to be visited, and all that."

Dr. Tuckerman looked embarrassed to the point of agony, and I wondered what modern psychology had to do with it. Fay swept along serenely, one manicured hand patting a silver comb.

"In a way, Herman, it will be lucky for you if Gail should finish the book, instead of Dr. Dahlberg. Not that you would have wished the poor man any harm. A brilliant addition to our little colony. It's poignant—his sudden death. But he was so unyielding, you know, so set in his ways. I'm sure Gail will be more understanding, won't you, dearie?"

I'd had enough of her vagueness. "Understanding about what?"

Fay's hands fluttered. "Well, you know, dearie. Things like it's not being Herman's fault his father was—the way he was. Confidentially—oh, don't look that way, Herman—there's no harm in being frank after all these years—confidentially, there was a distinct lack of rapport between Herman and his father for a long time." She sighed, with a faint sad motion of her head.

"You mean they didn't like each other?"

Dr. Tuckerman started to expostulate.

"Let's not be old-fashioned, dearie," Fay admonished. "The way he treated you and your mother I'd be shocked if you *hadn't* hated him. And don't you see—if Gail understands the background, she can absolve you in the book from all responsibility."

All responsibility except maybe parricide, I thought, and I wondered how much deliberate throwing of dear Herman to the wolves was behind her sweet reasonableness. But of course Fay didn't realize the significance of what she was saying. Or did she?

Dr. Tuckerman stood up, lips tight under his mustache, eyes suddenly old and bleak. His gnarled hands were shaking as they had the night Axel was killed.

"Fay," he said, "you take advantage of old friendship."

"Why Herman, I wouldn't have breathed a word if I'd thought—"

"Never mind," he said. "It doesn't matter. I have to be going now, anyway."

When he'd disappeared around the house, I gave Fay a hard look. "Those are probably painful memories for him."

Fay was all sweet remorse. "Oh dear. I just shouldn't say whatever comes into my head. But I didn't suppose after all this time—and his mother's been dead so long—he'd still—"

When she mentioned Dr. Tuckerman's mother an expression of bitter animosity flitted shockingly across her lovely face. She shrugged.

"Oh, well, he'll get over it. He always has. Why don't you run into the kitchen and make us a cup of tea, dearie? I'm roughing it here, you know, without a maid. It's that door to the left and everything's on the table. I was just going to brew a cup when Herman came."

She had the casual high-handedness of someone who has always been waited on. I considered asserting my independence, but I didn't mind a recess to think things over. In the kitchen I turned the dial of the electric stove under the tea-kettle. Waiting for it to boil, I looked around.

So Fay was roughing it! If your taste ran to kitchens, this was a humdinger. The clinical whiteness of all the super equipment—electric stove, big refrigerator, deep freeze, garbage disposal—was softened by a color scheme of turquoise and maroon. When Fay wanted to play house she had everything as painless as possible.

The kettle was humming—it didn't take long at that altitude—and I poured the boiling water into a turquoise pottery teapot. While the tea steeped I recapitulated. Point one: Fay did indeed take advantage of Herman Tuckerman's life-long devotion. Probably she always had.

Point two: As I had already suspected, there had been no love lost between Herman and his father, B. J. That hatred had been strong enough to start the old doctor's hands shaking after thirty years—had it been strong enough to motivate murder?

Point three slid into my mind so easily that it must have been lurking there all along. How about Herman's mother? Obviously more of a Mom than a wife. What if she had killed her husband and Herman knew it? Wouldn't he go to any length to cover her?

Point four: Fay had hated Dr. Tuckerman's mother and still did. Undoubtedly, jealousy had been involved: on Fay's part, a dog-in-the-manger resentment of his devotion to the other woman, and plain garden-variety Mom jealousy on the part of Mrs. Tuckerman.

Point five: Why had Fay contrived to give me the dope on the old doctor and his father? If Dr. Tuckerman had a guilty secret and Fay knew or suspected, why should she try to jeopardize him? And if Fay herself had something to conceal, why drag out the business about Herman and B. J.? Camouflage?

Maybe it had been merely delicate sadism on Fay's part. Maybe if a man hung around all his life waiting for a kind word, occasionally it would be impossible to resist giving him a kick, instead. In that case, my sympathies were all with the poor old guy, and I was annoyed at Fay.

I was still annoyed when I put the tea things on a gaily enameled tray and carried it to the terrace. And I wondered how Fay would respond to like treatment. I was sufficiently curious not to reflect that I might be tipping my hand.

I set the tray down, and I made my voice guileless, hoping my face looked as innocent as hers was while needling Dr. Tuckerman.

"Your conversation with Dr. Tuckerman reminded me of something," I said lightly. "That's what makes modern psychology so interesting, don't you think? The way one thing reminds you of another? I mean trains of thought and all that. But heavens, I guess I shouldn't have said trains, should I?"

Fay put down her cup with a little thump, looked at me sharply. "Are you feeling all right, dearie? Not light-headed? Why shouldn't you have said trains?"

I registered confusion. "Well, you know." I allowed myself to try one of her airy gestures. "Trains. Railroads. Narrow gauge. Everybody seems so upset when the Granger, Glory Cloud & Western is mentioned, don't they? But I suppose with the dreadful scandal and so much crookedness all around—oh dear, I'm not being terribly tactful, I'm afraid."

Fay picked up her cup, took a careful sip. "You seem to be laboring under a misapprehension, my dear. I believe I made it clear some time ago that my father was in no way connected with the mismanagement of the narrow-gauge railroad."

"I remember that's what you said." Very slight emphasis on said. Before she could catch me up, I rambled on. "But I really wasn't thinking about that at all. Your father's probably being involved, I mean. Of course, he *did* come out of it with plenty of money, didn't he, and poor old B. J. Tuckerman without a dime? However, that's beside the point."

"Very much so," Fay agreed. No mistaking the cold hostility in her voice now.

"What I was really thinking—you know, all mixed up with everything else the way a person will think sometimes if his mind isn't terribly disciplined—is how *odd* it was that B. J. Tuckerman shot himself. Of course I don't know anything about it and perhaps I shouldn't even speculate, but from all I've heard he just didn't seem the *type* to commit suicide, did he? Too much of an extrovert, you know. And I just wondered—"

"You wondered what? Or is your obviously confused thinking too vague to say?"

I said plaintively, "I don't see why you take such an unfriendly attitude, Fay. At least you *sound* unfriendly. And, after all, if someone did shoot B. J. Tuckerman for some silly reason, that's no skin off your nose, is it? Such a crude expression, but I mean surely nobody could ever have imagined that a young girl like you shot him or anybody connected with you did, so what difference does it make?"

Maybe I overdid it. Fay must have known that somewhere I would have picked up the information that B. J. had used St. Vincent's gun to kill himself. But at least I'd resisted the temptation to describe anything as poignant.

She probably saw through the mimicry too. As I had observed, Fay could slough off her zany manner when the occasion demanded as easily as a snake sheds its winter skin.

"I begin to see what you're getting at," she said, her tone more patiently sympathetic than hostile. She lay back and closed her eyes, continued slowly, thinking aloud. "You and this lad, Jeff Calhoun, are in a tight spot. Perhaps deservedly so. I couldn't say. You're casting frantically about for something—anything— to toss out as a distraction for the sheriff. Your minds worked this way. Axel Dahlberg was murdered. Axel Dahlberg was doing research on the narrow gauge. Everybody in Glory Cloud was sensitive on that subject. Somebody was especially sensitive because he had a guilty secret. Dahlberg discovered that secret. Dahlberg was killed. The person with the guilty secret killed him."

I listened to her exposition, and I felt a perfect fool for having treated her like one. She opened her eyes and gave me a level stare.

"And then you remembered having heard that B. J. killed himself with Papa's gun. And that there was a brief investigation which conclusively proved Papa's innocence. But you wondered. You wondered whether I was the one with a guilty secret. You wondered about Papa. You wondered about that gun. And you paid me a call to see what you could learn." She paused, added: "Didn't you think it might be dangerous, my dear?"

I was too chagrined to answer, and I suppose I showed it. Fay's smile seemed genuinely commiserating.

"I'll tell you about that gun, Gail. It was on Decoration Day in 1921 that a group of us here in Glory Cloud had a picnic late in the afternoon. That was about a week before the wreck on the Granger, Glory Cloud & Western, about ten days before Mr. Tuckerman killed himself. I remember Mr. Tuckerman had a new Hupmobile that spring, and he and Papa were having a friendly argument about whether it was a better hill-climber than Papa's Reo. We all drove to that high point beyond the mine—the same place you said you went Monday night.

"There must have been about ten in the party: the senior Tuckermans and Herman, my parents and I, Gilbert Hazlitt, my fiancé—" She sighed, and her gray eyes momentarily clouded with that romantic sadness.

"Milton Evans was with us, of course. Just a lad. He was simply an unfortunate mistake on Papa's part, you know. And yes, I believe Mr. and Mrs. Greenfield and their two children were along. So that makes how many? Twelve, doesn't it?"

I nodded. I was remembering Luella had mentioned some such outing.

"You know how men are, dearie—always excited about guns. The men in the party were practicing target-shooting—making a great racket. When it got dark we all went back to the Tucker-mans' for the rest of the evening. We chatted and we sang—Gil-bert played the piano beautifully, did you know that?"

I shook my head. And I started to speak, but Fay waved a shushing hand.

"You're still wondering about the gun. Well, darling, it was as simple as that. When the party broke up, Papa forgot to take along his gun. He didn't think much one way or the other about getting it back—he knew where it was. In fact, I believe he asked Milton Evans to stop in and pick it up, but Milton neglected to do so. And before Papa did get around to calling for it, Mr. Tuckerman used it to kill himself. I always thought he did it on purpose—tried to implicate poor Papa, I mean."

I wondered, if her story were true, why B. J. *had* used St. Vincent's gun. I wondered how Papa managed to square himself so readily. I thought of how many others might have known that St. Vincent's gun was still at Tuckerman's.

"But Papa was in Denver that night," Fay said. "The night B. J. shot himself. And there were lots of reliable witnesses to prove it. So you see?"

If Papa's alibi had been that iron-clad, why was she working so hard to convince me?

XI

That evening I dined at the inn. There was a reason. Jeff and I planned giving Murphy and Henderson the slip; it would be easier in a group.

Dinner was late, but nobody raised the rumpus Sarah did when one of us was tardy. Fay with her sherry, and Luella Greenfield with her fancywork, were having a low-voiced conversation near the fireplace. Milton Evans, with infallible poor taste, was drinking bourbon and ginger ale, expounding to Dr. Tuckerman what the doctor probably didn't know about the treatment of arthritis. Milt got his medical information from a column in the daily paper. Dr. Tuckerman, moodily silent, only half-listened. I noted, however, that he upped his customary single highball to three. Henderson and Murphy had struck a nice compromise between not drinking on duty and sitting with tongues hanging out: they had withdrawn to a far corner with beer.

I wanted to be on my toes tonight, but I didn't think one scotch would prevent that. I nursed it along, meditating on our progress. Jeff and I had held a second conference at my cabin late that afternoon, pooling our findings.

He had listened with dismay to the report of my call on Fay St. Vincent.

"Ye gods, honey! Why didn't you draw her a diagram?"

"Don't rub it in," I said. "I'm already aware my technique wasn't really inspired."

"Maybe it doesn't matter," Jeff said slowly. "I can't see Fay as a dangerous character, and you did learn quite a bit."

133

"Yes." I ticked off the items. "I learned that Fay hated Herman Tuckerman's mother, that Herman hated his father, that Fay has a catty streak behind her sweet facade, that Papa had an iron-clad alibi for the night B. J. Tuckerman died, that most of the people on our list were in a position to know the whereabouts of Julius St. Vincent's gun. And I also learned something about Fay's conception of the simple life."

Jeff said:

"One other person on our list could have known about the gun, too. Sarah Walker."

"Did she tell you that?"

"No. Milt Evans did."

"Why, you—! Poaching on my suspect!"

"Quiet, please. I only did my duty as I saw it. Sarah went to Granger today for supplies, so I had no chance to sound her out. But I did talk to Luella, Milt and Amanda. In that order. And wait till you hear about Amanda!"

"I am waiting."

But he insisted on making his report in chronological sequence. At the Greenfield cabin, he'd found Luella packing to leave. She didn't like the recent goings-on in Glory Cloud; she was going home to Pueblo. Maybe she would return later in the summer when her married daughter from California visited; she didn't know. Old Charlie had been on hand, helping close the cabin, checking the tires on her car, and so on.

"I didn't know Luella had a car here," I said. "I've never seen it."

"Well, it's an all-right car. A '47 Pontiac. But Luella's getting on toward seventy and she learned to drive late in life. Mountain-driving makes her nervous. So she just uses the car to come up from Pueblo in the spring and go back in the fall. That's around two hundred miles, and Luella takes about two and a half days for it. But all summer the car sits out in the shed except when her son or daughter visits her."

"But will Sawyer let her pick up and walk out?"

"I doubt it."

He had, he said, suggested as much to Luella, but she was adamant. She had said she would tell that young whippersnapper of a sheriff that she was getting too old for this kind of excitement, that her heart wasn't strong, and that, if he didn't let her go, he would be responsible for the consequences. There were several things she intended to tell the sheriff. With that, she had tossed her head and shooed Jeff from underfoot.

"So I went back to the inn," he said, "to work on those screens Sarah's been beefing about. Right away Milt Evans turned up and started straw-bossing the job."

"And you made the best of a horrible situation by quizzing him? Okay, I forgive you. Did you get any dope from the dope?"

"I got plenty of innuendo, back-biting and subtle slander. Despite his apparent friendliness with Fay and Doc Tuckerman, Milt managed to cast slurs on both their families. For the *pièce de resistance*, he intimated that Fay and the doctor have been having an affair for lo, these many years."

"Baloney. Fay's too much the eternal virgin for such peccadillos. She too much enjoys posing gracefully on her pedestal while Tuckerman worships from afar. Also, can you imagine her being untrue to her romantic memory of Hazlitt?"

"Frankly," Jeff said, "I don't know and I don't care."

"And was that the extent of the wisdom reaped from our know-it-all friend?"

"No. He filled in the background on Sarah Walker."

"Now we're getting some place! I suppose Milt hates her too."

"On the contrary. He thinks she's an admirable woman."

I was disgusted. "Nobody can be wrong all the time, but Milt sure tries."

It seemed Milt Evans and Sarah Walker had been high-school classmates in Granger. Sarah was a year older, but Milt had been the bright boy who skipped grades, and they were graduated in the same class. Milt lived in town with his family, while Sarah's home was in Glory Cloud. But during the worst cold weather she stayed in Granger, working for room and board in the home of a family named Walker.

"Walker?" I said. "How—"

"Sarah's maiden name was Foster," Jeff said. "And she married Jim Walker, the son of the household."

I kept hoping for some startling revelation and couldn't help being disappointed in the prosaic story. Sarah's father had been a prospector and had worked in the mines. The family never had much, but they were never actually down and out. They had a few acres and raised chickens and vegetables, and when work in the mines was slack, Foster did odd jobs for the wealthier residents.

"Much the sort of thing old Charlie does," Jeff said.

"When do we get to the part that makes her so admirable?" I asked.

"Don't you see why Milt Evans thinks that? It's the American success story. Poor girl from humble background marries above her station and makes good in the hotel business."

"You mean her husband's family was in the chips?"

"Only by comparison with Sarah's family," Jeff said. "Walker, senior, had a coal and feed business in Granger, and he owned the Glory Cloud Inn. Comfortably fixed, but far from wealthy. Summers, when business was slack in Granger, the family ran the inn. Sarah waited on tables sometimes—that's how she got acquainted with the Walkers."

According to Evans, Sarah had been an extremely pretty girl. That I could believe. She and Jim Walker had been married the September after she finished high school, and they lived briefly in Denver where he was studying for the ministry. But that winter Jim's father died from a heart attack, and Jim had to leave school for a term to handle family affairs. He never went back.

"Probably after living with Sarah he'd lost the call to religion anyway," I said. And I asked, "Why did you say Sarah could have known about St. Vincent's gun?"

"My own deduction. Milt said that after Sarah moved back up here in the spring, and before the inn opened for the season, she sometimes worked as a hired girl. Her older sister had been the Tuckermans' hired girl before she married and moved away, and Sarah inherited the job. The night of that Decoration Day picnic Fay told you about, and which Milt mentioned, Sarah was in the kitchen at the Tuckermans'. Milt remembers she was sensitive about her social status—not being included in the party, just being someone to wash dishes—and she made a point of staying out of sight. But she could have known about Julius's gun."

Even so, we'd found no reason for her to kill B. J. Tuckerman. Now, if it had been Jim Walker's father and they had inherited heavily, including the inn Sarah was so proud of—

"You say Jim's father had a heart attack?"

Jeff looked at me questioningly. Then he chuckled.

"You don't give up easy, do you? Old man Walker died in the Granger hospital where he suffered the attack while recuperating from an appendectomy. Jim and Sarah were in Denver at the time. Sarah's mother-in-law died of cancer three years later, and Jim Walker died a natural death about ten years ago. Natural in the sense that it wasn't violent. He got typhoid from drinking contaminated water on a fishing trip."

"You may jeer," I said, "but I notice you collected the information."

"Sure. We ought to think of everything."

"Then Sarah's only connection with the narrow gauge was the tenuous one of old acquaintance with most of the principals." I sighed. "I still think she done it. Woman's intuition. I think it was she and Milt Evans working together."

Jeff laughed.

And I said, "Maybe the narrow gauge doesn't have anything to do with it after all. Maybe Sarah killed Axel Dahlberg because of their disagreement about the divorce testimony."

Jeff said, "If he asked her to do something and she refused, wouldn't it be more reasonable for him to kill her?"

"Maybe he intended to," I said wildly. "Maybe she saw it coming and beat him to the draw."

"Honey, you've been eating loco weed. Leave out the question of whether Dahlberg would plan such a thing for such a reason—and where would it get him? Would he have strolled casually outside to get firewood, have accidentally run into Sarah in the yard and have decided he might as well polish her off then and there? A very slaphappy way for a man of Dahlberg's intelligence to operate. Come, come now."

He shook his head sympathetically. "As for your suggested conspiracy: the night B. J. Tuckerman shot himself, or was shot, June 10, 1921, was the night Milton and Sarah's graduating class was having class night exercises in Granger. It was on a Friday and the graduation exercises were Sunday."

"And they both attended Friday night?"

"I presume so." Jeff looked momentarily dashed. "One takes it for granted—"

"With those two I don't take anything for granted. If possible, I intend to find out. And I'm still waiting to hear your news flash on Amanda Plumb."

Jeff frowned. "That's the darndest thing yet. Amanda came rattling along about the usual hour. I knew she wouldn't want to waste time chinning, and Amanda's not one to mince words herself, so I just put it to her. 'Amanda, my friend,' I said, 'what do you know, if anything, about B. J. Tuckerman's alleged suicide back in the dark ages?'"

"Well!" I said. "Talk about *my* giving the show away!"

"Yeah. We're a couple of sharp operators. But hell! Amanda seems so on the outer edge of things, and what's more she's darned shrewd. If I'd beaten around, she'd have seen through me. The way Fay did with you."

"Let's skip the recriminations," I said. "What happened?"

"It wasn't so much what happened," he said slowly, "as the way she looked. I thought she was going to pass out. She started to tremble all over—and when Amanda trembles the car shakes—and she turned white as the snow on Mt. Evans. Next she got red and opened her mouth to bluster something, then turned white again and closed it. I could see the sweat standing out on her forehead and her eyes looked scared to death. By that time I was sorry I'd ever started it."

I gaped. "But didn't she say anything?"

"Yeah. She got sore. She exploded, 'Listen, you young squirt, I've got a job of work to do. The U.S. government don't pay me to sit around chewing the fat with crazy kids. You're attempting to deflect a federal employee from the enactment of his duties.'"

"But that's no answer."

"Isn't it? I think it is. Then she tramped the gas—I was leaning on the old jalopy—and started off with such a jolt it damned near knocked me off my feet. And I don't think Amanda would have cared if it had."

"You mean, it's an answer because it shows she must know something? That's true."

But for the moment I abandoned speculation about Amanda's reaction. All day I'd been toying with a vague idea, and now I said:

"You know, Jeff, I'd like to go up to that place near the Glory Cloud mine again. Where we had the fry."

"What for?"

"I don't know exactly. I just want to see it again without Sawyer or any of his deputies along."

"Easier said than done, baby. And what's the good of it?"

"I don't know. Call it a hunch. Call it a feminine whim. Remember how Axel insisted we go there and nowhere else Monday night? What if he had a reason? Don't ask me what, because again I don't know. It's the same place, too, where the gang went on that Decoration Day picnic back in 1921."

"Well, it's a nice spot," Jeff said.

"Sure. Maybe that's all there is to it. But just the same I want to go. Do I have to do it alone?"

"You're a stubborn wench. I think you're nuts, but I'll string along. Hey—when did I use that line before?"

We looked at each other and we both remembered his saying something like it the night I insisted on searching Dahlberg's cabin.

"That little inspiration didn't turn out so hot, did it?" he commented.

"This time will be different," I said. "And I don't want those nosey deputies on our heels."

Jeff concentrated. "Once a sucker, always a sucker. Okay, baby, how about this? You come to the inn for dinner—"

The before-dinner drinks that evening seemed to tighten rather than relax people's nerves. Tension hung over the dinner table, and awkward silent lulls alternated with bursts of chatter.

Part of it may have been caused by Luella Greenfield's running squabble with the deputies. She kept insisting that she was going home and that she was going tomorrow: she was all packed and ready. They argued back and forth till Murphy pushed back his chair and went to the phone, where he held a long conversation with Sawyer in Granger.

My edginess could be explained by the escapade we'd plotted. And the thought came to me that secret plans might be fermenting in other minds that night, releasing added nervous energy into the supercharged atmosphere.

Another factor contributed to the strains and stresses of the occasion: the fact that both Jeff and I had bungled things till everybody must know what we'd been up to. I sensed the same undercurrents of antagonism there'd been toward Dahlberg when he was the one digging into a past they all wanted to forget and have forgotten.

Sarah Walker moved in a personal aura of bland serenity, although her white skin was lightly flushed, the pupils of her dark eyes pin-pointed. When she leaned over to remove my salad plate I noted that her aura had more than serenity. I suddenly tumbled. Sarah had taken advantage of her shopping expedition to re-stock the cellar, and she'd been sampling the new merchandise. That was why dinner had been late.

At this stage, alcohol did kind things for Sarah, erasing the temper lines around mouth and eyes, sweetening her acid tongue, bringing back a brief glimpse of the pretty girl who had worked for board and room and married above herself. And I felt a fleet pang of pity for her and for all of us who find out sooner or later that life isn't such a bowl of cherries, after all.

Jeff was bringing in the lemon chiffon pie by the time Murphy returned to the table.

"Well?" said Luella.

Murphy swallowed an enormous bite of pie, washed it down with coffee. He shook his head.

"Nothing doing."

Luella set her stubborn little chin for battle. Fay and Milt Evans and Dr. Tuckerman had risen to go in by the fire, but Milt's long nose sniffed the delicious scent of trouble brewing and he lingered. Henderson tilted his long frame back in his chair, waiting.

"Dan Sawyer said," Murphy emphasized, "that under no circumstances are you to leave Glory Cloud until after he's come back. He will be up tomorrow and he'll talk things over with you then and possibly—just possibly—it might be okay for you to leave Sunday morning. That's what the man said, Mrs. Greenfield."

His tone carried a firm finality which Luella had to accept.

"He'll be sorry if I get all upset and have a spell with my heart," she said tartly. "If I have to wait till Sunday, I'll wait, but I demand that one of you young men walk home with me."

I thought Luella was laying it on a bit thick, and I suspected she was trying to spite them by her inconvenient request. From the look that passed between the two deputies, they suspected it too. Henderson stood up and stretched.

"I'll take you home, Mrs. Greenfield. Now, if you like. You can handle things here for a few minutes, can't you, Murph?" His glance touched Jeff and me lightly.

Murphy nodded. "Sure. I'm going to have more coffee anyway. I don't suppose there's another piece of that pie in the kitchen, is there, Mrs. Walker? That's the best lemon pie I ever ate."

Either the drinks or the flattery—perhaps both—brought out unaccustomed graciousness in Sarah. There certainly was another piece of pie and she would get it for him. She would have a second cup of coffee herself, and bask in his appreciation. Looking wry, Henderson went out with Luella.

Jeff's eyes were level, meeting mine. "Since we both have to be under the law's watchful surveillance," he said lightly, "why don't you help me clear the table, Gail? Many hands make light work, to coin a phrase."

"I don't see why I should." I stood up. "But I'm a slave to your every whim."

We made several round trips through the swinging door to
the kitchen, carrying dishes and glasses, clowning. At first we
passed each other coming and going, but after a few minutes we
were both in the kitchen at once. Jeff's quick look and gesture
were enough, and in a flash we were silently through the back
door. It was as easy as that. As rapidly as possible we put as much
distance as possible between ourselves and the inn, and we were
past Dahlberg's, well started on the steep pitch of the Alpine
road, when we heard the kitchen door slam open. Jeff pulled
me to the side of the road; we got our wind while we listened to
Murphy's shouts of outrage.

I giggled as another voice joined in, the words floating distinct through the clear night air. Milt Evans was saying:

"Now don't worry, Murphy—I'll take over. You should have
been on your toes, but you're lucky I can—"

Beside me in the darkness Jeff chuckled. "Hopalong Evans
rides again."

And I murmured, "With his help, they'll never find us."

For all that we achieved by that evening's expedition, we
should have stayed at home. It would have been better all around.
There was nothing, of course, in that rocky clearing on the hill-
top to show why Axel Dahlberg had insisted on going there and
refused to settle for any place else. Nothing to indicate why he
died later the same night. Or if there was, we didn't see it.

We were almost to the top of the rise out of Glory Cloud
when the moon appeared over the wall of forest and mountain,
two nights past full, making flashlights unnecessary. About then
we heard the grind of a motor in second gear climbing the hill
behind us, and we scrambled off the road into a thicket of jackpine. In the moonlight we saw an official Granger County car go
by, Murphy at the wheel, Milton Evans beside him.

"Headed for the same place," Jeff murmured. We waited, perhaps twenty minutes, before the car returned, moving faster on
the downgrade.

"They can't hope to find us at night, in these hills," Jeff said.
"They just want to tell Sawyer they tried."

Going back to the road, we climbed the rest of the way to the Glory Cloud mine. Jeff warned me to use my flash now and to watch sharp for the treacherous shafts.

In the moonlight the picnic site was a lighted stage with the dark forest a gloomy backdrop. From the far distance drifted voices of coyotes and I caught my breath, listening. It was very lonely up there, very cold. A wave of discouragement swept me.

Jeff shared my mood. Voice somber, he said, "Well, now that you're here, what next?"

"I don't know. Let me think."

Sinking down onto a log, I lighted a cigarette, and worked at making my mind blankly receptive. Maybe some forgotten impression made here earlier would become a conscious memory; maybe some clue to all the missing answers, all the loose ends, would emerge from the dark limbo of the unconscious.

But nothing came except the ghosts. Axel's ghost first, of course, a friendly sort of pipe-smoking specter with an earthy twinkle in the dark eyes. And after him flitted the older ghosts— ghosts of thirty years ago. Fay St. Vincent was there, with a motoring veil tied over hair not yet silvered, vivaciously lovely despite the outdated clothes. And Luella Greenfield, a bustling, clucking little hen with Jeb and her two chicks around her. Herman Tuckerman was there too, a gentle young man recently returned from abroad, setting up practice in Glory Cloud to please his mother and to be near Fay. His blue-eyed spirit looked melancholy as the girl he loved coquetted with Gilbert Hazlitt, a shadowy, romantic figure, faintly roguish.

I wondered whether Jeff was seeing them too. Was he noticing that fresh kid in knickers, Milt Evans at seventeen, familiarly calling B. J. Tuckerman B. J., slipping an onion into Jeb Greenfield's pocket?

The ghosts of Julius and Mrs. St. Vincent and of B. J. Tuckerman and Mom were more hazy. Julius was small and soft-spoken, smiling with quiet amusement at big, blustering B. J.'s extravagant claims for the new Hupmobile. They all seemed to be having a good time, unaware of disaster and scandal poised to strike.

My cigarette had smoldered down to burn my fingers. I dropped it, grinding the stub underfoot against the ever-present fire hazards of dry pine needles and dead wood. When I looked up again, the ghosts were gone. I strained my ears, but I couldn't even hear the men at their target-shooting.

Something clicked then. "Jeff," I said, "remember how cross Axel was when you suggested using the gun in his cabin? I wonder why? What if, by some wild chance—?"

After I finished Jeff said, "A good try, but it's no go. St. Vincent's gun was a revolver."

But I felt I had been close to something and I suggested we go over in detail everything the three of us had said and done Monday night. Re-enact the whole scene and conversation as accurately as possible. Jeff remained skeptical, but he played along. It would have been warmer and more cheerful to build a fire, but indiscreet. By the time we'd played back all the dialogue we could remember, our teeth were chattering. Several times I'd had that tantalizing sense of an idea just beyond reach, but it always slipped away before I could nab it. At last I said wearily:

"It's been a wild-goose chase. I'm sorry I brought the whole thing up."

Both of us were silent and dejected as we headed back toward town. Passing the abandoned Glory Cloud mine, I considered pausing there to poke around, but failure had taken the heart out of me for any further assaults tonight on the windmills of my imagination.

Murphy was waiting on the porch of the inn. When he sighted us he began to swear. I didn't see Henderson or Milt Evans. At some point in the search, Milt had disappeared and they had to struggle along without his invaluable directions.

"The sheriff's going to hear about this!" Murphy finished wrathily. I didn't doubt it. But right now I was beyond caring, dragged down as I was with fatigue and hopelessness.

Nor did the more restrained reproaches of Henderson, whom I found waiting outside the Barlow cabin, make a deeper impression. Drearily I agreed with him that it had been a dirty trick.

Sleep finally drifted over me after an hour of staring into darkness, of going over the day's achievements and frustrations, then going over them all again. I wasn't yet completely under when I heard the scream.

I jerked to alert wakefulness, muscles rigid, the sound ringing in my ears, before I remembered having heard that cry before. Only a mountain lion. But the shock had tightened my nerves again, and it must have been another hour before I lapsed into oblivion.

XII

Saturday morning my woodbox was empty, and the cabin was chill despite the brilliance of the day. At the woodshed I noted that my supply was dwindling; I'd have to speak to old Charlie about bringing me a load. Arms filled, I turned toward the cabin to see Milt Evans hurrying along the road.

More rampantly eager-beaverish than usual, he bustled toward me, and my surly greeting didn't discourage his following me into the kitchen.

I dumped the wood into the box. "Thanks for the help," I said. "To what do I owe this unexpected pleasure?"

"Have you heard the news?" His oily voice had that gloating tone I had observed before when trouble was involved, and shaking my head was lost motion. Wild horses couldn't have stopped Milt from spilling what he had to spill.

"Luella Greenfield's vamoosed," he announced triumphantly. "Skipped. Taken a powder."

I was stuffing papers into the cookstove, and I paused only briefly. I was a little surprised, but not as bowled over as he seemed to expect. Luella had made enough fuss about going home and now she had done it.

Milton digressed to tell me what I was doing wrong, and to explain the basic techniques of fire-building. But when I invited him to take over, he declined.

"So what if Mrs. Greenfield did leave?" I said. "I suppose the sheriff doesn't like it, but there are lots of things he doesn't like."

"Oh, the sheriff likes it all right," Milt chortled. "Why shouldn't he like it, having his case cracked for him? All he needs now is to pick her up and that shouldn't be hard. I was telling him how to go about—"

"Wait a minute. What's that about having his case cracked?"

"If you knew as much about criminal psychology as I do, you wouldn't need to ask," he said. "Don't you see what it signifies—Luella's taking it on the lam? That's a colloquialism, of course—it means—"

"Yes, Mr. Evans, I've heard the expression. But frankly, I *don't* see what her doing it signifies."

He fairly licked his chops.

"It signifies guilt. One of the primary tenets of criminology—"

"You're suggesting that Luella Greenfield took it on the lam, to use your clever expression, because she murdered Axel Dahlberg?"

"Why else? Personally, I wasn't surprised either. It's what I've told the sheriff all along. I kept saying, '*Cherchez la femme.*' That's—"

With four years of college French under my belt, I listened absently while he explained what that meant. I was considering his theory and rejecting it.

"How wacky can you get?" I said. "That's the silliest idea I've ever heard. Luella Greenfield's killing Dahlberg and fleeing from justice!"

Milton was offended. "Some people think they know everything," he observed acidly. "But Sawyer's got a head on his shoulders, even if he is young and needs an occasional word of guidance from someone more experienced. And he doesn't think it's silly!"

The kindling had finally caught, and I washed my hands. I was remembering that Luella had got the sheriff fired up about the knife missing from my cabin, that she had persistently intimated there was more between Dahlberg and me than met the eye, that she had been closely tied in with the Granger, Glory Cloud & Western, what with Jeb's being station agent and her long acquaintance with everybody in town. But I still couldn't swallow it, and I was surprised that Sawyer could. I said:

"She may be home by now. Have they contacted Pueblo?"

"Certainly they've contacted Pueblo. That was the first thing I had the sheriff do. She isn't there."

But of course she wouldn't be yet. I remembered what Jeff had said about Luella's driving.

"Her car's gone?" I asked.

"Certainly her car's gone. Also her baggage. Do you think a culprit planning a getaway would walk?"

I was feeling a desperate need of coffee, but I was darned if I'd make any with Milt Evans around. There was a cooking column in the daily paper too.

"Sawyer's out beating the bushes right now," Milt was saying. "He has extra deputies covering all the roads, and the word's gone out statewide and beyond to be on the lookout for her. I told him she had grown children in California and would probably head for there, so that end has been alerted too."

I suddenly realized this development would cause Dan Sawyer to lose interest in Jeff and me. His thinking processes were careful enough, God knew, but not subtle, and when a material witness in a murder case ignored an express command and dropped from sight, I suppose he would think it indicated guilt.

I was relieved to be out from under, but I wished it had happened some other way. With certain reservations I liked Luella Greenfield, and on the whole she had been kind to me. Her faults and foibles were forgivable ones, and I simply couldn't see her as dastardly. The business of beating the bushes and alerting the countryside to hunt down one jittery old lady with a passion for Culture seemed faintly ridiculous.

Jittery! I stared blankly at Milt Evans, and I didn't hear a word. Seconds passed and I missed innumerable gems of wisdom while I worked on my own explanation of Luella's taking a powder.

Luella had been wound up tighter than a toy locomotive ever since Axel's death. Even before. She had been nervous and jittery and steamed up over that darned filing folder, and she had been getting worse all the time till she finally wanted to go home. And when she was refused permission, she wanted an escort to her cabin.

Why hadn't I seen it before? Luella Greenfield had been scared to death. She knew something, or thought she did. There was her announcement yesterday that she had several things to tell the sheriff. There was her unwillingness to talk to Jeff when he had called and found old Charlie helping her pack.

And finally she had grown so frightened she simply bolted. She had gone into hiding, either till she was tracked down by the authorities or till her panic subsided enough to permit her to come back of her own accord.

My preoccupation with this reasoning, which seemed eminently logical, betrayed me. I had absently plugged in the hot plate and started to measure coffee, and now I heard what Milt Evans was saying.

"You probably don't know, but if you want to make good coffee—"

For the next few days Glory Cloud throbbed with more activity than it had known since the boom. It was the hub from which radiated all the excitement of a manhunt. Woman-hunt, rather. And although I remained unconvinced of Luella's guilt and felt sorry for her, taking cover in some hole like a quaking cottontail, the hue and cry was exciting.

Local authorities were on the lookout in Pueblo, of course, and in Denver and Cheyenne and Albuquerque and Omaha, and in Sacramento, where Luella's son practiced law, and in Santa Monica, where her daughter lived. Saturday evening at the inn Milt Evans had to turn on the radio, as he would, and we heard the announcer's voice over a Granger station:

"... for this woman who may be armed. Any person having knowledge of this woman's whereabouts or seeing anything of such a car is requested to telephone the sheriff of Granger County, collect. To repeat: the woman is about seventy, white hair, blue eyes, small but wiry frame. Height, five feet, two inches. Weight, one hundred and ten pounds. She is wanted in connection with a murder charge. The car is a 1947 Pontiac coupe, dark blue, bearing a Colorado license plate, number . . ."

Most baffling was the absence of any trace of the car. With highway patrols alerted and garages, filling stations, and motel proprietors issued special warning to watch for such a car, it seemed that somebody should come up with a lead. But nobody did.

One theory was that Luella might have ditched the car and gone on by train or bus, but an intensive search of every road and trail in the vicinity had so far failed to produce any sign of the missing blue coupe.

There seemed little doubt that she had been driving her car when she left Glory Cloud. Dr. Tuckerman reported hearing a car going along the main drag past his house shortly after midnight Friday. It turned down the Coyote Canyon road. He had been wakeful that night, suffering a neuralgic headache, and had arisen to take an Alka-Seltzer. Returning to bed, he heard the car and consulted his watch. Traffic in Glory Cloud at that hour was unusual. He hadn't looked out, but from the sound of the motor he thought it was Mrs. Greenfield's Pontiac.

And Saturday night a near-cloudburst did away with any possibility of discovering tire-tracks turning onto a side-road or into a thicket. The rain was preceded by an electrical storm; it was my first experience with such phenomena in the mountains; and so far as I was concerned, it could be the last.

Jeff and I had returned to the Barlow cabin and were wrangling as to whether Luella was the murderer. To my surprise, I found Jeff siding with Sawyer and friend Evans. He listened to my theory that Luella had hidden out because she knew something and was frightened, but he wasn't buying it. Maybe there were warning rumbles of the storm, but we were too absorbed to notice.

"If Luella killed Dahlberg," I was arguing, "why did she wait this long to skip? Why—" My mouth snapped shut and I bit my tongue, as an anti-aircraft gun went off just outside. I had barely realized it was a thunderclap of incredibly heroic proportions when there was a crackling, sputtering sound and the lights went out. Almost immediately a second crash followed, louder than the first.

I was in Jeff's arms without being aware of having moved. He was saying there was nothing to be afraid of, that the electricity always failed in a storm, but his deep voice was tense.

The blinding flashes of lightning kept on, snapping and hissing in the supercharged air; the stovepipe crackled and windowpanes rattled. The thunder was a battery of cannon, blasting away, and I knew what was meant by combat fatigue. Every second I expected one of those murderous bolts to strike.

The tumult reached a pitch of violence impossible to maintain, then maintained it. But at last came a perceptible lessening in the sledge-hammer crashes and longer pauses between the jagged streaks and the following explosion. Rain began to fall. The thunder and lightning sullenly withdrew, but the electricity didn't come on again for more than an hour.

When I recovered my wits sufficiently to think of anything but my own alarm, I remembered Luella Greenfield. I wondered whether she was holed up some place in these mountains where, alone and already terrified, she would have had to go through the same unnerving experience of the storm.

Early Saturday afternoon I had offered Dan Sawyer my analysis of Luella's disappearing act. His indifference couldn't have been more profound. He had a few words of rebuke for Jeff's and my escapade Friday night, but his heart wasn't in it. He didn't want to be bothered.

When I asked about the narrow-gauge filing folder, he opened his briefcase and handed it over, and when I asked permission to look around Luella's cabin, he casually granted it. Deputies had already examined Luella's place in the vain hope of finding a written confession.

Sunday morning was radiant after the storm, but I found the interior of Luella's cabin dusky, its shades drawn. I wandered aimlessly through the empty rooms. The house had an air of having been put in order by an inhabitant who expected to be gone—for how long? In the kitchen an enamel breadbox stood open, airing; mouse traps were spotted around strategically. The only thing out of place was a clean dish towel lying folded in the old rocker near the stove. I picked it up, stuck my finger on a needle.

Then I saw it wasn't a dish towel, but the bridge-size lunch cloth Luella had recently been working on. A corner of the material with an unfinished cluster of daisies was stretched taut by hoops and the needle was neatly secured there.

Frowning at the uncommunicative material, I gradually became aware of something screwy about the design. The completed frame of green cross-stitch was okay, and the partially completed spray of yellow daisies. But what were those random stitches scattered beyond the daisies? Blanket-stitch? Whatever they were, they served no purpose, decorative or otherwise.

I shook out the cloth, examining other corners where the design had been completed. No such aberration in either of them.

Maybe Luella had been so upset she simply hadn't known what she was doing. Maybe she had come home Friday night after hearing the sheriff's edict and had sat around her tidy cabin, wondering what to do. Probably everything was in readiness for taking off whenever Sawyer gave the word; nothing to do but kill time. So she rocked by the kitchen stove, going on with her fancywork.

But as she worked, she kept thinking about whatever it was that had her so scared, and she lost track of what her fingers were doing. Trepidation growing, she finally put down the embroidery, locked the house, drove away. She must have been still at work when the compulsion to leave overcame her, for the needle was impaled just beyond the last of the erratic blanket-stitches. Blanket-stitch didn't sound quite right. Maybe it was running-stitch. I was vague about such technicalities.

I wasn't entirely satisfied with my explanation. I wanted to take the lunch cloth home and puzzle over it at my leisure. But I wouldn't risk Sawyer's ire by filching even such an insignificant object. I clung to belief in Luella's innocence, and once Sawyer discovered she wasn't the murderer, after all, he would doubtless start breathing down my neck again.

So I stopped outside the front door, showed Henderson, whose trick it was this morning to watch for Luella's return, what I had.

"Do you think Mr. Sawyer would mind my borrowing this temporarily? I'd like to copy the design for some pillow-cases."

Henderson thought it would be okay. I headed for home, planning to start going through that controversial filing folder. Since getting it from Sawyer I hadn't yet had a chance to examine the contents.

When I had given Sawyer my theory about Luella's being scared out, and he had brushed me off, I hadn't mentioned our private detective work. He was in no mood for fantasies and hypotheses when he had a good, lively suspect who had run away. Perhaps now that I was at liberty to dig into material on the Granger, Glory Cloud & Western, I could uncover something more conclusive. It was my chance to make hay and, whatever Jeff thought, I was going ahead.

In the Barlow cabin I put Luella's berserk embroidery on the desk, took out the filing folder. It was loaded with material, and, since learning more of the background, I understood why Hazlitt had kept these things for possible use in writing. The set-up was rich in human emotion and dramatic possibilities. First I looked over the pix: eight-by-twelve glossy prints. News photographer's prints; Hazlitt must have obtained them from a pal on the Denver paper. Mainly on-the-scene shots of the wreck, uncomfortably graphic. I made myself study them closely, but I found no lead. Then I scrutinized a posed shot of the rescue crew at work, and among the overalled trainmen and roughly-clad prospectors, I spotted somebody in breeches and leather hunting jacket. A young chap with an inquisitive nose and a self-satisfied expression. Milt Evans. I put that one aside.

There was also a picture of B. J. Tuckerman, doubtless taken before the tragedy, for he was smiling broadly. He had Herman's hawk nose, but there the family resemblance ended. B. J.'s face was both stronger and more ruthless, with an aggressive jaw and wiliness behind the genial eyes. The high-pressure smile failed to disguise the greed of his mouth. I put that picture aside also.

Yet another picture held my interest, going into the group for special attention. Taken at the mass memorial services in Granger for the victims of the wreck, it was a heartbreaking thing. Far to the right, stood a younger and slimmer Amanda Plumb. Her face was drawn and haggard, but she wasn't weeping. She looked mad enough to spit nails.

I turned to the newspaper clippings. These were from both the Denver and Granger papers. The first long account of the wreck failed to provide fresh information. Nor were various follow-up yarns more productive. One was a feature story from the Denver paper, human interest stuff, with a by-line: Gilbert Hazlitt. The editor's note explained that Mr. Hazlitt had been until recently a staff member, but was now on leave of absence to write a book. Residing in Glory Cloud, he had been asked to cover this angle because of his close association and acquaintanceship with many of the key people.

I read that yarn with an eagle eye. And though I didn't immediately discern anything useful, I put it into the growing reserve pile.

Next I read the stories on the Tuckerman suicide. Here was where I hoped to hit pay-dirt, and I was glad Hazlitt had saved the whole front page of the Granger paper. A two-column cut from the earlier picture of B. J. Tuckerman beamed incongruously at the reader, and the story ran the full right-hand column to be continued on page eleven. That page also Hazlitt had saved entire.

And on page eleven another item snagged my interest. An account of Granger high school class night exercises, pushed back to page eleven by the more spectacular news of the Tuckerman suicide occurring the same night. Jeff had mentioned that both Sarah Walker, née Foster, and Milton Evans were members of that graduating class, and he had taken it for granted they had been present on Friday night. But he didn't know.

I read the item carefully and this time my persistence paid off. Following a recital of the opening address, the songs, the poems, the assorted shenanigans, came this paragraph:

> "The next event on the fun-filled program was the delivering of the June, 1921, class prophecy. The prophecy was read by sweet girl graduate, Sarah Foster of Glory Cloud, altogether charming in her sheer white frock with a blue sash. The prophecy was written and originally scheduled to be read by a fellow class-member, Milton Evans of Granger, but at the last minute young Evans was unavoidably detained in the mountains and was unable to attend. However, Miss Foster pinch-hit very creditably and many of the witty prognostications brought down the house."

No doubt! And bright boy Milt had been detained in the mountains. What crisis could possibly have prevented Milt Evans from turning up that night to bask in the audience's amusement at his witty prognostications? Not even a broken leg would have deterred Milt from swaggering around in that limelight.

Nor would a mere electrical storm have been enough to keep him from the stage of an auditorium. The account of Tuckerman's suicide mentioned a violent storm in the mountains that evening. Both Mrs. Tuckerman and the son, Dr. Herman Tuckerman, had been in the house at the time the shot presumably had been fired, but both had been upstairs in their respective rooms and had blamed the deafening thunder for their failure to hear the report. Remembering last night's display, I accepted that. Accordingly, B. J.'s body had not been discovered till the following morning.

The widow had been too prostrated to see reporters. The son, however, young Dr. Tuckerman, had described the family's activities during the preceding day. He himself had been busy all afternoon with calls on patients and, as the Tuckermans were sitting down to dinner, he had been summoned to treat a local patient for food poisoning. Hence, he had been late for dinner; otherwise, there was nothing out of the ordinary about his routine.

His father, B. J. Tuckerman, had been silently brooding during the meal. This occasioned no question on the part of his family, as he had been moody since the wreck of the week before, particularly since prosecution had been discussed. Perhaps he had been more deeply depressed that Friday night than previously; the son couldn't say.

When Mrs. Tuckerman and Dr. Herman Tuckerman had retired about ten-thirty the storm was brewing. They left B. J. at the desk in his downstairs study where his body was found next morning, Julius St. Vincent's revolver in his hand. According to the medical examiner's estimate, the fatal shot must have been fired at approximately the time the thunder and lightning had been at their worst.

Upon being questioned, Mr. St. Vincent alleged that he left his revolver at the Tuckerman home some time before, and that he was in Denver Friday evening, attending a banquet of Colorado mining men.

I put down the paper, and, opening my notebook, I wrote a list of questions.

1. Did B. J. Tuckerman commit suicide or was he murdered? Only murder could lead to present situation.

2. If murdered, who was in position to do it? And who had motive?

a. Mrs. Tuckerman was in house. Could have slipped down and shot husband, unheard by Herman because of storm. Or maybe she was heard and Herman is still covering her. Motive obscure except that I have gathered Tuckermans were not devoted couple. Mrs. T. resented being dragged to outposts of civilization. No doubt outraged by disgrace husband brought on family. Did B. J. have insurance?

b. Herman Tuckerman also in house. Could have gone down and shot father under cover of storm as well as Mrs. T. could. Motive? Known to have hated father. Maybe killed to avenge shame brought on dear old Mom.

c. Milton Evans was "detained in mountains" and missed hour of glory at class night. Detained how? Could have entered house from outside during storm. Knew St. Vincent's gun was there; had been asked to pick it up and neglected to do so. Neglected on purpose? Motive—well, Milt was caught at dirty work in St. Vincent's Denver office later. Maybe it wasn't his first endeavor in free enterprise. Maybe he was on verge of being caught in something crooked by B. J. Pot calling kettle black. Milt would have thought it clever to point finger at his "friend," Julius St. Vincent.

d. Amanda Plumb may have been in Glory Cloud that night. Why did she act so strange when Jeff asked her about Tuckerman suicide? Must know something. If murderer herself, motive would be revenge. A primitive type.

3. Where was Fay St. Vincent Friday night? In Denver with father? Where was Mrs. St. Vincent? Gilbert Hazlitt?

4. If Axel Dahlberg found clue to assumed murder of Tuckerman, what did he find and where? Reasonable to suppose it was something in folder just examined. It was after he acquired same that things started popping. If so, what have I missed? Is it still here? Did murderer find and steal? Did Axel hide it? Where?

5. Did Luella Greenfield find same thing Dahlberg did? Why didn't she tell anybody? Is that why she was frightened and ran out? If so, whole problem will be solved when we get in touch with her. Incidentally, where was Luella Friday night, June 10, 1921? Husband lost job as station agent when narrow gauge blew up. Did family suffer more significant loss or consequence?

6. Re Dahlberg's murder the following so-called clues have turned up:

a. Fay St. Vincent's comb.

b. Prescription slip given Jeff by Dr. Tuckerman.

c. Knife from my cabin planted to look like murder weapon.

d. Amanda Plumb's credit card.

e. Flakes of red enamel, alleged by sheriff to be nail polish.

Why such an assortment? Have they all been planted? Has murderer simply collected everything handy and thrown it in to confuse issue? If so, must be somebody not indicated by above clues. Or must it? Maybe murderer planted one clue pointing to self if sufficiently sure he could disclaim. Pretty risky. Or maybe he just overlooked something.

I leaned back, flexed my fingers. Just then a knock sounded and Jeff popped his dark head through the doorway.

"Hi. What do you know?"

"Very little," I said. "What do you?"

"Nothing that amounts to much." And he told of all the high-tailing around Sawyer and his deputies had been doing. "They'll get Luella before long," he added. "How can they miss with Milton Evans supervising?"

"Which brings us to an interesting point. Remember your assumption that both Milt and Sarah Walker were alibied for B. J.'s death because their high school class was having class night? Milt wasn't there. He wrote the prophecy and was supposed to read it, but at the last minute Mr. Nosey-know-it-all didn't turn up."

"How do you know? Did you ask him?"

I gave him a résumé of what I'd learned from the pix and news stories, then showed him my questions.

"Haven't you forgotten a few things?" he asked, after reading them.

"Such as?"

"Such as why did Milton Evans come back to Glory Cloud this particular summer? Such as what bearing did the information Dahlberg gave you about Evans' owning property here have, if any? Such as what was Dahlberg about that last afternoon when he dragged you on an apparently pointless stroll through the woods to a ruined cabin and didn't even go in?"

I didn't know those answers either.

"You realize," Jeff added, "you've strengthened the case against one pet suspect at the expense of the case against your other pet?"

"You mean that Sarah Walker, *née* Foster, was at class night?"

"It looks that way, doesn't it?"

"Well, according to the paper Tuckerman died at approximately eleven-thirty. Class night was probably over by ten. Couldn't Sarah have made a fast get-away, returning to Glory Cloud in time to do it?"

"With a storm raging and taking these roads in a '21 vintage car?"

"I don't see why not," I said stubbornly.

Jeff chuckled. "I'm sure glad you didn't take an instant dislike to me."

"Let's get on with your additions. What else?"

"Okay. Why has Fay St. Vincent been perturbed about this projected book, if her father was so lily-white? And why did somebody try to scare you off twice within your first few days in Glory Cloud?"

"That proves my contention: it all goes back to the narrow gauge. You suggested yourself it was because of my connection with Axel Dahlberg and his book."

"I wonder," Jeff said slowly. "I wonder. Have you done much on your Hazlitt thesis yet?"

"How could I? I've been too busy fending off Sawyer and trying to figure things out."

"Well, look, didn't Fay tell you that Hazlitt died from falling into an old mine shaft?"

I nodded. "But isn't that reasonable? Everyone says open shafts are dangerous."

"Sure it's reasonable. A good reasonable way to dispose of anyone and have it appear accidental. Happened that same summer, didn't it? Quite a record for a quiet little village: a disastrous wreck, a suicide and a fatal accident all in one season."

My mind was working on about one cylinder by now. "You're implying that Gilbert Hazlitt might have killed B. J. Tuckerman?"

"No, no. You're tired, honey. But suppose you're right about its all hinging on the narrow gauge and about B. J.'s being murdered. Hazlitt was right in there with the rest of the outfit. He might have seen or known something. He might have been victim number two!"

XIII

In some ways it added up. It was in Hazlitt's cabin I had come upon the folder of narrow-gauge material. Hazlitt was the known subject of my own research, and the two tries at scaring me had been made before I said anything about taking over Dahlberg's book. Even before Dahlberg was killed. But then why was he killed instead of me?

Clammy fingers trailed across the back of my neck and I voiced the question.

"Don't you see why?" Jeff said. "Because it was Dahlberg who found whatever he found. I don't see Gilbert Hazlitt's murder, if it was murder, as apart from the narrow gauge and B. J. Tuckerman. I see them all tangled up together, with Hazlitt the second victim and Dahlberg the third."

I suddenly thought of Fay St. Vincent, and I wondered whether the sentimental grief over her lost love wasn't just a touch over-played.

"What else do you see?"

"Just trying it for size," Jeff said, "how would this fit? Gilbert Hazlitt had some lead on who killed Tuckerman. What did he intend to do with his information? Sell it? He was chronically broke, wasn't he? Work it into a short story or a novel or a ballad? That wouldn't be good. Give it to the authorities? Not good, either.

"Or maybe," he said carefully, "he just thought things over and couldn't bring himself to marry a killer. Maybe that's the real reason the June wedding was postponed."

Funny how impossible it had been to see Luella Greenfield as a murderer, and how easily Fay slipped into the part. Perhaps it was because of the glimpses I had caught of claws under the velvet touch.

"Or it could have been," I suggested, "that Hazlitt didn't like the idea of marrying a murderer's daughter."

Jeff nodded. "Except that would entail Fay's being our current killer to protect her father's memory. And I don't see Fay taking chances like that for anybody's but her own sweet sake. Not even for poor dear Papa's."

I mentioned the silver comb near Axel's body, and how Dr. Tuckerman had tried to prevent its being found. Jeff nodded again.

"He's probably been stooging for Fay so long it's second nature. I wouldn't care to be in his shoes on several counts."

"I wish I knew what was said last Sunday night when Axel dined with Fay."

"We could be moving too fast," Jeff said. "If Hazlitt were murdered, Fay's not the only one who might have had motive and opportunity. How about Herman Tuckerman? If he had killed his father, or knew his mother had, and Hazlitt applied pressure, don't you imagine Herman would have enjoyed polishing off his rival? He never made the grade with Fay anyway, but at the time it might have looked like two for the price of one. Getting rid of a threat and a rival both at once."

"How about Milt Evans? And Sarah Walker and Luella Greenfield? And Amanda Plumb? Would any of them have had reason to do in Hazlitt?"

"Remains to be seen. Any one of them would have reason if they had killed Tuckerman and Hazlitt knew it."

I sighed. "This mess we're brewing gets worse. Now we have two hypothetical old murders to deal with. Do you realize that, if we're right, we're up against somebody who has killed three times already? Somebody who must be getting nicely used to it by now? I have no desire to be number four."

"Nor I." Jeff was silent, reflecting, then said: "I've got it! Let's talk to old Charlie. He's lived here forever, he knows everybody and everything about them. And he loves to talk."

"Sounds good except for that last item. I agree that Charlie himself is safe as a church, but what if he gabs to somebody who isn't?"

"Oh, we won't tell him what we're up to. We'll just get him started on the good old days and see what develops. Play it smooth this time."

Smooth!

It was Monday evening before we paid our call on old Charlie. Meanwhile the authorities continued the hunt for Luella Greenfield's hide-out. Incredible that both she and the car could have vanished without a trace. To Sawyer, it was more than incredible. It was a personal affront reflected in the coldly determined anger beginning to overlay his usual passivity. Observing the splash of publicity resulting from the search, the district attorney had suddenly taken keen interest in the case, an interest that expressed itself largely in giving interviews and in hounding the young sheriff. His concern didn't extend to making the drive up to Glory Cloud, but he kept Sawyer shagging back and forth between there and Granger.

Old Charlie was garrulously hospitable when we presented ourselves at his door Monday night. Our alleged mission was to order firewood for my cabin, but Charlie didn't have many callers and he wasn't allowing a potential audience to leave at once.

Later I realized that the inundation of gossip had included no fragments of information about Charlie himself. Not that it was important; old Charlie's life and background were irrelevant to our interest; it just seemed a little odd such uninhibited loquacity could reveal so little directly personal.

And how much of what he said that night was important? We couldn't determine. Was there significance in the fact that Herman Tuckerman had interned in Chicago during 1911 to 1913? Remembering that Gilbert Hazlitt originally came from Chicago, I adroitly discovered that Hazlitt had still been there during those two years. I kept telling myself Chicago was a big town, but I also kept having a hunch Tuckerman's and Hazlitt's paths might have crossed before they met in Glory Cloud.

The rest of the fill-in on Tuckerman didn't seem to mean much. That he had been Mommed we knew already; and that Mom had been badly cut up over the disgrace and scandal of the narrow gauge and of her husband's suicide, as well as infuriated by the lack of cash in the bank when everything was over. We learned that following the debacle, Herman, over Mom's protests, had set up practice in Granger, but that she had refused to leave Glory Cloud. Herman had to commute. We learned he had done well, that he was a good doctor, that Mom eventually died too late for Herman to know what to do with his freedom, that he had been all set for retirement when the war came along and the shortage of younger men kept him in practice till a couple of years ago. Now he had retired, although he still helped out when anybody in the vicinity needed a doctor.

Nor did anything Charlie contributed about Milt Evans or Sarah Walker seem to matter. I still wanted to get something on those characters, but I wasn't much interested in what a fine feller Jim Walker had been and how crazy he was about Sarah Foster and how he had served in the Navy during World War I and how Sarah had made him a good wife and a fine little helpmeet. Too bad they'd never had any youngsters. Sarah's only sister—lived in New Mexico somewheres—had ten. Charlie cackled. Too bad Sarah had taken to the bottle so hard—maybe it was not having any younguns of her own that started her. I thought it a shrewd bit of homespun psychoanalysis, and I wasn't startled to hear that Sarah had been completely potted Friday night. That was the evening after her trip to Granger when at dinner I had observed she was feeling no pain.

As for Milt Evans, it was obvious old Charlie didn't love him, but who did? "A slimery smart-aleck I wouldn't trust around the corner." I remembered Jeff's question about Monday afternoon when Dahlberg had dragged me on that pointless hike to an abandoned cabin and made an equally pointless remark about Milt Evans' owning property in Glory Cloud. So I queried Charlie about that shack and about Milt Evans' property. I didn't get what I half expected, but I got something.

What I got was the approximate time and exact place of Gilbert Hazlitt's death. We knew only that Hazlitt died during the summer of 1921 from falling into a mine shaft. But Charlie said the fatal shaft was beside that path Axel and I had followed. I remembered noticing what seemed a boarded-over well. They found Hazlitt on August 14, but because of water in the shaft, Dr. Tuckerman, who examined the body, had been unable to say exactly when Hazlitt had died. It had been deduced he died the night of August 11; nobody remembered having seen him since.

Hazlitt had spent the evening of August 11 with his fiancée, and the date had broken up early with a quarrel. Fay hadn't mentioned that in telling her sad saga. Charlie knew about it because that had been Fay's stated reason for not making a fuss over Gilbert's absence sooner. She had been waiting for him to come around and make up. Other people had been aware he was missing—after all, he was supposed to be taking care of the post office—but Hazlitt was erratic, and everybody assumed he had got some bee in his bonnet and unceremoniously taken off for Denver. Later, they believed that on the evening of August 11, after his tiff with Fay, he had gone for his usual stroll, and in the darkness had missed the path, falling to his death.

The afternoon of August 14 Fay had pocketed her pride and gone to Hazlitt's cabin to make peace. His dog—a big hound— had been shut up there, hungry and thirsty. Fay took care of him, but the dog refused to eat. He drank, then started whimpering. When Fay let him out he snuffled around the yard till he picked up his master's scent, and he led Fay to the shaft with its broken-through boards.

No amount of probing could elicit from Charlie anything but respectful admiration for Fay St. Vincent. A real lady.

Luella Greenfield was a lady too, not as high-class as Fay, but a right good-hearted soul. Charlie didn't think she'd killed Axel Dahlberg and run away. He didn't know why she had run away, but he didn't think she'd done it.

An occasional guiding question was all we allowed ourselves, casual questions that wouldn't betray our aim of playing it smooth. We came up against a blank wall only when we tried to find out more about Amanda Plumb.

The conversation had meandered back to B. J. Tuckerman when I threw in Amanda's name. Old Charlie clammed up. He had nothing to say about Amanda except that she was all right. Salt of the earth. He was so vehement and oddly defiant that we dropped the subject. But I wondered. Why all the protests?

It was close to midnight by the time we had squeezed old Charlie dry. At the door he was profuse about his enjoyment of the evening. He grinned, a gleam in his rheumy old eyes.

"Ain't many younguns that'll pay attention to an old duffer like me—listen to him chew the fat. Ain't many of these young squirts that give a durn about the old days and what happened to people they never even knew like B. J. Tuckerman and Gilbert Hazlitt. Just shows you're an extra smart pair, I reckon." Walking away from Charlie's, along the Coyote Canyon road, we were silent. Finally, Jeff spoke.

"Extra smart, it says here. I wonder."

Next morning I carried my coffee into the living room and curled up on the davenport. My brain refused to function fully this early, and I picked up an ancient copy of *Life* from the coffee table. Nobody ever accused me of being excessively domestic, but even I was revolted at the clean spot thus revealed, framed by a thick coating of dust. That was how Jeff happened to find me wielding mop and dust cloth.

"Expecting company?" he asked.

"I hope not. But a place ought to be cleaned once a year, whether it needs it or not."

He glanced around the now-shining room. "The finishing touch would be a bowl of flowers on the mantel."

"Flowers! What flowers would have the nerve to bloom in this year-round climate? Year-round winter."

"I know where we could get lilacs. Do you like lilacs?"

"Love them. My favorite flower."

"What are we waiting for? She shall have lilacs."

"Just a minute," I said. "Whose yard are you figuring to raid?"

"These flowers I have in mind don't belong to nobody, lady. They're growing wild. In Quartz."

"Quartz! I'm not that crazy about lilacs. How many miles is it down there?"

"Only a couple by road, but I know a shortcut. A trail over the ridge that makes it just a good hike. We could go down this afternoon."

It occurred to me that perhaps the sheriff wouldn't want us leaving town, even on such an innocent errand, but Jeff said Sawyer needn't know, that he was too steamed up about finding Luella to notice or care what we did.

That afternoon I discovered that Jeff's idea of a good shortcut was incompatible with mine. It was rugged. Narrow and rocky and so steep in places that at the summit I collapsed. When I could speak again, we re-hashed last night's session. Jeff kept harping on Amanda Plumb, and I was gnawed by curiosity about the quarrel between Fay and Gilbert Hazlitt.

When we started on, I found going down almost as rigorous as climbing. Jeff went first, promising to let me land on him, and we slithered along, digging in our heels, grabbing bushes. Finally we emerged behind the sole business establishment of Quartz, the tavern. Jeff glanced at the big sign for Coors beer across the porch of the brown frame house and then glanced at me.

"Why not?" I said, and we went in. The place was dark and cool and deserted, nobody behind the bar, the juke box silent.

We perched on bar-stools, lighted cigarettes, waited. Presently a little girl of five emerged from a door leading to living quarters. Regarding us gravely, she said Daddy had gone fishing, but Mother would be here in a minute. Then she helped herself to a five-cent bag of potato chips and munched them, looking us over.

Just when her sober scrutiny was beginning to make us uncomfortable, Mother appeared. A tired-looking woman in her late thirties, no more of a conversationalist than her daughter. Silently she produced two bottles of Coors, rang up Jeff's

change. He was reading a sign that announced roast beef sandwiches could be had for a consideration, and before the woman
disappeared, he said:

"How about a couple of those roast beef sandwiches to go?"

She agreed, and he added: "Better make it four."

When she and the child had gone to the kitchen I said: "What
gives?"

"Aren't you getting hungry?"

"Yes, I guess I am."

"Okay. We'll take the sandwiches and potato chips and more
beer and have a picnic."

"If we horse around too long," I said, "we'll have to go back
in the dark. And what will Sarah Walker say when you don't turn
up for dinner?"

"I've a flashlight in my pocket and we can go back by the road.
As for Sarah Walker, she can fire me any time. I wouldn't have
stuck with the old hellcat this long if you hadn't come along."

When we emerged from the tavern with our paper bag, the
sun had disappeared and there was a sharper nip to the air. In
the canyons darkness came earlier than in Glory Cloud. Wisps
of smoke rising here and there from wooded hillsides suggested
supper being cooked in invisible cabins.

I said, "I'll bet you are going to swipe those lilacs. I'll bet
you're just waiting for darkness."

"You wrong me, honey. You really do." We had been following the side road which branched off toward the village of Bitter
Creek, but now he touched my elbow, turning me toward the old
bridge across Coyote Creek. "This way."

The bridge seemed stout enough, although it couldn't have
been used for years, but Coyote Creek was still swollen with
melting snow from the high peaks, and it churned and bubbled
enthusiastically. I hurried across to the flat clearing on the other
side. Then I said:

"Why, this is the old roadbed of the narrow gauge."

Jeff nodded.

"Would you mind telling me what you're up to?"

"Getting lilacs for my girl. Along the roadbed a little way downstream we come to where the railroad station used to be. The station agent lived upstairs and his wife planted lilacs in the yard. The building is gone now, but the lilacs have kept growing."

Below the fork in the Coyote Canyon road, but on our side of the stream, we came to the site of a building. Only a few foundation stones remained, but the lilac bushes sprawled in untended profusion. The blossoms were in their prime, although lilacs had stopped blooming a month ago in balmier localities. Jeff chuckled as I sniffed the scented air. "You look just like Ferdinand."

"You say the sweetest things," I replied, but my heart wasn't in it, any more than my heart was in gathering lilacs now we had found them. It chilled my spirits to realize we stood on the roadbed where a runaway freight car, loaded with dynamite, had sped along, gathering momentum. Leaving murder out of it, if you could, the subject had a gruesome fascination: I expected to see more ghosts in the rapidly failing light, and I shivered.

"Cold?" Jeff asked.

"A little."

"I'll build a fire," he said. "Let's hike down the roadbed till we can't be seen from Quartz—they're fussy about where you build fires in the hills."

So we went down the canyon, finally rounding a curve. The old roadbed was easier walking than Jeff's shortcut. Grown-over with grass and weeds, it still had enough solidity to support a car, if anybody had wanted to drive his car in such a crazy place.

I kept remembering what had happened along this right of way and how many lives had been changed by what happened, and I kept walking after Jeff pronounced it safe to stop. At last he protested.

"Hey, do you realize this is all downhill? And that going back will be a climb?"

"I want to see the tunnel."

"What for?"

"To see what it looks like. Is it much farther?"

"Shouldn't be. But why not wait till after we eat?"

"It will be dark then."

"It's practically dark now." But he had enough small boy in him to be getting excited about the idea. A cave, a tunnel, an underground house—oh boy!

When we reached the tunnel entrance, a great gash in a mountainside of solid rock, I had seen enough. The vision of that June morning was already unpleasantly vivid, and the darkness inside the tunnel looked impenetrable. But Jeff stepped inside, beaming his flashlight over the rough stone walls and ceiling, along the rubble-strewn roadbed. I waited outside, shivering again, eager now to get away, to build a fire, drink some beer, forget it.

"Gail! Come here a minute!" Jeff's voice, sharp with command, came from farther inside. Reluctantly, I stumbled along to where he stood aiming his light at the ground. Some of the radiance fell back on his face, and he was tight-lipped. I looked at the roadbed, and I didn't see anything but dirt and small stones and weeds. I kept looking and then I saw it.

A patch of ground comparatively bare of grass and refuse. Firm underneath, but damp on top from the frost slowly leaving the ground here where the sun never warmed it. And on that patch of ground car-tires had etched their tread, sharp and distinct.

And I knew where Luella Greenfield had left her car. Who would think of looking in the abandoned tunnel of the old railroad? For that matter, who would think of hiding a car there, except someone very close to the narrow-gauge business, someone to whom it was still fresh and vivid? I began revising my ideas about Luella's innocence.

"Come on." Jeff headed deeper into the tunnel. Some twenty feet on, the tunnel curved slightly, and when we rounded that curve we found it. Luella's dark blue Pontiac looking fantastically impossible in its rough-hewn hide-out.

I still clutched my armful of lilacs and sniffed them, ridiculously, unaware of what I was doing. By the faint light, I saw Jeff's nostrils twitch, an expression of growing horror on his face. He told me to stay where I was, and he walked toward the

car like a man forcing himself to something he'd rather take a
beating than do.

Ignoring his command, I followed right on his heels. That
was why I didn't have to ask what was wrong when he wrenched
open the door, threw his light into the car, sucked in his breath.

Luella Greenfield wasn't sitting behind the driver's wheel
where she'd always been so nervous. She lay on her side, curled
up as if she had grown tired and decided to nap. That is, I supposed it was Luella lying there. Those were her clothes and that
was her once-bustling little figure, but the head hung at such a
grotesque angle her face wasn't visible and the back of her skull
was split open.

I held on long enough for my gaze to follow Jeff's flashlight
beam to the floor of the car, where it lingered on a prospector's
short-handled pick. Then I passed out.

XIV

Luella Greenfield's murder couldn't be handled as casually as Axel Dahlberg's. Luella's prestige as a native Coloradoan; the hue and cry of the search; the D.A.'s profound statements; the body's dramatic hiding-place: it was a big yarn. At whatever cost to resort owners and local businessmen, the press splashed it. Reporters from Denver and Granger were in Glory Cloud that same night.

Probably I was one of the few casualties in the mountains ever resuscitated by beer instead of brandy. And probably I would have passed out again if Jeff Calhoun hadn't carried me outside the tunnel even before he tried bringing me to.

The tavern at Quartz had a telephone, and Dan Sawyer was in Glory Cloud when we called. The sheriff looked me over, and he didn't insist on my going along when Jeff guided him and the deputies across the bridge and down the old roadbed. I waited, huddled in a tired Morris chair.

Perhaps fifteen minutes after the sheriff's group left, the door swung open and Milt Evans' inquisitive nose poked in. I knew he would spot me, even in my inconspicuous corner, and that was when I pretended to be asleep.

Jeff and I were certainly geniuses—at doing the wrong thing. Our little trick of ditching Murphy Friday night flew back and hit us in the faces when Doc Bailey, the coroner, decided Luella Greenfield had died that evening. By now the condition of the body made it impossible to narrow time of death to even the usual approximation, but the coroner was willing to go on record

173

that it had been Friday night. That fitted with Luella's being gone Saturday morning and with Dr. Tuckerman's having heard the car shortly after midnight Friday. It occurred to me there was no proof Tuckerman had heard the car; he might have his own reasons for cooking up such a story.

The scene at the inn that Monday night when Axel Dahlberg had been killed was being repeated. But with a difference. More tension now in the group awaiting the sheriff's questioning; more of something else, too. Fear. They had found Dahlberg's death easy to take; he had been a thorn in everybody's side and a specific menace to at least one person. Only old Charlie had even pretended grief for Axel.

But Luella Greenfield, her skull split with a prospector's pick, was another story. Luella had been inside the circle; she was one of them. There had been a summer when old Dr. Tuckerman saw her children through both measles and whooping cough; she and Fay St. Vincent were friends in the guarded, sparring-for-position manner of two women interested in the same man; she had watched Milt Evans and Sarah Walker growing up. There was grief that night, as well as strain, but more than anything there was fear.

Fear—of being the next victim. And for one person, panic. Who was experiencing that panic? I wished for a psychic Geiger counter to tell me. The murderer, I thought, must be thrown off balance and into desperation by our discovering Luella's body so soon, when conceivably it might never have been found.

And suddenly, with smothering certainty, it came to me that of all that group I was the one with most reason to be afraid. My stomach turned to lead and my bones to cellophane as my conviction grew that I must be a marked person. On a knife or on a chunk of pitch pine or on another prospector's pick my name must be written. Gail Rawson. Gail Rawson needs a bit of lethal attention.

I had been asking for it. I was the one who had snooped, pried, hinted. I was the one who had proclaimed my intention of finishing *Narrow Gauge to Gold;* I was the one to whom Dahlberg would have entrusted important information; I was the one who had turned up the folder in the Hazlitt cabin. For that matter, I was the one writing a thesis on Hazlitt, advertising in the *Saturday Review* for unpublished material concerning him.

And I wasn't cheered because I had been half-right about Luella's disappearance. Right in believing she wasn't the murderer, that she had vanished because she possessed dangerous knowledge. Last Friday night when she agreed to stay till Dan Sawyer's return, when she declared her intention to tell him several things, she was pronouncing her own death sentence. Whatever Luella knew, the murderer wasn't chancing its being told. Did I know it too? Did the murderer think I knew it? The fear solidified into an icy certainty that Glory Cloud, Colorado, was for me no longer a safe place. "Safer than you'd be in Denver," Jeff had said my first night, but he couldn't say it now.

The terror that moved in with me that night we found Luella's body stayed a long, long time. From then on, during all my days in Glory Cloud, I never ceased to be afraid. Oh, I learned to live with my fear, as one must; there were times when I almost forgot I walked in peril, times when I laughed and downed with Jeff and believed I had eluded my shadow. But always the fear was there, lurking in my unconscious, patient, biding its time. Even now, it returns at the most unlikely times and places: when mists roll in from the Pacific, smelling of salt water, quite different from clouds invading a mountain village, but still fog, mysterious and concealing; when the Sierras are bombarded by a summer storm, and I hear again the sizzle and snap of lightning at high altitudes, and the cannonade of thunder; or when, on a moonlit desert night, the coyotes sing their eerie serenade. Then the old fear comes skulking back.

The night the panic first caught me, I snapped out of it soon enough. Dan Sawyer helped me. He restored my equilibrium, started me off again on the treadmill of conjecture, simply by showing me exactly the spot I was in.

I kept saying: "But if I had killed her or had anything to do with it, why in the world would I have gone down there and then have called you?"

Sawyer regarded me stolidly. "It wouldn't be logical, would it, Miss Rawson?"

"No, it certainly wouldn't."

"You're great on logic, aren't, you, Miss Rawson?"

"Is that bad?"

"People who have a high opinion of their own reasoning powers, Miss Rawson, are inclined to underestimate the intelligence of others."

"Like Milt Evans, you mean?"

"Like quite a few people around here." Silence, uneasy on my part, thoughtful and waiting on his. Then: "What was it you and Calhoun were up to last Friday night?"

"I've told you. Over and over."

"Tell me again."

Registering pained resignation, I told him again. I didn't mention the ghosts I'd seen that night; I felt sure Dan Sawyer wouldn't believe in ghosts.

"Murphy and Evans drove up there," he was saying. "They didn't see you there or along the road."

"I told you we heard them coming and ducked out of sight."

"And after you came back, what did you do?"

I sighed. "We told Murphy we were sorry. Also Henderson. I went home to bed."

"That would have been—?"

"Around eleven o'clock."

"And did you go right to sleep?"

I tried to remember. Then I gasped, my vertebrae prickling.

"What is it, Miss Rawson?" For a slow-moving guy, he could pounce.

"I just remembered something." I told him how I had been nearly asleep when roused by a scream. How I had been alarmed until I realized it was only a mountain lion. "But now—"

Sawyer nodded. "Now you're suggesting it was Mrs. Greenfield screaming."

"It must have been."

"Thus establishing," Sawyer continued, "that you were home in bed when she was killed. Is that the best you can do?"

I didn't argue. If he thought I was spinning a yarn, let him. I had been through a lot that night, and now the fear was returning. I thought of Luella Greenfield on Friday night, rocking in her cozy kitchen, struggling with her own fear, the fear that had become a compulsion driving her to leave Glory Cloud. I thought of someone entering that kitchen, someone Luella knew and greeted cheerfully, someone, perhaps, for whom she brewed a late pot of coffee. And I thought of the final inescapable moment when Luella realized what was coming and uttered that terrified shriek. And I broke out of those reflections to say:

"Mr. Sawyer, couldn't you arrest me?"

For once, Sawyer looked surprised. But his voice was grim enough. "I certainly could."

"Then will you, please? Won't you take me to Granger and put me in jail? Tonight?"

"Is this a confession?"

"It's a confession that I'm scared. Plenty."

"Innocent people have nothing to fear," he said ponderously.

I exploded. "That's the brilliant remark of the century! Innocent people have nothing to fear, for heaven's sake! Axel Dahlberg and Luella Greenfield—what were they guilty of? It's the innocent people who have cause to be afraid with a half-witted sheriff going around with his eyes shut!"

Dan Sawyer blinked.

"Tell me more about your being so scared, Miss Rawson."

So I told him what Jeff Calhoun and I had been up to. In a general way. He listened, pale blue eyes skeptical.

"And you see," I finished, "I don't really know what we've found out. I don't know what it means or what the answer is. But how can the murderer be sure I don't understand or that I won't eventually catch on?"

"You want me to take you into protective custody?"

"Yes, I do. I've heard about miscarriage of justice, but someone who isn't guilty has a fighting chance to get out of jail. But a knife in your back is so final."

I could tell he thought it was some elaborate hoax to engage his sympathies. And I knew he put no stock in my theorizing about the narrow-gauge railroad disaster having a connection with recent occurrences or about murder striking B. J. Tuckerman and Gilbert Hazlitt.

Even knowing, my heart sank when he shook his big head. "No. I guess we won't arrest you right now, Miss Rawson. Too bad you're so frightened. But you'll be safe enough. My deputies and I will be right here."

"I don't see why you won't."

"You're too eager, Miss Rawson."

Daylight was breaking when Sawyer dismissed us that Wednesday morning. The inquest would be Thursday at ten; nobody was to leave Glory Cloud; everybody was under suspicion; same old routine.

Wednesday afternoon was distinguished by two items: a session with the reporters, and my brainwave about Luella Greenfield's embroidery. And, of course, by the fog. Noon was but little brighter than dawn, and the prospect of another sunless three days intensified my depression.

Jeff arrived with the reporters and photographers. I didn't know whether he came with them to my cabin to give me moral support or because the red-headed chap from the *Granger Record* turned out to be young, brash and attractive. His name was Cy.

What they wanted, of course, was a first-hand account of our discovering Luella's body. Young love, lilacs, murder—I could imagine the linotypes clucking over such tidbits, and the presses thundering approval, and the newsboys yelling on Champa Street, and the people on the suburban busses gobbling it down.

"Tell me, Gail," the red-head said chummily, "what is your opinion about these murders? Do you think there's a connection between your pal Dahlberg's death and Mrs. Greenfield's?"

Ah, yes, Dahlberg. My pal Dahlberg. The commuters were going to enjoy that.

Jeff's face had darkened; he shook his head in warning. But I ignored him and gave Cy a high-powered smile. I had just thought of how I could fix Dan Sawyer's wagon, and I started talking before examining pros or cons.

"Since you want my opinion, Cy," I said sweetly, "I'll give it to you."

Whereupon I spilled my deductions that everything went back some thirty years to the Granger, Glory Cloud & Western. At least I had sense enough not to mention names or to voice specific suspicions. I merely pointed out that life in Glory Cloud had been beautiful until Axel Dahlberg started research on the narrow gauge, and emphasized the abundance of emotional potential in the old scandal.

"You understand," I added, "that the sheriff doesn't agree with my ideas. But of course he *is* quite young, isn't he?"

The Denver reporters were looking dubious, and the older of them shook his head. "Better leave it lay, boys. The St. Vincent interests wouldn't like it, and that means the business office wouldn't either."

But Cy was smiling broadly. "I like it, Gail. I'm not saying you're right, but it'll make a sweet spread."

Jeff's face looked like a thundercloud as he sped the reporters out into the murky afternoon and turned on me.

"Have you lost your mind? Thanks to you, that red-headed screwball will dig into the morgue and have a Roman holiday."

"So what if he does? Maybe it will give Mr. Dan Sawyer something to think about."

My cockiness wilted at his next words.

"Maybe it will. And maybe it will give the murderer something more to think about where you're concerned, too."

The gentlemen of the press had helped themselves to cigarettes from my pack on the coffee table, so I crossed to the desk where I kept a carton. A folded square of white material caught my eye. It had lain there several days, but suddenly it registered.

Luella Greenfield's unfinished embroidery. I remembered how puzzled I had been at her deviation from the stamped pattern and how dissatisfied with my tentative explanation. Now that I knew Luella was dead, the problem roused more than idle curiosity. I snatched up the cloth, draped it over the davenport.

"Look. Here's something for your master mind to chew on."

Jeff gave it one disdainful glance. "What kind of pansy do you think I am? Maybe that red-head does fancywork, but I don't."

"Okay, wise guy. Now listen."

I told him where and how I had found the lunch cloth. I told him how Luella's embellishments had baffled me and how I had brought it home to study. By now he had alerted out of his sulks, and when I offered the theory that Luella had been too scared to know what she was doing, that didn't satisfy him either.

He bent to scrutinize the embroidery. "I don't get it. Without knowing the first thing about such matters, even I can tell it's not according to Hoyle. What did you say that funny stuff is called?"

"Running-stitch, I think. At first I thought it was blanket-stitch, but then I remembered blanket-stitch is used along edges."

We stared at it. The unaccountable corner looked like this:

At last Jeff said: "Suppose your idea was right up to a point. Suppose Luella did go home that night, all set to leave town, having nothing to do but wait for the sheriff's high-sign. Suppose she did settle down in her favorite rocker there by the kitchen stove with her fancywork to help kill time. But suppose instead of her just getting increasingly frightened and bolting, somebody came. Somebody she knew. And then suppose that while they sat talking, Luella's fingers busy, as always, she gradually realized this person intended to kill her."

"I thought of that last night. And if I'm right about the murderer hunting something, he or she probably thought Luella had what he was hunting and demanded it."

"But in a spot like that why didn't Luella come across?"

"Maybe she did. Or maybe she couldn't because she didn't actually have whatever it was. Either way, by then the murderer would have to bump her because she knew too much already."

Jeff nodded. "So Luella knew she was going to catch it, but she was a spunky little number, and she determined to leave a clue to the murderer's identity. She stalled for time, probably pretending she would deliver any second, and she kept working on this lunch cloth."

"But why didn't the murderer take along the cloth when he hauled Luella away?"

Jeff shook his head. "Even a murderer must be under a slight nervous strain at such a time. We can't figure out what this means ourselves, and he probably didn't give it a thought."

Again, I remembered the scream I had heard that night, and I asked, "Do you suppose she was killed right then and there?" I told him about the cry of terror.

"I don't know," he said. "The murderer could have knocked her out, dumped her and the bags into the car and driven off. Wasn't it around midnight old Tuckerman heard the car?"

"Shortly after. He said."

"Yeah. He said. Well, whenever it was, the murderer drove Luella's car down to Quartz, across to the old roadbed and into the tunnel. There he hauled out the prospector's pick—they're common in a mining town. Then he hiked back to Glory Cloud, maybe using the shortcut, and went home to bed."

"Why couldn't it have been this way?" I asked. "The murderer drove from Granger to Quartz. There he hid his car and hiked on up to Glory Cloud. The picture here is just as we've outlined it. After driving Luella's car down to Quartz and into the tunnel, the murderer got back into his own car and returned to Granger. Obviously, I mean *her* own car."

"Obviously, you mean Amanda Plumb. Sure, it could have been that way too."

I looked again at Luella's busywork. "But what does it mean? Can you think of anybody those stitches might refer to?"

"When a doctor performs an operation he stitches up his patient."

"Oh, honestly! Try again."

"How about those flowers? Aren't they daisies? I'd describe Amanda as a daisy."

"Maybe so, but they're part of the regular design. If any part means anything, it's that last stuff she dashed off."

"Wait a minute. You said she dashed off. When you were a kid did you have a toy telegraph set? I did."

"That's for boys. What about it?"

"But you know what Morse code is?"

"A means of communication, Mr. Evans. Any fool knows that."

"Yeah, sure. But what are those means? I'll tell you what they are—dots and dashes."

I looked down at the embroidery.

"But this is all dashes."

"No, it isn't. See how much longer some stitches are than others? Is that how it's supposed to look?"

"No," I said. "Even I know the stitches should be uniform in length and spacing."

"And these aren't uniform! The long ones are dashes and the shorter ones dots!"

If he was right, it meant we had the murderer's name literally in our hands.

"Well, get going," I said. "Translate. What does it say?"

But Jeff shook his head. "I don't remember enough of the code to read it." He concentrated, frowning. "I believe she meant the first letter to be an H. I guess we'll have to get Dan Sawyer in on this."

"Nuts to that! He would just say I did the work myself. Henderson could tell him I've had this here since Sunday."

"Doc Tuckerman has an unabridged dictionary. That would give the code."

"Consulting it might be risky if you're right about the first letter meaning H."

"This whole business is risky," he said. "Hold on. How do we know Luella Greenfield was familiar with Morse code? It's not a common accomplishment."

"But I'll bet you anything she was. Her husband used to be station agent for the Granger, Glory Cloud & Western and sometimes Luella helped with his duties. I've heard that from several sources, including Luella. And what are a station agent's duties?"

"Yeah. Among other things, sending telegraph messages. So that's okay. All we have to do now is dope it out."

It sounded simple. Tenderly I folded the cloth and I said: "This goes in the family vault. Where should I hide it?"

We decided what was good enough for Edgar Allan Poe was good enough for us. We placed it in a linen drawer in the kitchen hutch.

Jeff couldn't wait to consult Tuckerman's dictionary. Before leaving, he put his arms around me and held me tight.

"You know, honey, we've guessed that Axel Dahlberg found something and hid it. Likewise, Luella Greenfield. If anybody comes around—anybody—and wants what we've just hidden, give it to them. Don't argue."

I locked the door behind him, but something had slipped into the cabin along with wisps of fog. It was my new companion, the featureless face and shadowy form of my fear.

I didn't see Jeff again till just before the inquest Thursday. But somebody left a copy of that morning's *Granger Record* under my door. Later I learned it had been Milt Evans' way of throwing my lack of discretion into my face. Sawyer had ordered Amanda Plumb to be on hand for the inquest, and she had driven up early, bringing along the papers.

I spread out the *Record* on the kitchen table. Cy had said my interview would make a sweet spread and he had been so right. The morgue had yielded plenty of background stuff, including pix, and my first thought was that the yarn might contain facts I didn't have. My second thought was that Cy had really let himself go in referring to "Gail Rawson, beautiful and perspicacious Doctor of Philosophy," who had tipped off the *Record's* reporter to the real inside story. That must have been the easiest Ph.D. ever achieved by any graduate student.

But my third thought was the disconcerting one. It came when I read that the *Record's* representative had approached Miss Fay St. Vincent and Dr. Herman Tuckerman for statements, and that both had refused to be quoted. Cy hadn't dared say or imply too much, but even in the carefully-worded account it was apparent that cold hostility had greeted his inquiries. I realized at whom that hostility was mainly directed.

And I sensed at once that my popularity was way below par when I arrived at the schoolhouse for the inquest. Disapproval started with Henderson whom I found waiting outside the Barlow cabin to accompany me the short block through the clammy fog. We made the trip in silence. At the door Murphy gave me a hard look and muttered a single word. "Blabbermouth!" Inside the crowded little room Dan Sawyer and Doc Bailey suspended a quiet conference to stare at me with blank, unfriendly eyes.

None of that surprised me. I had known when I shot off my mouth to the reporters that it wouldn't promote cordial relations between me and the sheriff. What I wasn't prepared for was Fay St. Vincent's aloof disdain, Dr. Tuckerman's glance of quiet reproach, Sarah Walker's tight-clamped mouth and flashing eyes, Amanda Plumb's hot stare of hatred. There was nothing Milt Evans enjoyed more, next to blowing about his own cleverness, than a good mess of trouble, but behind the gloating amusement, his shifty green eyes were worried.

Even the strangers from Pinto and Quartz eyed me askance.

But when I glimpsed old Charlie on the other side of the room, he grinned his toothless grin and gave me a little wave, and I felt like running over and throwing my arms around him.

Just before the coroner got under way Jeff slipped in to sit beside me. I whispered:

"Nobody loves me. I wonder why?"

"Yeah. I wonder."

But I forgot my failure to win friends and influence people when he told me he had looked up Morse code. I asked whether he had doped out Luella's message.

"How could I? I didn't have the cloth. I made a copy of the symbols and we can work on it when this is over."

We stopped whispering then; Doc Bailey was pounding for order. There was a stir at the door as several reporters hurried in. After Cy had hailed me with a smirk and a wink, the frigid temperature dropped several more degrees.

As first witness the coroner called me to describe the finding of Luella's body. Next Jeff. I expected to be questioned concerning my interview with the press, but the Granger, Glory Cloud & Western was never mentioned.

Nobody would admit having seen Luella Greenfield after Henderson took her home Friday evening. Fay and Tuckerman and Milt and Sarah had all been at the inn when she left there, and each, in turn, swore that was the last time he had seen her alive. Amanda Plumb testified she hadn't seen her since the afternoon before, Thursday, when Mrs. Greenfield had been at the mailboxes when Amanda came along. One might have expected that on Friday afternoon, when Luella was preparing to pull out, she would have made a point of seeing Amanda to arrange for her mail's being forwarded. If that had happened, Amanda didn't admit it.

Nor did questioning people concerning their Friday night activities produce any real alibis. Everybody could account for his movements up to a point, but nobody could prove it would have been impossible for him to go to Mrs. Greenfield's around midnight and kill her. Herman Tuckerman had been at the inn till after ten when he accompanied Fay home. Milt Evans had been supervising the deputies' search for Jeff and me till after nine, when he disappeared. His story was that he had taken it upon himself to hunt for us in some of the abandoned cabins.

Milt confined his remarks to answering questions, volunteering neither advice nor wise pronouncements, and I thought this indicated his nervous state.

As for Sarah Walker, she had been at the inn all evening, most of the time in the kitchen. She testified she had been "indisposed." No doubt in people's minds, judging by their expressions, as to the nature of her indisposition. And old Charlie, accounting for his activities, revealed that he had gone to the inn around ten because Sarah had asked him to drop in to talk over some work. He testified he had found Mrs. Walker dozing at the kitchen table, head on arms.

Charlie grinned. "I guess she was just plumb wore out."

Amusement ran over the room and Sarah Walker's black eyes snapped, but the coroner wasn't interested in spicy details that shed no light on what had happened to Luella.

Amanda Plumb was outraged to be questioned at all. She had been home in Granger all evening, alone.

Nobody admitted ownership of the prospector's pick; nobody was willing to go on record as having seen it before or knowing where it came from.

The verdict: ". . . at the hands of a person or persons unknown."

When I left my cabin that morning I hadn't locked the door, and when Jeff and I entered the kitchen after the inquest we found I'd had a caller.

Jammed into a milk bottle on the table was a fragrant mass of lilacs. Under the bottle, a scrap of paper torn from a pocket notebook, bearing one word: Cy.

I laughed. Not a young man to let grass grow under his feet. But as I bent closer to inhale the scent, I sobered. In imagination I held again the lilacs we had picked Tuesday night, and I saw Luella Greenfield's car in the dimly-lighted tunnel. And I knew it would be a long time before I could again enjoy the smell of lilacs.

Jeff hadn't laughed. The tempery expression I was learning to dread came over his face.

"That heel! Trying to muscle in—"

"Oh Jeff, don't be childish. It's only a gracious gesture."

"I'll gracious gesture him!" Jeff headed for the door.

"Not so fast, son. We've work to do."

Jeff reached in his pocket, handed me a folded sheet. "There's the code. You can get started. I intend to catch that guy before he leaves town—give him a heart-to-heart talk on the subject of poaching."

I took the paper. "Go ahead. If you must make a fool of yourself, don't let me influence you."

"I won't." He strode out.

I was completely out of patience with him. This flying off the handle at no provocation was a different thing from a little healthy jealousy. It was his foolish outburst at Axel that had first put us on a spot. Now people had been murdered in this town; we were both in danger of arrest; we had our hands on something big, something that promised to solve everything; and the big lug went storming out like a hot-blooded adolescent.

Nuts to him. I would figure it out myself and he could go jump off a mountain. I took the cloth from the hutch and spread it on the kitchen table, the code beside it.

It was slow going, but Jeff's thought that the first symbol was meant for H seemed correct. My excitement mounted when an E followed. Lunch forgotten, my eyes raced between Luella's work and the code, and I jotted down letters as I went along.

That I had jumped to a premature conclusion became evident when the third grouping of short and long stitches turned out to be a J. I scanned the code, sure Luella had meant an R. But no. R was dot, space, dot, dot, and this was unmistakably dash, dot, dash, dot. J.

I was still wrinkling my brow over this surprise when a knock fell on the door. It was old Charlie, twisting his corduroy cap between wiry hands. I thought he had come about the firewood and felt impatient at the interruption.

But Charlie had something else on his mind. He wanted to talk, insisting it was important. I led the way to the living room, gloomed by the fog, and switched on the lamp, then turned to find I had lost Charlie en route.

He was standing by the kitchen table. I called, "Shall we sit in here and be comfortable?"

He started.

"Pretty flowers," he grinned, coming into the living room. But his eyes had been on the lunch cloth and the code sheet, and I upbraided myself for not having put them away. I didn't want him spreading the word of what I was up to before I knew myself.

Charlie's loquacity was strangely cramped today. He looked sorry he'd come. I chatted, trying to put him at ease, wishing he would get to the point and leave.

It seemed that the night Jeff and I called on Charlie, the old fellow had a pretty shrewd notion of what we were driving at. But he hadn't been sure till he saw this morning's paper. Since Monday night he had been thinking it over, and now he had concluded it was his duty to tell me what he knew.

"Never bothered me too much about old B. J.," Charlie said wryly. "He was an ornery son-of-a-gun anyway. But I liked your perfessor feller and poor Mrs. Greenfield was always good to me."

"You mean you have some idea who might have killed Axel and Luella?"

"Not exactly that. But I know something I never told nobody about the night B. J. shot himself."

"If it's evidence," I said, "the person to tell is the sheriff."

But Charlie shook his head. "No, sir. I don't want to get this person in no hot water if I'm wrong. That young sheriff—he's kinda slow but he'd hang on like a bulldog once he got an idea. And it ain't rightly evidence, I reckon—it's just something I seen."

"What did you see?"

But Charlie couldn't be hurried. He made me promise I wouldn't tell Sawyer unless I felt it was really necessary, and he went back to describe the night of B. J. Tuckerman's death. He told about the storm that evening, a real humdinger: lightning, thunder, rain coming down in buckets. Charlie had been walking along the main drag of Glory Cloud, head down against the storm, hurrying home.

As he passed the Tuckerman house somebody slipped out the door, hurried across the porch, disappeared down the road in the rain. Just as this person descended the steps there was a brilliant flash of lightning and Charlie recognized who it was. Apparently, he wasn't seen himself. He felt only mild surprise and curiosity till the next day, when he learned it was at that hour B. J. Tuckerman was presumed to have shot himself.

"And you never reported seeing this person there?"

Charlie looked wretchedly guilty, but stubborn. "No, I didn't. I figgered she could have had a perfectly good excuse for being there, but nobody would ever believe her then, and like I said, whatever happened, old B. J. only got what he had coming. I didn't want to make no trouble for anybody over him."

So it had been a woman! I asked quietly:

"Whom did you see that night, Charlie?"

He twisted his cap, looking acutely miserable. But when he finally blurted out the name, it wasn't the one I expected.

"It was Amandy," he said unhappily. "Amandy Plumb."

XV

I wondered whether old Charlie had invented this. But then I knew he hadn't. This explained why he defended Amanda so tenaciously Monday evening, why Amanda was so rattled by Jeff's question about the night B. J. died. I thought of Amanda's credit card turning up in Dahlberg's cabin, of her feeble alibis for Dahlberg's and Luella's murders. And I thought of her husband meeting violent death in a tunnel, meeting death because of one man's negligence and greed. B. J. Tuckerman's.

Impulsive sympathy stirred me as I pictured that stalwart, self-sufficient woman striking out against the man who had ruined her life. Striking with the terrible, straightforward vengeance of the frontier: a life for a life.

But then I realized that, if this were true, it had been four lives for a life, one of them Axel Dahlberg's, and the sympathy faded.

Charlie seemed to feel better now that he had passed on his burden. Probably for thirty years he had searched his soul as to whether he'd done right in not telling. Now he tossed the responsibility in my lap; he could afford to be cheerful.

But could he? I frowned. "You've never mentioned this to Amanda?"

"No, I ain't. At first I figgered to ask her some day what she was up to that night, and then the years kept going by and I pretty near forgot it. You think maybe I ought to ask her now?"

"No!" My voice was sharper than I intended. "I think you ought to keep forgetting it. Unless the sheriff asks you about it."

191

"You promised not to tell the sheriff."

"Unless I had to. I may have to. Don't you see that both you and I might be in danger, just knowing it?"

Charlie chuckled. "Shucks, I ain't scared of Amandy. Could be she knows something too she ain't telling, but Amandy's no killer."

"Maybe not. However, I'll feel better if you don't quiz Amanda or anybody about it yet."

Looking solemn, old Charlie agreed.

It no longer seemed important, but I mentioned a question that had worried me. I didn't really expect him to know the answer, but he came close enough to surprise me.

"Look, Charlie—this is just plain curiosity. Do you have any idea what Fay and Hazlitt quarreled about their last night together?"

"I wasn't there," he drawled, sharp old eyes thoughtful, "but I got a pretty good idea on account of I'd already heard 'em spatting before that. Fay was riled because he hadn't give her no engagement ring."

Charlie read my mind. "You're thinking she wasn't so crazy about him if a little thing like a ring mattered that much to her. But she was crazy about him all right. I reckon she was just kind of used to having her own way—spoiled, you know. And then, girls bein' the way they are, it probably bothered her because Sarah—Sarah Foster she was then—was flashing a pretty engagement ring around town and Fay didn't have none."

All my suspicion and antagonism toward Sarah Walker surged back, and I wondered how Jim Walker, a ministerial student, had been able to splurge on a showy diamond. But Charlie corrected me. Not a diamond, but the handsome old-fashioned amethyst I'd seen Sarah wear. And Jim Walker hadn't bought it; it had been left to him by a doting aunt.

"His ma's sister in Cheyenne," Charlie said. "She was an old-maid schoolteacher and Jim was her only nephew and she knew he was fixing to get married. She had Bright's disease and she died that summer—I remember Jim and Mrs. Walker went up to Cheyenne for a couple of weeks—it was while Sarah was visiting her sister. And the aunt left her insurance to Jim—don't know how much, but enough to help with his schooling and she left him that ring that had been her grandmother's. Fer that matter, Sarah did kind of prance around putting on airs—can't say you could blame Fay for pouting a little."

After sorting out the aunts, grandmothers, sisters, and what not, I still couldn't make the story mean anything against Sarah Walker, except that coming up in the world, according to her lights, had gone to her head. I asked:

"Why do you think Hazlitt didn't get Fay a ring? Even if he was hard up, couldn't he have bought one on time?"

"Oh, he was hard up all right. Most times Fay kind of bragged about how he was poor but proud. Claimed he was a genius and that everybody would know it some day. Once I heard him say he wanted to give her his ma's ring, only it was in a Chicago bank deposit vault and it'd take time to get it."

What Charlie had just told me about Amanda seemed to make Fay's love life none of my business anyway; I dropped it.

The fog was steadily growing denser. As I watched from the open door, old Charlie de-materialized in about three feet. The late afternoon had a brooding, ominous silence, normal, every-day sounds muffled by the gray cotton batting. I felt weary and very much alone, and I hastily closed and locked my door.

I returned to my project, but I couldn't concentrate. I kept asking: where did Hazlitt fit in, if Charlie's story about Amanda meant what it appeared to? Simplest was the explanation Jeff offered when he first suggested Hazlitt could have been murdered too. That Hazlitt had a lead to Tuckerman's murder.

Perhaps that stormy night Charlie hadn't been the only one to recognize Amanda. Possibly Gilbert Hazlitt had also been abroad in the rain and lightning, and perhaps he had not refrained from questioning Amanda. Perhaps Hazlitt had decided how to raise the money for Fay's engagement ring.

From all I had heard, I didn't think Hazlitt would have been above blackmail. But would Amanda have had the money to buy his silence? Would there have been compensation as a result of her husband's death? Perhaps, but not enough to insure peace and safety for the rest of her life. Only one way to do that: arrange for Hazlitt's body to be found in an old mine shaft.

But the problem remained: what clue to the sequence of blackmail and murder could Axel Dahlberg have found after thirty years?

I gave up. Pulling the shades, I sat down at the table again and turned to Luella's lunch cloth. It might tell me everything I needed to know. There was no longer any question but that her erratic stitches represented the dots and dashes of Morse code.

Much later I threw down my pencil and scowled at what I had written. I had made a number of false tries, but this final result was checked and double-checked.

And I knew no more than at the beginning. So far as I could tell, Luella's attempt to leave a clue didn't mean a darned thing. It had to be what I had made it: HEJULY201921DESMOIN. And what was that? A great big nothing.

Of course, when I stopped trying to force the letters to spell Herman Tuckerman, I saw at once the date and the place: July 20, 1921, Des Moin(es). Luella hadn't finished the final word, but it could only be Des Moines. And I wouldn't have been more amazed to have Peru come into it than Iowa. So far as I knew, nobody in Glory Cloud had any connection with Des Moines.

I leaped at 1921, the year of scandal and sudden death in Glory Cloud. But July 20? I was sure such a date hadn't turned up before, but I found my notebook and checked. The wreck on the Granger, Glory Cloud & Western had occurred June 6, 1921. B. J. Tuckerman had shot himself June 10. June 10 was also the date of the class night exercises which Milt Evans had missed.

I should have other specific dates, but even while I leafed through my notes, I knew that July 20 was not among them. The picnic when St. Vincent left his gun at Tuckerman's took place May 3o, 1921. Gilbert Hazlitt's body had been found August 14; it was assumed he had died August 11.

Things had been popping in Glory Cloud in June, 1921, and in August, but what had happened in July? Presumably, of course, whatever it was hadn't even happened in Colorado, but in Iowa.

But why had Luella taken the trouble and risk of leaving an obscure message? Why hadn't she simply coded the murderer's name? I tried to put myself in Luella's shoes, God forbid! Wouldn't anybody in her situation go right to the heart of the matter, indicate the murderer's name?

I wished Jeff were here, and I wondered why he wasn't. Almost dinnertime and I hadn't eaten since breakfast. I opened the refrigerator and gazed blankly at the meager larder, all the time thinking why, why, why?

Food was what I needed. When I had eaten half a sandwich, the answer hit me. Only one reason why Luella wouldn't have put down the murderer's name. Because she knew or feared that the murderer also was familiar with Morse code.

So who in Glory Cloud did know Morse code? As Jeff had pointed out, it wasn't a common accomplishment. However, it didn't matter whether the murderer actually knew code or whether Luella simply thought he did. Either way, she was too cagey to put down a name—that might snag his attention; she put down a date that might or might not mean something to the murderer, but which would be less obvious than a name. An element of chance in that, too, but Luella had little to lose by trying.

Now my thinking came full circle. What if Luella, as I'd first assumed, had started to spell Herman? What if she had got as far as H E, remembered old Dr. Tuckerman knew code and switched her tactics? Or maybe the H E wasn't the beginning of Herman or of anything; maybe it stood alone. He. He did something. He knew something. He was up to something on July 20 in Des Moines. In that case, the H E could refer to Tuckerman or Milt Evans, or, for that matter, to Julius St. Vincent or Gilbert Hazlitt.

On the other hand, it might be the beginning of a word different from Herman. And abruptly I knew what that word might have been. Help. When Luella started to use code, her unconscious mind would have gone back to the days when her fingers automatically tapped out the message to be transmitted, and in her panic she started to signal for help. But then she realized the futility of that.

I tried to connect Amanda Plumb and July 20. Was that when Hazlitt first approached Amanda? Then had she stalled him with promises till early August? But where did Des Moines come into it?

I kept running into blank walls, going up blind alleys. I felt I must have the key, either in my notes or in my head, and be neglecting to use it.

What had I said when I originally sold Jeff my hypothesis about the significance of the narrow gauge? Something about Axel Dahlberg. I had said Axel was the catalyst in the situation.

If Axel had known that Amanda Plumb had been seen leaving the Tuckerman house on the night of June 10, 1921, would he have gone to Granger, notified the authorities? Or would he first have given Amanda a chance to explain?

But if Charlie weren't lying about telling only me, how could Axel have known?

The answer emerged smoothly from the tangled facts and imaginings in my memory. Earlier I had theorized that damaging evidence had turned up in the filing folder from the Hazlitt cabin. Now I was sure of it. Axel knew about Amanda because he had stumbled upon the information in that folder. And I hadn't found it because Axel had removed it.

It all stacked up. Gilbert Hazlitt, as well as old Charlie, *had* seen Amanda that night. And he had not only accosted Amanda but had also made a written record of what he had seen and slipped it into that filing folder to reinforce future demands.

When Luella took the folder to examine before letting me lend it to Dahlberg, she found and read that notation. She had been puzzled and worried. She hadn't realized precisely what it meant. But it upset her, and she kept fussing at me about the folder. And after Axel was killed, she kept speculating about that notation and growing increasingly disturbed. Luella, poor soul, had been an inveterate chatterbox and she had probably sounded out the wrong person.

So who had last possessed that deadly bit of paper Gilbert Hazlitt had filed? Dahlberg or Luella? I thought it would have been Dahlberg. I thought he wouldn't have let it out of his hands. That fitted in with Luella's pestering me about the folder after

Axel's death: she wanted to get the notation again, to study it further. And that was what the murderer had been seeking in my cabin and in Axel's, and demanding of poor Luella the night she died. But it wasn't in the folder now.

If I could dope out where Dahlberg had concealed Hazlitt's blackmail evidence and get hold of it, then July 20, 1921, Des Moines, would take care of itself. Maybe Hazlitt's note carried that date. Des Moines I still didn't get, but the main thing was to find the note.

I thought of my bewilderment over Axel's trip to that abandoned cabin Monday afternoon. Now I knew why he had gone there. He had been so far ahead of me that he was reconstructing Hazlitt's murder, probably seeing Hazlitt and Amanda making a rendezvous at that old cabin for her pay-off, seeing Amanda waiting along the path beside the mine shaft in darkness.

I had already gone over everything Dahlberg had said and done during his brief time in Glory Cloud till I was punchy. But somewhere along the line I must have missed something. I still had a stubborn hunch that Axel's activities the night he was killed, the night of our fry, held the answer. Doggedly, I started all over.

We had met at his cabin around seven. Everybody had carried something and we had started up the Alpine road. Halfway up, we stopped to rest while Axel went to look at the marker showing the Divide.

Wait a minute. That little scene was one I had overlooked. He said some silly thing about wanting to see whether Mt. Evans was still on the job, and he hadn't particularly seemed to want us along. I remembered the gesture I had feared betrayed a pounding heart. Had that been unconscious verification that something was still safe in his pocket? And he had been gone such a short time, but looked so pleased with himself when he returned. What had been said then?

Jeff had asked if the mountains were all in their proper places or something of the sort, and Axel had said: "Everything's right where it should be."

I remembered how the bronze marker showing the peaks of the range was bolted to a flat-topped stone. Would there be room between the marker and the stone to insert a folded paper? I thought there would be. I thought Axel Dahlberg had carried Hazlitt's note in his pocket that night, had gone up the path and tucked it between the stone and the marker for safe-keeping, perhaps planning, in case he went to Granger the next day, to stop on his way and pick it up.

One thing about it. If that was where Axel had hidden the note, it would still be there. Because Jeff Calhoun and I were the only ones who knew anything about the incident.

And, feeling so sure it was there, I intended to get it. Now. Tonight. I would have preferred Jeff's company, but if he wanted to sulk in his tent, I wasn't going around to make conciliatory noises.

But suddenly I was no longer alone. Jeff wasn't with me, or Cy, or old Charlie. It was the something new that had recently been added; it was my uninvited guest, the fear, lurking just out of sight beyond the door to the living room.

"You idiot!" it jeered. "You dope. You mean that you intend to go out at this hour—it's almost eleven, you know—into the dripping fog up to that remote spot, alone, unarmed? Didn't you tell the sheriff you were afraid because you knew too much? Don't you realize that now you know even more? Are you out of your mind?"

I listened to the voice of fear, and my resolution wavered. But then I argued. "Of course I'm afraid. You should know. I'm afraid wherever I am, whatever I'm doing. I'm afraid right here in my own cabin with the door locked. Sure, I know too much. Sure, the murderer has his eye on me. But what's to prevent his slipping down here this murky night, killing me in my bed? Maybe he's on his way right now. Maybe getting out of this trap and melting into the night is the smartest thing I can do. And the only help for knowing too much is to know more. When I know enough the sheriff will have to believe me."

My companion subsided into mutters, slunk away. But I knew he wasn't gone for good.

I snapped off the lights in the kitchen, left the lamp burning in the living room. I was wearing flannel slacks and I put two sweaters under my heavy jacket, tied a scarf over my page-boy, picked up the flashlight with mittened fingers. Summer in Colorado!

I slipped quietly outside, locking the door. Then I discovered my companion had returned; the fear wanted to go along.

At first, I was grateful for the blackness and fog. I didn't care to encounter Murphy or Henderson or Dan Sawyer, and I definitely didn't care to encounter anyone else. Unless it would be Jeff returning. I hadn't been spoofing when I thought that the murderer could be creeping toward the Barlow cabin to settle with me. It was a night made for stealthy activity, and once I'd entertained the thought that my cabin was a trap I had felt a breathless urgency to get out of there. Quick.

I used my flashlight as little as I dared. By now I knew my way around well enough to follow the road running east and west past my place. About half a block beyond Luella Greenfield's I would reach a crossroad where I could turn right to hit the main drag. I don't know why I didn't follow my usual route—south to the schoolhouse corner and then left—I just felt better doing it this way.

But my feet misjudged the distance. I kept plodding east, and suddenly I knew I had gone too far, that somewhere I had missed my right turn. I found myself no longer on the hard-packed dirt road of the street, but on rough, rocky ground, slick with weeds and sparse grass. I thought it must be the end of the road since I had made no change in direction.

For a cautious moment I snapped on my light. The beam failed to pierce the opaque fog for more than a few feet; its radiance fell back in a small circle of hazy light. But I saw enough to know that a few more steps would have taken me to the drop-off into a canyon, the same canyon that yawned behind Dahlberg's cabin and beyond the lookout point. If I had stumbled over that down-plunge, anybody who wanted me out of the way could stop worrying.

My hands were shaking as I turned around and when I thought I had retraced my steps far enough to hit the crossroad

I used the light again to check. This part would be tricky. Going along Glory Cloud's main street, past the Tuckerman house, past the inn, past Dahlberg's, past the intersection with the Coyote Canyon road leading to old Charlie's place.

As soon as I started to climb noticeably, I would know I was on the Alpine road. A pitch, they called it in these parts. What I would describe as a long, steep hill was termed a sharp little pitch. Maybe it was easier to live with the grandeur of the Rockies if one employed such understatements, referred to the mountains merely as the hills. So once I was on that sharp little pitch, the only remaining problem would be locating the point where the trail led to the lookout spot and the marker.

Ever since venturing forth my nerves had been trigger-edged, ears straining for the slightest sound, eyes narrowed in a futile effort to peer behind the misty curtains of the black night. And then, just as I passed the Tuckerman house, its lights dimly visible through the opalescent darkness, I sensed, or thought I sensed, another human presence very near. My heart lurched and I thought instantly, "It's Jeff. He's coming back to make up with me."

I halted, snapped off my light, called his name softly. Just once. "Jeff?" But the word had barely crossed my lips before my companion snarled: "What makes you think it's Jeff, you fool! Run! Run fast and run silently. Make yourself scarce."

As one runs in a nightmare, straining, straining, but seeming never to get anywhere, I sped past the lighted inn, past the dark crossroad where Axel Dahlberg's cabin stood. There had been no answer to my tentative call; there were no footsteps thudding along behind. Probably there had been no unseen presence back in Tuckerman's yard—it was only that I wished so heartily for Jeff's company.

Now I knew I was on the Alpine road, definitely going uphill. I was winded and I slowed to a walk. I thought: "Well, I got through town without anybody trying to stop me. Now I can relax."

This infuriated my companion. "Oh yeah?" it sneered. "These hills are filled with creatures that prowl at night. The hills and the night belong to them. You're the intruder. The coyotes and the bears and the mountain lions have a right here—what right do you have? Listen! What's that padding behind you?"

I whirled, swung my light. But again, the beam failed to penetrate, producing a pitifully small circle of veiled illumination, droplets of moisture shimmering in the subdued rays. And I held my breath and listened, but I heard nothing.

I snapped off the light, continued climbing. But fear wasn't so easily defeated. It kept pointing out things I should see, but couldn't. What were those two tiny points of green light glowing off there to the right? Were they eyes? They looked like cat eyes, didn't they? You could call it a puma or a cougar or a mountain lion or any one of several other names, but it was still a great big cat, wasn't it? A cat that could kill a horse with a single snap of its powerful jaws. So people claimed that a mountain lion seldom attacked a human being, did they? Would you like to test that? And how often is seldom? The same people also say a cougar will trail a person, don't they? Will follow and watch and wait. What do you suppose it's waiting for? Do you suppose it's waiting for some silly girl to get far enough away from the village alone, to intrude far enough into alien territory? They say a mountain lion is afraid of people. They say, they say, they say. But what if the lion doesn't know what they say? What if it only knows what its wild cat-blood tells it? To stalk, to pounce, to kill.

My heart was galloping at such a rate I found it hard to breathe. Of course, it could have been the altitude. And the running. And the climbing. I must be nearly to the trail. I used my light again, merely to determine my location, not because I thought there were any mountain lions around.

My companion didn't like the light. Fear snarled, "Douse it. You're just showing where you are. Do you want to make it easy for them?"

And I said, "Watch your antecedents. Whom do you mean by 'them'?" But I knew all right. "Them" referred to all those denizens of the night watching and resenting our encroachment. It referred to all those residents of Glory Cloud who were so belligerent toward strangers poking into their private business, so determined to let the dead past bury its dead. It referred to the one of those residents who might not have been eluded tonight, after all, who might have been lucky enough to glimpse my flashlight heading this way. Was that why the back of my neck prickled so uncomfortably? Fool that I was, I preferred thinking a human animal was trailing me instead of a wild one. You could always reason with a person, couldn't you? Gail's a fast talker—she can talk her way out of it.

I was so disgruntled with my companion I decided to keep the light on just to show it. Besides I must be getting very close to the trail leading to the marker and I couldn't possibly locate it without help. So I hugged the left-hand side of the road and I kept my flashlight turned on the ground, watching for a narrow path branching off. As best I could, I ignored my conviction that someone or something was following me. There was no point in constantly looking back; no point at all; I couldn't see a thing and it was all imagination and my fear anyway. This was positively the last time I would do it.

Even with the light I almost missed the path. Maybe it was because I was wondering about Amanda Plumb. Because for the first time I was seriously considering that her leaving the Tuckerman house that night might not mean she had killed B. J. Tuckerman, but that she had just witnessed somebody else killing him. Amanda was close-mouthed; if she had seen somebody firing that gun or somebody laying it down to creep out the back way, she would have kept her trap shut. I wished my mind would stop serving up words like trap and gun and creep.

When I spotted the trail there was no question about needing to use the flash. Without it I could walk right off the precipice beyond the marker and goodbye, Gail. And as I came closer to my goal, anticipation of what I expected to find thwarted my companion and my caution. I forgot all about being afraid. I even conceived a crafty plan. If the note were where I was convinced it would be, I wouldn't take it along tonight. I would just read it and put it back. And tomorrow I would bring Dan Sawyer up here and present it to him with a flourish.

Now I reached the end of the path, and saw the flat-topped stone with the bronze marker bolted to it. But when I bent down to peer eagerly, all my fine ideas collapsed. There wasn't space enough between the stone and the bronze plate to insert a hair. However, the stone wasn't perfectly smooth—maybe on the far side there was enough unevenness to form a niche. I walked around there, treading cautiously the narrow space between the great boulder and the edge of nothing. Sure enough, a paper could have been slipped in from this side, but, if it had been, I couldn't locate it, even with my nail file which I had brought along for just such a purpose.

I had been so sure that when I looked here I would learn what Axel Dahlberg had known. So certain beyond any doubt or misgivings. Now I felt sick defeat. I snapped off the light momentarily, realizing this expedition had been quite in vain.

With let-down, I became abruptly aware of what my companion had been shouting for some seconds. Fear was warning me. It was screaming: "Look out. Look out. He's coming closer. He's almost here."

And for the first time tonight I really trusted what fear had to say. There was such a ring of conviction in this warning. Rigid, I stared into the gloom around me, afraid to use my light, afraid to move, afraid to breathe.

I saw nothing. But such compensation as the blind know sharpened my ears and I heard something. Gravel crunching under a stealthy foot. There was another wayfayer coming along the path and I knew with sudden instinctive terror that it was a creature more deadly than any native of the woods.

It occurred to me that standing on the edge of a precipice was a poor place for a social encounter with a murderer and I started silently to work my way back around the marker. Then I halted, spotlighted briefly by a flashlight snapped off almost at once.

But it had been long enough for the hunter to make sure of his quarry. Long enough to judge the distance and estimate the strength of the push that would be needed.

All I heard then was a quick intake of breath. No time for me to struggle; no time to use my light. I opened my mouth to scream, not for help, but just because one is apt to scream at a time like that. But I hadn't time to get it out before there was a muffled onrush and determined hands struck my shoulders with brutal strength, shoving me off-balance, forcing me backward. With almost objective astonishment I heard my own despairing cry as I went over the edge, scrambling and clutching at nothing.

XVI

I couldn't say whether drowning men re-view their lives on the television screen of memory as their lungs fill with water and they gasp their last gasp. But this I do know. You can do mighty fast thinking in a brief span when you believe that span is all you have left for thinking or anything else. When you take off from the high edge of a Colorado canyon, headed non-stop for eternity, your mind takes off fast too.

And what my mind was pounding at, during those seconds, left me feeling I didn't much care anyway. It must have been only the stubborn instinct for survival that kept me grabbing and clutching for something to halt my descent. For I was convinced it had been Jeff Calhoun who sped me on my way.

And I didn't expect anything to stop me till I became a greasespot on the bottom of the canyon. When my clawing right hand suddenly fastened on something, it clamped with no conscious volition of mine. The rest of my body kept traveling; the subsequent jerk wrenched my shoulder and tore the flesh of that clutching right hand, but its grip didn't loosen.

As soon as I realized that I had actually stopped falling, I brought up the other hand to reinforce my hold on God's beautiful little jackpine. And I knew with a cold sweat of horror that my feet were airily suspended over empty space.

My mind continued working fast, flashing me a picture of the terrain as I had seen it by daylight. Immediately beyond the marker, the ground fell away at a sharp angle for some feet before the sheer drop-off. On that steep slope grew a few tortured shrubs and stunted trees. They clung to the rocky soil with that pitifully persistent will-to-live which growing things show under the most hostile conditions. I didn't need to visualize the rocky soil. I was all too well aware of it abrading my cheek.

Now let me see. I was five foot six, and my feet dangled over the edge, but just above the ankles I felt terra firma under me. What was that old blackface joke? The more firma the less terra. So the blessed little jackpine must grow approximately five feet from the edge. My assailant hadn't shoved quite hard enough. For a hopeful second I thought perhaps he hadn't really meant to kill me, but the silent laugh which that produced turned into a muffled sob.

As soon as I caught my breath, I would work my feet up from their dangling. But quietly. Better to be quiet and rest for a while anyway. He was probably standing up there, listening, peering into darkness, wondering if a cry would float back from the canyon floor. If the fog hadn't been so impervious to flash-light beams, he could have picked me out, clinging there, and could have finished the job. Even as this occurred to me I saw a blurred light searching from the lookout point, wavering through moisture-laden atmosphere, and I lay immobile, trying not to breathe. But the rays were thwarted; soon they disappeared.

But I wasn't taking chances. I had done that. From here on, I was playing it safe. Reason told me that by now the murderer would be dusting of his hands, heading back to the village. But something stronger than reason told me to keep still, to continue hanging there.

So with hands chafed by the rough trunk of the jackpine and silent tears falling across my cheeks and trickling down my neck, I sprawled face-down in the night, remembering how I had sensed Jeff Calhoun's presence back there in the Tuckerman yard, how I had given myself away by calling to him.

How long is a night? How far is down? It must have been nearly midnight when I took my swan dive, and dawn came early this time of year. But the hours of darkness while I huddled, cold and miserable, on that steep slope were long enough to permit a lot of thinking.

My flashlight had departed during my downward plunge, probably landing where the murderer had intended I should land. After waiting what seemed hours, I hauled and worked myself farther from the edge, finally achieving a cramped position bulwarked by the jackpine. I waited again to see whether the noise of my scrambling and the rattle of pebbles had been heard. When there was no sign from the shelf above, I eased off my wide leather belt. Slipping it through a loop on the waistband of my slacks, I buckled it around the slim tree-trunk. The flannel loop on the slacks could pull loose, but I felt less precariously perched.

Then I felt through my pockets, found a folder of matches. Although it might be risky, I lighted one to look at my watch. But it was broken, the crystal smashed, and I saw a dried smear of blood from an unnoticed cut on my wrist. Since the match flicker hadn't drawn attention, I chanced a cigarette, keeping the tip shielded in a cupped hand.

Even if the murderer was home in bed by now, I would be doing business at this stand till daylight. The mountainside was steep as a mansard roof, and treacherous with loose gravel and pocked with drop-offs; and unstrung as I was, I would not chance trying to regain the ledge. Delayed shock was hitting me now; my teeth chattered and I couldn't make them stop; and under the layers of sweaters my skin felt at once icy-cold and damp with sweat.

The cigarette helped; when it burned down I lighted another from the stub. Chain-smoking. That's bad. You should take better care of yourself, Gail. Maybe you should give up drinking coffee, too, and carrying on flirtations with murderers.

But with the gradual lessening of tension came some slight return of common sense. And I saw the fallacy of my assumption that it must indisputably have been Jeff I had encountered at the marker, and that he was the one whose presence I sensed in the Tuckerman yard. Or thought I sensed.

But someone had been waiting in the murky night; I knew that, now. Someone had heard that call, had followed me, had shoved me off the point. But not necessarily Jeff; it could have been anybody. Anybody who happened to be out prowling around already, perhaps headed for the Barlow cabin.

Had it been Amanda Plumb? She was sufficiently sturdy to persuade three of me over the edge, although actually it wouldn't have required any muscular marvel to do a job like that. However, in view of old Charlie's story, Amanda was my liveliest suspect, so I went on thinking about her.

I had tried logic and I had tried itemizing data and I had tried asking questions. Now I tried something different. When you're such an outdoor gal that you spend the night roosting on a rocky hillside, it helps pass the tedious hours to tell stories. I made up a little story to tell myself. Amanda Plumb played the heroine. Or the heavy, however you wanted to look at it.

It went like this. In the spring of 1921 Amanda Plumb was a robust young housewife, happily married, her husband working as brakeman on the Granger, Glory Cloud & Western. Not the best job in the world, but not the worst either. Enough to support a wife and any kiddies that might come along. Enough to keep the kitchen of a little place in the hills stocked with groceries, enough to buy an occasional calico for the missus to wear at Saturday night square dances. They were young, and life and love stretched ahead for a good long time.

Suddenly, early in June, all this changed. Amanda Plumb became a widow and her husband became a martyr, killed in his attempt to avert the consequences of another man's selfishness. Amanda didn't like it very well, and why should she? Her face as it looked in that shot of the memorial services floated back to me through the mist and the blackness. Grim, brooding, vengeful.

Amanda kept brooding till she decided something should be done about such injustice. And one wild, stormy night she hiked up to Glory Cloud, went to B. J. Tuckerman's house, told him what she thought of him, and boom! Then she felt better. It didn't bring back her husband, or any of the others, but B. J. Tuckerman got what he had coming.

I continued the story, including every morsel of information, following through with the attempt of Gilbert Hazlitt to blackmail Amanda and his subsequent demise. Then the long quiet years when Amanda found a job to do and did it well. Then fresh turbulence when Axel Dahlberg came across information that Amanda thought nobody would ever learn. And so on to the bitter end, the bitter end being my present plight. Although, of course, this couldn't be the real end. When and if I turned up tomorrow in Glory Cloud, steps would have to be taken, and fast. She couldn't know how completely ignorant I was of my assailant's identity.

It made a pretty good yarn. A few holes in it, here and there, but mighty interesting. And it helped take my mind off the creeping cold that numbed my fingers and it kept me from listening for a twig snapping underfoot. I hadn't forgotten mountain lions and bears, but there's a limit to how scared you can get and I had about reached my limit. I didn't want to freeze and I didn't want to fall off the cliff, but beyond that I felt a sense of philosophical detachment.

I wondered how the same technique would work with other people. How convincing a story could I make up about Dr. Tuckerman? Or Sarah Walker or Milt Evans or Fay St. Vincent? Or Jeff Calhoun? Time to try was what I had the most of. I lighted another cigarette, squirmed into a position no more comfortable, but uncomfortable in a different way, and went on spinning.

By the time I had gone through all those stories I was half-paralyzed with cold and, despite myself, I was growing drowsy. I thought there was the faintest possible lessening in the intensity of the blackness, but the air was still heavy with fog and it was hard to judge. And no longer was I so sold on my story about Amanda. One or two of the other stories I had dreamed up suited me better, although they too had their blank spots. Not that it made much difference. I was beginning to feel that I had been born here and that I would grow old and die here.

I even concocted stories about Gilbert Hazlitt and Julius St. Vincent and, of all people, old Charlie. But I was fighting a losing battle against sleep. Hazily realizing what was bound to happen, I checked the sturdiness of the clasped belt and wound both arms around the little jackpine before weariness took over and I slept.

"Stop here. We'll get some hot coffee into her."

Jeff Calhoun gave the order and, without argument, the sheriff pulled the station wagon up in front of the inn. There were people, quite a few of them, in the main room, watching, and I heard a buzz of conversation as Jeff and Dan Sawyer half-led, half-carried me into the cheerful red-and-white kitchen, warm with the cookstove fire, fragrant with fresh coffee. But I was beyond noticing whether anybody looked surprised or disturbed at seeing me.

When I had wakened back on that mountain, it had been daylight. But the third day of fog obscured the sun and everything else. Impossible to judge the time, or how long I had slept. My arms ached from hugging the tree and my throat was raw, my fingers stiff. I still couldn't see the ledge overhead, and I wondered whether I dare try to reach it in the haze.

Then I heard a car laboring up the Alpine road. Every so often its horn sounded and I could hear voices shouting. The car reached the summit before I thought incredulously, "Why, they're looking for me."

Centuries passed, centuries of silence and nothingness, while I gathered my strength, listened for the hum of the motor returning. After an eternity I heard it, far up the hill. But then the throb of the engine died away and my hopes sank, only to rise anew when the horn sounded and voices called. Faint and far away. This was followed by several seconds of stillness, punctuated by the squeal of brakes on the sharp pitch.

Then I knew what they were doing. They had shut off the motor so they could hear better, and they were coasting down, braking from time to time, signaling with the horn, calling.

I didn't wait for the car to come closer. I started yelling. No telling what I yelled. Help, I guess. Help, help, help. Maybe occasionally a silly thing like, Here I am, or Jeff, Jeff, but mostly just Help.

They finally heard me. Sounds carry in that rarefied atmosphere. I wouldn't let myself think that maybe one of the searchers knew where to look. After all, when I heard voices directly above me and when I shouted more hysterically, it was Jeff who scrambled down the slope, a rope around his waist, to drag me to safety.

It was Jeff who kept pouring steaming coffee into me now and who cut a slice of warm coffee cake I couldn't eat and who ordered Sawyer to lay off questioning till I felt better. And when sudden weakness assailed me and I leaned over to put my head between my knees, as we'd been taught in First Aid, and I could tell it wasn't going to help, it was Jeff's arms that caught me.

This time when I roused, I couldn't imagine where I lay. Certainly not in the Barlow cabin. One of the rooms at the inn? I doubted it. This was pure luxury: these fine percale sheets, this heavenly mattress, those hand-blocked linen drapes drawn against the gray day. And what in the world did I have on?

Through the open door I heard quick, light footsteps, treading more softly as they approached the bedroom. In a moment Fay St. Vincent stood there, less tailored than usual, very beautiful in a long blue silk hostess gown. She smiled and exclaimed:

"Well! Awake! That's better, dearie. You lie quietly and rest while I get you a cup of broth."

She disappeared and I obeyed orders, feeling no inclination to do anything but lie quietly and rest. So that's where I had acquired the lace and chiffon confection.

There was a murmur of voices outside my door and presently Jeff came in. He stood by the bed, looking down at me, and his high-cheekboned face showed concern. But he looked angry, too, and I wished I could stop thinking things like maybe he was angry because he hadn't done a better job.

I managed a sheepish smile. "Just a real outdoor kid—ready for anything."

"You need somebody to take care of you," he said.

"Brother," I replied, "somebody darned near did take care of me. For good."

"Don't think about it, honey."

I asked Jeff what time it was and he said 3:30 P.M. He told me it had been around ten that morning when they found me; that they had been searching for a couple of hours. According to him, he had gone to my cabin early, wanting to make up after yesterday's tiff over Cy, and he had been alarmed when he couldn't raise me and when he noticed the light still burning in the living room. He and the sheriff had forced that door on the sleeping porch.

"Look, baby," he said, "Will you promise me not to do any more chasing around alone from now on? To be extra careful and not to trust anybody?"

"Including yourself?"

He sighed. "I ain't just a-woofin', honey. Don't you see the spot you're in? Somebody meant to kill you and fluked it. Somebody doesn't know how much you saw or heard or sensed before you went over that edge. Somebody is bound to try again. Soon."

I watched his face and I said, "Are you trying to scare me?"

He flushed. "You should be scared, you little fool. If you don't have brains enough to worry about your own neck, I'll have to do it for you."

"Oh, I'm worried, pal," I said. And I was. And I just couldn't shake the aftermath of that intuitive flash which had come to me last night when I started falling. Probably because it was rooted in emotion rather than logic. I kept thinking that Jeff had gone from Dahlberg's cabin out into the night and had returned to say Axel was dead. And I kept remembering the time Sawyer dragged us back to the site of the steak fry: Jeff had pointed out that either of us, if we had wanted to kill Dahlberg, could have shoved him off that high point from which we viewed the lights of Denver. It was a method that had suggested itself to Jeff's mind. I wondered when and where he lost the prescription slip Tuckerman gave him, if he had lost it. And I kept thinking how instinctively certain I had been last night that it was Jeff's presence I sensed in front of Tuckerman's house.

Now I said slowly, "You never did give me the details of how your father happened to lose ten grand in the narrow gauge."

He stared at me. Then his flush deepened.

"Boy, are you pig-headed! Once you get an idea in that pretty noggin, it settles down for life."

"Some people call it persistence," I said coolly. "Or determination. Admirable qualities."

But I wondered if I were being pig-headed about the narrow-gauge railroad, among other things. Certainly if I could junk that theory, it would make last night's story about Jeff Calhoun read more smoothly.

I heard bustling in the other room and Fay returned, bearing a tray, followed by Dr. Tuckerman, complete with little black bag. He was working hard at a cheery bedside manner, but his kindly old face looked drawn, and there was shock in the shrewd blue eyes.

"How's our patient? Feeling better now? You're looking better. Let's just see how our pulse is and take our temperature."

He fussed and fiddled around and finally concluded I would survive. But he was stern about my staying in bed for the rest of the day and he left a sedative in case I needed it.

"You'll be all right," he said, relief in his voice. "Just rest and quiet for a while. I've advised the sheriff to wait before questioning you. We can't be too careful. You're in good hands. Miss St. Vincent generously insisted on bringing you here where she can keep an eye on you. She's a fine nurse—you'll be good as new in no time. Now let's just drink our nice broth and go back to sleep."

The thought of food was still repellent, but rather than make a row about it, I did what he wanted. To my surprise the hot clear liquid tasted wonderful, and after draining the cup I felt relaxed and content. I must have been more exhausted than I had realized; I didn't anticipate needing sleeping tablets. Dimly I heard everybody tiptoeing out, talking in hushed voices; then I didn't hear anything for quite a while.

But this slumber was more troubled. I drowsed, but I dreamed. I kept going through last night's experience and I knew it was all a dream, but I couldn't make myself wake up. When at last I fought my way to full consciousness and opened my eyes, darkness had fallen and the house was silent.

I snapped on the bedside lamp and called to Fay. No answer.
Then I saw a slip of paper beside the lamp.

> "Gail, dear. If you awaken before I return, please
> stay in bed and rest. I'll be back soon to fix your
> dinner. Maybe I'll bring you a little surprise. Fay
> St. V."

Petulantly I thought that all these characters who had pro-
fessed such concern for my welfare were darned blithe about
traipsing off and leaving me there by myself, asleep. But probably Tuckerman and Jeff had assumed Fay would stick around. I
wondered where she had gone and why. I wished I were back in
my own cabin. The troubled dreams had suggested something I
wanted to check against my bulky notes.

And I thought what an opportunity this would be for anybody who wanted to ransack my place again. But they would be
wasting time and energy. Whatever it was that they sought, and
that I had sought under the marker, it wasn't in the Barlow cabin.
I felt convinced of that.

Wanting to go home must be a sign of recovery. I suddenly
couldn't endure doing nothing another minute. I threw back the
covers, shivering in the bridal delight I wore, even though a small
electric heater glowed from a corner of the room. A warm-look-
ing robe of pale green flannel lay across the foot of the bed, and
I slipped it on.

Then I headed for the living room where I could hear the
crackle of a fire and sniff the spicy fragrance of cypress logs.
Fay's thoughtfulness hadn't extended to slippers and I didn't see
my own tired saddle shoes. So I went barefoot, and in the other
room I curled up on a davenport by the open hearth, tucking my
feet under me.

Staring into the flames had a mesmeric effect; the mood of
my dreams crept over me. I tried to throw it off, without success.
Strangely enough, what now disturbed me wasn't the memory of
the dark mountainside or of my awakening to the gray day. It
was the memory of being nearly out on my feet while they tried

bucking me up with coffee. It was something about Jeff. I didn't want it to be, but I knew it was. Something Jeff had said or done had made only a faint impression on me in my semi-coma, but now it kept returning to plague me. There hadn't been much. Was it something he had said? Something he had done? All that I remembered was concern and sympathy.

Deliberately, I shook myself out of that brooding, and padded over to the low bookshelves, seeking distraction. Something to read while waiting for Fay's return, something as frothy and removed from reality as Fay's conversation. But when, on the deep bottom shelf where the reference books were ranged, my gaze encountered a late atlas, I forgot my desire for escape reading.

Before opening the maps I decided to see whether there was any sign of Fay's returning. No reason why I should feel surreptitious about consulting an atlas, but I just thought I'd look.

I opened the door, glanced out. No light twinkled through the darkness and I heard no voices or approaching steps. The fog had lifted partially, but an overcast still obscured the stars, and the night air had a sullen, threatening quality as if a storm churning in the high range might have an appointment in Glory Cloud tonight. The raw cold bit into my bones and I hastily closed the door.

Back by the fire I opened the unwieldy book. I wanted to examine the map of Iowa. Maybe some brilliant thought would hit me about Luella's reference to Des Moines. And I also wanted to correct my vague conception of Colorado geography, to check the location of Pueblo, Luella's home town, its distance from Denver and Glory Cloud.

Colorado came first alphabetically and I studied that map. I found Pueblo. I found Denver and Glory Cloud and Granger. Also, believe it or not, Quartz. Painstakingly, I went over the whole area, puzzling, conjecturing, discarding. And when I gasped, it was because what snagged my attention was something totally unexpected. Something I wasn't even looking for. I did a double-take. What I had seen was still there. You live and you learn.

I couldn't under-estimate the importance of what I had just learned. And I couldn't over-estimate it. It was an item I had desperately needed to know. It was an item that enabled me to pull together a miscellany of odds and ends and to make of them a unified whole. It fitted so neatly into one of last night's bedtime stories that the story had to be right, had to be the story Dan Sawyer should hear. When I had it complete.

And I had it very nearly complete now. For under this fresh stimulus my belabored brain came across with a clear definition of what had been nagging me in the recollection of this morning's activities. I knew now what that hazy memory had been, why it troubled me. And the knowledge fitted the story too.

The mantel clock showed seven-thirty. Fay's punctilio would doubtless include dinner at eight. Could I find my clothes and get out of here before she returned?

My slacks and sweaters and shoes were, of all places, in the bedroom closet. I scrambled into them, refusing to acknowledge the weakness that returned with my frenzied activity, refusing to gaze longingly at the inviting bed. Once I heard a rumbling noise and I froze, thinking it was somebody at the door, somebody in the house. But silence followed.

I didn't make gestures toward being a considerate guest. I left the bed tumbled, and I neglected to hang up the borrowed gown and robe.

And I made it. I went out the kitchen door, and immediately outside I heard the distant rumble again. This time I knew what it was. The overcast was heavier; faint flashes of lightning flickered in the distance.

But it would have taken more than an electrical storm to stop me now. I was on the home stretch, a fire-horse heading for the barn. But an apter figure would have been a runaway freight car loaded with dynamite plunging toward a tunnel.

XVII

Behind the cabin I paused, remembering the low-walled terrace with the drop beyond. I wanted no more truck with jumping-off places. On my way through the kitchen I had picked up a flashlight, and now I snapped it on, locating the path that twisted off through the woods. The wind was rising, the trees tossing.

Dousing the light, I lingered another minute. Should I have taken time to scribble thanks to Fay for her hospitality? I wouldn't want to hurt her feelings, would I?

But I'd had enough of Fay's luxurious domicile. It was fine for roughing it in comfort; one could live the life of Riley in a set-up like that; but I wasn't interested in living the life of Riley—just the life of Gail Rawson.

There was a possibility I'd meet Fay—or somebody—along the path before I reached the road, but it was a chance I'd have to take. As yet, no light was approaching, and I used my own only as often as needed to keep from straying.

One thing I needn't worry about: being quiet. What with the wind and the brewing storm, you couldn't have heard a bear crashing through the underbrush. I hoped I could get home before the storm broke. That mountain lightning was nothing to fool around with. The thunder wouldn't hurt you, unless the roar of its big guns deafened you.

Guns! Why did I have to keep thinking about guns? Guns were implements of destruction, of force and terror and death. Men took guns and went into the woods, and the panic-stricken little cottontail learned the meaning of a gun. There were all

kinds of guns and they all spelled trouble. There were guns that
weren't loaded and little boys played with them and suddenly a
playmate or a parent dropped dead. There were guns such as the
one a man snatched up in a moment of fury at a wife's nagging
tongue. Or men couldn't agree, so they took guns and stood up
and shot at each other to decide whose opinion was correct. Just
two men didn't do it that way any more; they'd decided it wasn't
civilized.

Guns! I never did like the things. There had been a gun belonging to Julius St. Vincent, and B. J. Tuckerman's life had been
blotted out with it. It was Julius' gun, but Julius was in Denver
that night. Jeff Calhoun didn't feel the way I did about guns.
He liked using them for target practice. There had been a gun
mounted on the wall in Axel Dahlberg's cabin and Jeff had wanted to borrow it. That was another trouble with guns—when they
were around men were always itching to use them. But Axel said
oh, no, that gun is too valuable. Don't you fool with that gun.
What made him think that old thing was so valuable? Axel knew
a lot about a lot of subjects, but he didn't know much about
antiques. He didn't know what made an old gun really valuable,
things like its being a muzzle loader in first-class condition, or
being the only model of its kind, things that Jeff knew about
guns and had told me.

Maybe Axel had said that because he didn't want to be responsible for Jeff Calhoun's having a gun. Or maybe because that
old gun was valuable to him, if not to anybody else. But it wasn't
even his—it came with the cabin. What value could it have to
him? Axel didn't even like to shoot rabbits. And what good was a
gun except for shooting? There was nothing constructive about a
gun: you couldn't wear it or eat it or read it. I suppose you could
hang it on the wall to conceal a spot on the wallpaper, but Dahlberg's cabin didn't have wallpaper—it was knotty pine.

Conceal! Guns! I halted as if I'd smacked into a stone wall.
The lightning was throwing its brilliant illumination over the
pine woods, and I felt as if it had penetrated my skull, illuminat-
ing the darkness in there, too. Conceal. That was the word that
did it. Conceal and guns.

If you had something you wanted to conceal where it couldn't be found, but where it would be handy when you needed it—a letter, say, or a memorandum—what would be wrong with rolling it up and poking it into the barrel of an old gun? The answer was that nothing would be wrong with it; it would be a darned good idea. And if that slip of paper meant a lot to you, and even more to somebody else, just knowing it was there would make that gun pretty valuable in your eyes, wouldn't it? You'd know it was valuable because you yourself had made it so. You wouldn't want a couple of slaphappy kids taking that gun down to shoot up beer cans, would you? You'd tell them to leave it alone. And if you had an ironic sense of humor, like Axel Dahlberg, you'd find it amusing, as he had seemed to the night of our fry, when something was said about a barrelful of trash. You'd chuckle at what you knew about a barrelful. But not of trash.

I thought of the ransacking Jeff and I had given the Dahlberg cabin, never once considering that gun on the wall. I thought of my harrowing journey last night to the lookout point. I thought of how I had racked my brain to imagine where Axel might have hidden the evidence he found and I asked myself why I had never before considered the gun. But I knew why. Because it was an object taken for granted in such a set-up. As a hiding place it had the time-honored virtue of being obvious. If that gun had hung on the wall in Fay St. Vincent's swank Denver apartment, it would have been noticeable. It would have been out of place, but in a mountain cabin it was completely orthodox. You didn't give it a thought.

I wasted little time wondering whether Dahlberg had really hidden his precious scrap of paper in the barrel of that gun: I felt as sure of it as if I'd been an eyewitness to his doing so.

Had the murderer thought of examining the gun? Or had he overlooked it as completely as I had? If he was still searching, how soon would he try again? How soon would he—or she—be lucky enough to look in the right place? Could I get there first?

Last night I had been afraid. But not now. The unseen companion who had thrown in with me the night we found Luella's body tried to muscle in on this expedition. But I was through with all that nonsense. I was too coked up about getting to Axel Dahlberg's cabin where a valuable old gun hung on the wall. I wasn't even frightened by the oncoming storm. I hoped I could beat it, but I wasn't afraid.

And when I whipped past the Barlow cabin I didn't consider stopping for my raincoat or my notes. I no longer needed those notes. All I needed was to get my hands on that valuable old gun.

As I had the night before, I continued straight down the road past Luella Greenfield's before turning right to the main drag. But tonight it wasn't because I was afraid and thought there was less chance of meeting anybody that way. It just seemed faster, and my sense of urgency carried me along without conscious thought about routes. And anyway, nobody in his right mind would be out charging around on a night like this. I was in my right mind, more or less, but I had a mission. Everybody else in town would be inside battening down the hatches.

But everybody wasn't. When I reached the main drag and turned left, I glanced in both directions, up and down the road. And the lightning, almost constant now, showed somebody running west along the road, rounding the corner by the school-house. Too far away to make out who it was—it almost looked to be two people. But I thought only that they too were trying to beat the storm, to reach shelter.

Now I broke into a run myself. Around me the thin atmosphere crackled; lightning snapped at my heels. When I raced up onto the little back stoop of Dahlberg's cabin my breath was coming in choking gulps.

The door was locked. Naturally. Of course. But I was wearing heavy-soled saddle shoes, and the upper part of the door was glass. Even if anybody had been around to hear the glass shatter under my sharp blow, the explosions of thunder would have covered it. Just as the thunder had covered the sound of a shot the night B. J. Tuckerman died.

Very carefully I reached in through the jagged hole, located the key in the lock, turned it. Still carefully I brought my hand back outside. And I slipped my shoe on again before I stepped in, treading gingerly over bits of broken glass.

Through the dingy kitchen where Dan Sawyer had shown me a long sharp knife that wasn't the right long sharp knife. Into the living room where Axel Dahlberg had drawled something about the male being belligerent during the mating season. My flashlight beam raked the knotty-pine wall above the front door and I expelled pent-up breath. At least the gun itself was still there.

But I couldn't reach it. Even standing on tiptoe and stretching, I could barely touch it with my fingertips. So when my light fell on a straight-backed chair I dragged that over and climbed up on it. I knew that was a foolish thing to do. I had always been taught that a person could get hurt, climbing up on chairs to reach for things.

Tenderly I lifted the old musket from its brackets. It was heavier than I expected. And it was long—must be five feet. Awkwardly I eased myself back to the floor, holding the gun as gently as a two-weeks-old baby. If what Axel Dahlberg had hidden here was still safely concealed and I found it, I might revise some of my harsh thoughts about guns. I might have a kind word for guns in general and this gun in particular.

The fireworks outside were booming and sizzling to a crescendo, and one part of my mind thought vaguely it was about time for rain to begin, but most of my mind held only a big question mark. Is it still here?

First I checked to see whether the gun was a breechloader. If it broke where the barrel joined the stock, Axel could have inserted a paper at that point. I held my light on the gun, squinting to read the worn lettering on the metal plate screwed to the wooden stock: 1864. U.S. Springfield. Then I tried, tentatively, to break it. But it seemed awfully solid. Maybe it wasn't supposed to break there or maybe I just didn't know how. A muzzleloader? Yes, now I observed the ramrod fitted snugly along the bottom of the barrel.

So anybody hiding anything in this gun would have had to insert it from the business end. I didn't like staring straight into the muzzle of a gun. Another good way to get hurt. But I did it. A difficult business, trying to hold my light so it shone into the barrel and trying to look in at the same time. I sat down, braced the stock on the floor between my feet, and with the heavy gun leaning toward me at an angle I peered into the barrel.

At first I thought this was another fiasco, that the barrel ran like an empty tunnel all the way, but then I noticed that the walls of the tunnel were white. I probed my little finger into the barrel, contacted paper, pulled my finger out, dragging along the single thin sheet of neatly rolled paper.

I unrolled the little cylinder, rolled it again the opposite direction, smoothed it. It was what I expected: a letter. No envelope, but the inside address was what I knew it would be. I frowned at the date: July 21, 1921. It should be July 20. That was the date Luella had given on her embroidery.

I ran my eyes swiftly over the page. It didn't take long; it wasn't much of a letter. Only enough of a letter to start a train of consequences that would wind up almost thirty years later with Axel Dahlberg departing life, his work just well begun, with Luella Greenfield meeting the end in terror instead of with peace and dignity.

Outside, rain was beginning to pour. I doused my light and sat in darkness, the letter in limp fingers. Even if details remained to be filled in, this letter and what I knew would be enough for Dan Sawyer. He could make an arrest and probably under the white light of a room at the Granger sheriff's office the details would come. And once more people could walk the dark roads of Glory Cloud unafraid.

Unafraid! What would that be like, really to feel unafraid again? To be carefree and brash and unconcerned? You can think you're not frightened; you can be too excited and too eager-beaver to acknowledge your stealthy companion, the fear. But then, if you're sitting in a mountain cabin once occupied by a Mr. Dahlberg—by a Mr. Dahlberg sometimes called Doctor and sometimes Professor and sometimes even Perfessor—if you're sitting in such a spot, fondling a very valuable Civil War musket, some little thing can happen to show you how mistaken you've

been. When you've achieved what you set out to do, when you're
the gal who made good, then comes the let-down. Then comes
reality, the rude awakening, the horrid truth. You know then,
and for sure, what terror can be. The authentic article. One hundred percent, sterling silver, gold-plated, solid-brass, 18 carat,
honest-to-God terror. The real thing.

I had thought I was afraid last night. But now, sitting in this
dark cabin with the rain pounding down outside and a letter from
Des Moines, New Mexico, in my hand, I realized how wrong I
had been. I realized that the whole subject of fear was one I had
only flirted with, that there were vast unexplored reaches in that
dread no man's land, virgin territory I was even now preparing to
enter. For, with the lessening of the racket outside, my ears had
picked up a sound inside. Somebody hadn't expected that broken glass just within the back door. It crunched when somebody
walked on it.

So this was it. This was what I had been heading toward
ever since that cold morning in late May when I first drove up
to Glory Cloud. For this I had left my happy home and loving
family. To achieve ephemeral notoriety in the Colorado press as
the latest victim of what by now they were calling Mysterious
Mountain Murders. And if the papers said I was beautiful, or a
Ph.D., or that I wore a ring in my nose, none of it would make
any difference to me. I would be pushing up the petunias and I
wouldn't care what they said. Dr. Herman Tuckerman would be
bustling around, ministering to stomachaches and head-colds;
Sarah Walker would be cooking heavenly food and insulting her
guests; Fay St. Vincent would be closing her rustic retreat and
returning to more worldly pleasures; Milt Evans would be telling
people what they probably didn't know; Jeff Calhoun would go
on drifting around the world, collecting little moss but having
a hell of a good time; Amanda Plumb would be whipping her
old Ford around hairpin curves. And what would Gail Rawson
be doing? Why, pushing up the petunias. You remember Gail—
she always did have too much curiosity for her own good. She
always was too independent, too self-sufficient, too much to
think she could take care of herself. But there was one time when

she couldn't. That last time there in a dark mountain cabin in Colorado she couldn't take care of herself, after all, and now she's pushing up the petunias. Along with her pal Dahlberg and that old lady, Mrs. J. Reed Greenfield.

The steps were closer, wary, determined, a flashlight stabbing the darkness ahead of them. And I knew that hiding was out of the question and running away was out of the question. I knew that, like B. J. Tuckerman, I was about to get what I had coming. I knew I couldn't squirm out of this one. Even if I'd felt right up to par, there was no way out of this one. And I didn't feel up to par. How could you, with a swollen tongue in a dry mouth that tasted of rusty nails, with hands as icy as a trout stream and as quivering as aspens in the wind?

But I could go down punching. I could be like the cougar in the cul-de-sac. So I placed my flashlight on the table, pointed it toward the door of the kitchen, snapped it on. And I picked up the heavy old gun and aimed it in my best imitation of a determined manner.

When she stepped into the ring of light, holding her own flash, and saw that gun describing circles in the air, she just laughed. Sarah Walker always did have a nasty laugh. And she sniffed and tossed her head, and the wire curlers that would produce a cherubic halo of curls in the morning jangled, although a gay printed scarf was tied over them. Raindrops glistened on the scarf and I caught the smell of damp wool from the old jacket she wore.

You couldn't blame her for laughing at me and my poor old musket. The gun she carried was a business-like service revolver her husband had kept around.

"You little fool," she said, "do you think I'm afraid of that useless old thing? You thought you were smart, didn't you? Thought you could stir up trouble for everyone and get away with it. Chase around after married men and get away with it. But this time you aren't getting away with it."

That made me sore, her insistence that there had been something questionable between Dahlberg and me. It would have been smarter to play it smooth, appeal to her vanity. Sarah had always been a sucker for flattery. But I couldn't stop myself.

And the anger made my voice cold and controlled. When I spoke she couldn't have known about the smothering sensation high in my chest that made speaking at all such an achievement.

"I don't blame you for feeling outraged about Axel Dahlberg and me," I said. "I suppose having husbands all over the country gives a woman quite a stake in the sanctity of marriage."

Her face changed. It showed fury, but it showed relief too. "You found it."

"Yes, I found it. In this useless old thing."

I started to set the gun down, but when I saw her eyes and the quick tightening of her grip on the revolver, I suspended motion, continued holding that musket.

"I found the letter to your dear fiancé, Jim Walker," I continued. "The letter sent July 21, 1921, from Des Moines, New Mexico, telling Jim to go jump in the lake. Telling him that you had been married the day before to a perfectly wonderful guy who operated the merry-go-round concession at a carnival. Pete, that was the wonderful guy's name, wasn't it? It wasn't a very nice letter, Sarah. It would have given Jim quite a shock if he'd ever received it."

"Well, he didn't receive it. I saw to that."

"No," I said gently, "the postmaster, Gilbert Hazlitt, saw to that and then you saw to him. How did you work it, Sarah? You must have been awfully clever."

I was determined to keep the conversation rolling as long as possible, whether by flattery or insult. I was sure she wouldn't kill me till she got her hands on that letter. And I was sure she didn't know the letter was hastily thrust into the hip pocket of my slacks, that she could kill me first and then get it.

And I was clinging to the tenuous hope that Fay just might have returned to her cabin and found me gone and raised the alarm. Of course, they'd never think to look for me here, but you have to have something to hope for or life isn't worth living. I repeated:

"How did you work it?"

She sniffed, tossed her head again. "There was nothing to it. I simply called Gilbert Hazlitt, long distance, and asked him to intercept and destroy the letter. I told him I'd written it in the heat of a lover's quarrel and I'd said things I shouldn't have and that now I was sorry." Her eyes glittered and the mouth that had once been a rosebud was a dried-up prune. "He promised to destroy it without opening it. But men are all alike. You can't trust one of them. He opened it and read it and kept it. He was a double-crossing snake in the grass."

"And he wanted you to buy it back, didn't he? He always needed money and you had been bragging about Jim Walker's inheritance. Flashing a valuable ring. Hazlitt told you to put the bite on your affluent boy-friend, to hock your ring, if necessary, and give him the money. Wasn't that about it?"

Her face told me I was right. The outrage of that old grievance at Hazlitt's perfidy still smoldered in her black eyes. She also looked as if she thought this chit-chat had gone on long enough, that it was time to get down to business. Time for me to produce the letter and make any last statements I wanted posterity to remember me by.

"Look," I said hastily, "just between us gals, how about giving me more of the low-down before we go our separate ways? You want that letter and I'll see that you get it. You also don't want me to pass any of this on and you'll see that I won't. We understand each other perfectly. So how about letting me get rid of this super-cargo I'm holding and let's pull up a couple of chairs and have a nice heart-to-heart talk? What ever happened to the merry-go-round magnate? And your other husbands? Did you bump them too?"

The crack about her other husbands was a mistake. Gail could talk herself out of anything, all right. She just about talked herself right out of this world with that line. Sarah was so mad I thought she was going to forget about her gun and slug me with the flashlight.

"You *are* a fool," she snapped. "No, we won't sit down and you can just go on holding that gun you're so crazy about. I never did have husbands all over the country. Only Pete, and he left me after two days when the carnival moved on. He deceived me and he broke my heart and he left me. The little rat! That marriage really didn't count."

Axel had been so right about her sex antagonism.

"So you came back to Glory Cloud and married Jim Walker in September, according to schedule. And even if the marriage to Pete down in New Mexico really didn't count, it was still bigamy, you know. Why didn't you get a divorce?"

"Divorce?" she said. "Are you crazy? Jim would have dropped me like a hot potato if he'd known anything about Pete. He was an idiot anyway. Jim, I mean. A sanctimonious idiot. Nobody ever knew. Not even my sister I was supposed to be visiting in Albuquerque. She was always stupid—it was easy to fool her."

One might have said that Sarah Walker viewed her fellow men—and women—with a jaundiced eye. Sitting back calmly in a psychology laboratory, one might have been amused at the abandon with which she used words like fool and rat and idiot. But under this particular set of circumstances, I wasn't exactly convulsed with mirth. I was convulsed by a sense of urgency. The sands were running out. I could tell by the weakness in my bones, by my conviction that they were filled with air and water instead of good healthy marrow. But I forced myself to solemn sympathy.

"Sarah," I said, "you got a raw deal all along the line. Going to visit your stupid sister in New Mexico and falling in love with that no-good Pete who ran out on you. Then having Gilbert Hazlitt double-cross you so that you had to kill him. And being married to a sanctimonious idiot all those years till you had to take a little nip now and then to relieve the boredom."

The lethal determination in her eyes hadn't wavered, but she was listening to my recital with grim satisfaction, nodding agreement.

"And then, as if you hadn't already had enough trouble, that smart-aleck Dahlberg had to run across the letter Hazlitt kept. And Dahlberg was low enough to try using it to persuade you to give evidence about his wife's infidelity. And Luella Green-field, who was a silly old gossip, also saw the letter. She didn't understand it, but she knew something wasn't right and she questioned you, didn't she? You had to kill her because you knew she wasn't quite satisfied with your answers. By the way, Sarah, do you know Morse code?"

"Morse code?" Her eyes narrowed. "Why?"

"I thought you might know it. How about Jim? Wasn't he in the navy during the first war?"

"So what?"

"So what did he do in the navy, Sarah? He wasn't by any chance a wireless operator?"

"Maybe he was," she said shortly. "Not that it's any of your business. Maybe he thought it would be cute to teach me Morse code, till I convinced him I didn't give a damn. What do you care?"

"I don't care. But poor Luella cared. She wasn't sure how much code you had learned."

I shouldn't have said poor Luella. Sarah's indignation flared again. "Poor Luella, my foot! She was over-due to kick off, anyway. And I don't see what Morse code has to do with it. We've had enough gabble now, young lady. Give me the letter and turn around unless you want that pretty face spoiled."

She moved closer and the revolver came up. You could tell she hated me for being young and pretty, as well as for my other sins. And she didn't like it because I wasn't acting more scared. But she must have got some satisfaction from the quaver I could no longer keep out of my voice.

"Okay," I said hastily, "I'll show you where it is. But there's one more thing. One last request. Why did you kill B. J. Tuckerman?"

Her jaw dropped. And under the steady beat of rain I thought I detected a sound on the front porch. Not really a sound. More the suggestion of a sound. I wasn't sure. But I started coughing as noisily as I could with a throat that felt stuffed with old nylon stockings. And I scuffled my feet because if there really had been a sound I thought things would work out better all around if Sarah Walker didn't hear it.

"Stop that fidgeting," she ordered. "What do you mean, why did I kill B. J. Tuckerman? What are you talking about? I never killed old Tuckerman. He shot himself. He was going to land in jail anyway because he was a crook."

It was my turn to gape. She knew I'd never tell. Why should she deny killing Tuckerman? She hadn't been reticent about her other murders.

"Oh, come on now, Sarah," I coaxed. "You know you killed old B. J. He was a crook and he had it coming, didn't he? I don't blame you a bit—it was just what you should have done. But why? What had he done to you?"

"I didn't," she persisted. "I was in Granger that night, reading the class prophecy, and I can prove it. I didn't have anything to do with B. J. Tuckerman's killing himself."

So we stood there and argued. And I kept thinking how fantastic it was and I kept wondering how soon she would arrive at the same conclusion. But I also kept saying she must have killed Tuckerman and she kept insisting that she hadn't, and heaven knows why I cared, except that my last wisp of possible salvation was to keep the conversation going. And heaven knows why she cared: what difference would one murder, more or less, make by this time? You'd think she could have taken an extra one right in her stride. You'd think she wouldn't care whether I floated into infinity tattling to headquarters that she'd been responsible for four deaths or five, but she seemed to care a lot.

Finally, though, she had enough of that foolishness. My stubborn tenacity exasperated her out of all patience and maybe she caught on what I was up to. Her face hardened till there wasn't even a suggestion of faded prettiness left, and she moved so close I could tell she'd had garlic for dinner.

"Shut up," she said. "What's it to you who I killed? Shut up and give me my letter and turn around."

I shut up. I dug out the letter and tossed it on the chair beside me. I turned around. And I was still holding the heavy musket because Sarah hadn't trusted me to put it down without a false move and my arms were weak from the weight. That must have been what weakened them although it was odd my legs should be affected too. And as I turned, I let the heavy wooden stock pivot with me, swinging in a wide arc a little more than waist-high.

It was a careless thing to do. It just shows how people are always getting hurt fooling around with guns, even when they're not loaded. The stock smacked Sarah Walker hard just below the shoulder. Hard enough to make a thud. It was her left arm, the one holding the flashlight, not the revolver. So the blow only caused her to drop the light. It didn't prevent the revolver's exploding instantly in the sudden darkness with a roar deafening in the small room. But it did throw her off-balance enough to spoil her aim.

And I ducked my shoulders like an All-American halfback and I scuttled for that big old chair Axel had liked, still carrying my trusty musket because I didn't have the sense to drop it. Before I gained the chair's dubious shelter Sarah's gun exploded again, but again her aim was spoiled. What spoiled it this time was Dan Sawyer's gun, speaking in unison with hers through the front window.

Then the door burst open and the lights came on and Sawyer stood there, rain dripping from his wide-brimmed Stetson, pistol in his hand, and Jeff was dashing around like a rooster with its head off, making wet tracks all over, hunting me. I stayed right where I was. It was nice and comfortable on the floor behind that big chair. I thought I might get hold of a blanket and a coffee pot and set up housekeeping there.

Sawyer's pistol went back into its holster. He had shot Sarah Walker through the right shoulder and her gun was on the floor and blood was slowly seeping over the plaid jacket. She wouldn't be doing any more shooting tonight. Probably she wouldn't ever be doing any more shooting. Or knifing or bopping or wielding prospector's picks or shoving people down abandoned mine shafts.

Sarah must have known all such wholesome pastimes were lost to her forever. Along with a great many other things, besides. In any case, when I finally rose from behind the chair, Sarah's eyes fastened on me and any little sign of ill-temper I had observed in her earlier was as a placid June day to a raging blizzard. And she called me things she never learned from a husband who had studied for the ministry.

XVIII

Saturday was one of those idyllic summer days in the mountains that often follows a storm. Fay and I ate a late breakfast from trays on the terrace. We didn't talk much. I felt ashamed of the things I had thought about Fay, and she was stricken with remorse for her carelessness in leaving me alone the day before. She had made such a fuss last night that I surrendered to her insistence and returned to sleep in the guest room.

But it hadn't been Fay's fault that I had climbed out of bed during her absence, had charged around the country. Her going to the inn and inviting Jeff to dinner had been the romantic gesture you could expect of Fay. Her contact with reality was always a bit hazy; she was amazed when Jeff hit the ceiling at learning I'd been left alone. It was they I had seen running up the road before the storm, and it was they who had started looking for me, trying first the Hazlitt and Barlow cabins.

Then they had notified the sheriff, and Luella Greenfield's cabin had been searched before anybody thought of Dahlberg's. And long before that, Sarah Walker, who had been standing at an upstairs window of the inn when I hurried along the road, with the lightning putting the finger on me, had picked up her revolver and followed me.

Fay still didn't know the score, and I didn't tell her. I thought Sarah Walker was lucky to be safe in jail. I shouldn't have wanted to be in her shoes and be anywhere but behind bars when Fay learned what had really happened to Gilbert Hazlitt.

Once Fay said, "But dearie, I just don't understand. It's all so dreadful and so poignant. Why did—"

"Fay," I said wearily, "there are things I don't understand myself. Let's skip it till I've talked to Sawyer later today."

That afternoon Sawyer sat behind the old library table in his headquarters at the inn, gazing somberly at Jeff and me. He held a blue-handled bread knife in his hands, turning it over and over. Finally, he said:

"You were right, Miss Rawson, in your suggestion to me last night about this knife. I checked with Sarah Walker on the way down, and it happened the way you thought. This is the knife she used to kill Dahlberg. And it did have a red-enameled handle to match the other implements, but the enamel was flaking off. And that day when I questioned you about nail polish and friend Evans kept busting in, he listened outside the door. He learned about the traces found on Dahlberg's jacket. And he told Sarah Walker. Not because he realized the matter made any difference to her—just because telling it made him feel important.

"And Sarah wondered how long it would be before I decided, as you did, that flecks of red enamel could come from something other than fingernail polish. She was afraid to try hiding the knife, but she re-painted the handle. She didn't have red paint so she used blue. And yesterday morning when we brought you into the kitchen, Calhoun sliced coffee-cake for you with this knife. Unconsciously, you were jarred by that blue handle in a red-and-white kitchen. But you didn't know till late yesterday afternoon what had jarred you and why. Then you guessed correctly that the knife had been re-painted and for what reason."

He paused, then asked:

"Would you mind telling me, Miss Rawson, what else contributed to your decision that Sarah Walker was the murderer?"

"It was really her own fault. Because she pushed me off the lookout point and I had to spend the night out there with nothing to do but think."

I told him how I made up stories to help pass the time.

"Her story had flaws in it, like all the rest," I said. "But it also had points the others didn't. For one, Dahlberg wanted something from Sarah Walker. He wanted her to sign a sworn statement of his wife's infidelity to discourage Nedra's demands for exorbitant alimony. That was an important point, one we overlooked too long. Axel didn't want anything from anybody else in Glory Cloud. There was nobody else on whom he would have had reason to put pressure.

"Another point was the clue Luella Greenfield left in her unfinished embroidery. I told you about that too last night. July 20, 1921, Des Moin . . . It had only two possible meanings. First, that someone had done something in Des Moines on July 20, 1921. Something he shouldn't have done, something he still didn't want known. Of course I was thrown there by assuming it meant Des Moines, Iowa. I didn't know till I saw the map yesterday that there was another Des Moines. But the page showing Pueblo and southeastern Colorado also showed northeastern New Mexico.

"The second meaning that clue might have was that somebody had written a letter from Des Moines on that date. A letter containing information so important that to keep it quiet the writer would do murder even after thirty years.

"Both possibilities were right. Sarah Foster was secretly married in Des Moines—New Mexico—on July 20, and she wrote the letter jilting her fiancé on July 21.

"But even before I understood the New Mexico angle, Sarah fitted the picture best because so far as I had been able to learn she was the only person now involved who had been away from Glory Cloud during July. It had to be someone who had been away, either to do something in Des Moines or to write a letter from there. And old Charlie told me one afternoon that during July, Jim Walker had gone to Cheyenne for his aunt's funeral and that at the time Sarah Foster had been visiting her married sister. And a few days earlier Charlie had mentioned to Jeff and me that Sarah's sister lived in New Mexico. So when I learned there was a Des Moines there as well as in Iowa it all clicked. I still didn't know what she'd been up to that she shouldn't have, but it was too pat to be coincidental."

"If you had told me about that embroidery business," the sheriff said, "we might have saved time. I knew there was a Des Moines, New Mexico."

"Your attitude just then wasn't encouraging to confidences," I said. "You might have been less friendly if I'd had leprosy. I'm not sure."

A dull flush crept over Sawyer's fair skin, but he only said: "How did your story about Sarah Walker go?"

"I started with general background. In the spring of 1921 Sarah Foster was a pretty high school girl on the verge of graduation. Poor but honest parents. Envious of the people who had it easier. Pinning great hopes on her engagement to Jim Walker. His father was a substantial businessman and Jim attended college. Real class. I included what old Charlie told me about Jim Walker's having been in the navy. Just playing around with ideas, as I was, the navy made me think of ships and SOS calls and, of course, Morse code. I wondered whether Jim could have been a wireless operator and whether he might have taught Sarah enough code to tap out her own name or some such foolishness.

"And I included that Decoration Day picnic when Sarah worked in the kitchen at the Tuckermans' while the others had a good time. I asked myself how much she resented the set-up. How much did B. J. Tuckerman patronize her? What could have been said or done that night to fuel her envy, spark her quick temper? At any rate, she was there. She would have known about St. Vincent's gun being left.

"The murder of B. J. Tuckerman was the conspicuous hole in my story about Sarah. It still is. Apparently, she was really in Granger that evening attending class night exercises. But I thought she could have worked it some way. I thought it might have been collusion with Milt Evans. He was mysteriously absent from the class night festivities, and I thought he might have done the actual shooting, but that Sarah was somehow in it with him. Still, I couldn't see any motivation other than the vague possibilities I've just mentioned. But I thought that somehow she might have been mixed up in the narrow-gauge scandal. Her father worked occasionally in the St. Vincent mines.

"And I don't know yet what happened that night—for some reason Sarah was too stubborn to admit anything—but considering the way everything else worked out, there must be an explanation for that too."

I paused, looked inquiringly at Sawyer.

"There's an explanation, Miss Rawson. Later."

"Well," I continued, "I left the problem of Tuckerman's murder temporarily in abeyance. And my story went on to deal with Sarah Foster and Gilbert Hazlitt in much the same fashion as my story about Amanda Plumb and Hazlitt. He was always strapped for money, and whatever he knew about Sarah and however he learned it, he tried selling his knowledge to raise cash, and he got himself killed. At first, I thought he might have seen Sarah the night Tuckerman died, just as old Charlie saw Amanda—"

I stopped abruptly. I hadn't meant to spill that about Amanda, because, with Sarah Walker signed, sealed and delivered, it no longer seemed vital.

But Sawyer didn't look surprised. He gestured for me to continue.

"Okay. That's what I first thought. And Sarah would have been a better prospect for blackmail than Amanda, for while she didn't have much money, she could probably get some from Jim Walker. But I remembered my conviction that Dahlberg had come upon concrete evidence, and that it had probably been a letter from or about Des Moines. And I already knew Sarah had to be the one in that connection because she was the only person who was away from Glory Cloud during July. She admitted last night that she called Hazlitt long distance, asked him to catch and destroy her letter."

"Yes," Sawyer said, "she told me all about it. She knows she's got nothing to lose now. In July, 1921, Sarah visited her sister in Albuquerque. Jim Walker didn't much want her to go, but she was set on one last fling before settling down. And she had quite a fling.

"A little one-horse carnival was playing Albuquerque, and one afternoon Sarah took her sister's kids. She didn't especially like kids, but the sister apparently believed in letting Sarah help earn her keep. She met Pete when the kids rode the merry-go-round, and that evening Sarah went back alone. When the carnival moved on to Las Vegas she and Pete fixed it up to meet in Raton later and be secretly married.

"She told her sister she was homesick—lonely for Jim Walker. Her sister put her on the train in Albuquerque, bound for Denver. Sarah got off in Raton. Pete met her and they were married in Des Moines where the carnival was playing by then.

"I don't think Sarah originally planned to keep the marriage secret indefinitely—just till the carnival moved farther away from Glory Cloud and Jim Walker and her parents. She played it slick and she would probably have got away with it if she could have resisted telling off Jim Walker. But her vanity and her vindictiveness tripped her up—writing that letter. Because Pete soon learned he'd got hooked up with a wildcat and he quietly moved on. Alone.

"Then Sarah was really in a spot. She had broken her engagement—and done it as insultingly as possible. She had been left high and dry by the new bridegroom, and, for all she knew, she might be pregnant. Her only out was to fix things up somehow with Jim Walker, and the best way was to see he never received her letter. So she called Gilbert Hazlitt. He agreed to oblige her, but the story must have sounded queer to him. Or maybe, being a writer, he had a lot of curiosity about people and no principles. Anyway, when the letter came he opened it and read it."

"I'll bet Sarah was plenty mad when she got home and learned that," I said. "Probably Hazlitt just said come across or else, and she stalled him long enough to make her plans."

Sawyer nodded. "Yes, she told him she needed time to get money from Jim Walker and to hock the ring, but she finally made a date with him at that old prospector's cabin off in the woods. Neither of them wanted to be seen confabbing—Hazlitt didn't because of Fay St. Vincent and Sarah didn't because of Jim and because she intended to kill Hazlitt.

"Sarah told me last night, with never a blush, that she offered to pay Hazlitt off another way. By going to bed with him. Hazlitt chuckled and said that would be fine too. When he said 'too' she realized that so long as he lived she would never be safe from his demands. So before their rendezvous, Sarah sneaked up there and weakened the boards across that old mine shaft to make sure they'd break. And that night she was waiting by the path with a rock in her hand when Hazlitt came along."

"That's another thing I remembered," I said. "The day Dahlberg was killed he and I hiked up that path, looked over the whole lay-out. Later I knew he must have been reconstructing Hazlitt's murder. And I remembered that Sarah Walker was looking out an upstairs window of the inn that afternoon and saw us headed that way. She too would have realized what Axel was thinking. And Axel had been talking of going to Granger next day so she must have known the time was short and she had to act fast."

"She decided to kill him that night," Sawyer said. "She was lucky because you were gone, Calhoun, and the gathering at the inn broke up early. Nobody could prove her whereabouts. She didn't anticipate you kids going in with Dahlberg after the fry—she thought you'd go home to neck. So she hung around the cabin, waiting to get Dahlberg by himself. She meant to demand the letter before she killed him, but when he came out alone after firewood, the chance was too good to pass up. And it had the added advantage of putting you kids on the spot. So she hit him over the head from behind and used her knife. She thought that once he was out of the way she could take her time about finding the letter because nobody else knew about it.

"So on Wednesday night, while you were up on the hill with me, she searched your cabin, Miss Rawson. And the next night, Thursday, she got her first chance at Dahlberg's. That was the night you were supposed to go to the square dance, but you and Calhoun stopped to do some searching on your own. She very nearly got caught that night. No wonder she was sore at you two—you gummed things up right along."

"There again," I said, "when I thought it over it seemed odd that Sarah let us use the station wagon that night. She wasn't distinguished for generosity—why did she suddenly change? So I wondered if she'd wanted to make sure we were out of the way while she ransacked Dahlberg's cabin."

"And she knew I'd gone to Pinto," the sheriff added. "I'd announced it for everyone to hear. I suspected that as soon as our guard was pulled somebody would try to get into that cabin. Only I expected it to be you two."

Jeff, heretofore silent, snorted, but Sawyer ignored him. "Go on with your story, Miss Rawson."

"Sarah got a shock when she learned Luella Greenfield also had read that old letter. Luella didn't understand what it was all about—she only knew that, to the best of her memory, Sarah had been married just once. To Jim Walker. Luella had never heard anything about a previous marriage and a divorce. But she assumed Sarah would have a reasonable explanation. Sarah's explanation was undoubtedly an evasion while she decided what to do.

"Meanwhile, Luella kept pestering me. She wanted to get the folder back and study that letter further. And she began to wonder if it was only coincidence that Dahlberg had been killed within a few days after reading the letter. The more she thought about it, the more upset she became.

"But Luella had known Sarah for years—she couldn't believe her a killer. So finally she decided to wash her hands of the whole thing and go home. If you had let her go, Mr. Sawyer, Luella Greenfield would probably be alive today."

"Maybe," the sheriff said grimly. "And Sarah Walker might still be at large. And some time next winter maybe Luella would be found dead at her home in Pueblo. Mrs. Walker told me last night that she didn't intend to let Luella live long enough to figure it out and tell anybody. Sarah Walker's a mighty determined person."

"At any rate," I said, "when Luella announced on Friday night that she intended to tell you several things next day, Sarah knew what she meant. Once again she decided to act fast. And that time our shenanigans gave her a break because everybody was too excited about our running out on Murphy to pay much attention to Sarah. And she really had a few drinks before dinner—her breath was alcoholic, but she pretended to have drunk a lot more than was really the case. She had asked old Charlie to stop by and he found her at the kitchen table, head down, apparently completely crocked. She knew if you started asking people about Friday night, Charlie would tell that, and she knew it was better than trying to establish an iron-clad alibi. It wouldn't look faked because it fitted her well-known weakness.

"So after Jeff and I returned and things quieted down she took her father's pick and went to Luella Greenfield's. She demanded the letter, but Luella couldn't give it to her. Luella didn't have it, didn't know where it was. She'd only seen it once—the day she gave me the folder to lend Dahlberg. But at first she didn't admit her ignorance. I imagine that as long as possible Luella let Sarah think she would eventually produce the letter, meanwhile putting a clue to the killer in her embroidery.

"We'll never prove it now, but I'd be willing to bet Luella's mind worked the way I decided. Her first instinct was to signal for help, and she got down H E before she realized that was futile. She hesitated to code the killer's name, but the next most important point in her mind—the point that had made such an impression on her—was the date and place of Sarah's marriage to Pete.

"Before the clue was quite finished, Sarah saw Luella had no intention of coming across. But she couldn't afford to let Luella live and talk. I don't know whether she used the pick then and there or later."

"Later," Sawyer said. "In the tunnel. She knocked Mrs. Greenfield out in the cabin."

"Luella must have seen it coming and must have uttered the scream I heard that night."

I shivered. Jeff pm his arm around me.

"Yes," Sawyer said. "Mrs. Walker said Luella screamed once. She was furious about that and furious because she still hadn't found the letter. She put more of her fury into swinging the pick than she really needed.

"But Sarah had a smart idea there in Luella's cabin. She made it appear that Luella had followed through on her threats to go home. She knew that, if it appeared Luella had defied my orders and run away, we would assume she was guilty. Such an assumption would make things easier than having another victim found in Glory Cloud.

"So Sarah loaded Luella's unconscious body into the car, threw in the luggage and drove to Quartz. Dr. Tuckerman heard her going by. After driving down the old roadbed into the tunnel and killing Luella, she hiked back to Glory Cloud over the short-cut. Again, she had reason to be sore at you because if you kids hadn't snooped into the tunnel, Mrs. Greenfield's body might never have been found. Did the fact that you knew Sarah's father was a prospector enter into your story about her, Miss Rawson?"

"I didn't give it too much weight. Almost everyone in Glory Cloud had been connected with mining, one way or another. With Sarah, I was influenced by the things I've mentioned, along with her being at the nerve center of life in Glory Cloud. Omnipresent, but unobtrusively so because she ran the inn. In a position to know everything that went on, what we were all doing, and even, by a little eavesdropping, what progress the investigation was making. And she was in an advantageous position to pick up articles belonging to others and plant them as clues. You've made cracks about my logical mind, Mr. Sawyer, but logic told me most of the clues to Axel's murder had to be planted."

"Why?"

"There were too many. And they didn't point exclusively to one person. What would have been simpler than for Sarah to enter Jeff's room and filch that prescription slip? That was a honey because it could point to either Jeff or Tuckerman. And what was simpler than for Sarah to pocket one of Fay's little silver combs that are always slipping loose? She could have got Amanda Plumb's expired credit card any one of several ways."

"Amanda threw it into the fireplace at the inn the same day I found it in Dahlberg's cabin," Sawyer said. "But there wasn't any fire."

"Exactly. I imagine Sarah didn't much care at first which of those alleged clues you swallowed. She sprinkled them around at random to confuse the issue. And because she didn't approve of my project in Glory Cloud, for obvious reasons, she gave me special attention by taking the knife from my cabin and planting it in Dahlberg's kitchen. She must have gone up and taken it while we were on the fry, planting it before our return. Planning to use the other knife on Axel, she knew what a bad light it would put me in when the Barlows' knife was found where we found it.

"It was like Sarah, under-rating other people, to think you would never discover the blade wasn't stained by human blood. I thought of Fay St. Vincent's deep-freeze and I thought of poor Luella's finding a mangled chicken behind the shed. Eventually I thought of who had the simplest, most obvious access to a supply of fresh meat."

Sawyer sighed. "There's something to be said for logic. Sarah Walker admitted she scattered an assortment of so-called clues to confuse us. But the knife was another mistake. Because when I learned it had to be a plant, the case against you became weaker instead of stronger."

Jeff spoke for the first time. Angrily.

"But how about Sarah Walker's attacks on Gail? Gail hadn't threatened her with any letter."

Sawyer shook his head. "Miss Rawson must know as well as I do that she was threatening Sarah Walker from the moment she arrived in Glory Cloud. The very first night at dinner Miss Rawson spoke of advertising in the *Saturday Review* for Gilbert Hazlitt's unpublished letters and documents. And she mentioned she would be going over the material in Hazlitt's cabin. How did Sarah know what Hazlitt might have written some correspondent in 1921 about the juicy scandal he'd uncovered in Glory Cloud? A scandal involving proposed bigamy. How did Sarah know what memorandum Hazlitt might have left among his papers to start Miss Rawson wondering and asking questions about his untimely death? She didn't expect her own letter to turn up after all these years, but she didn't like any part of Miss Rawson's project. Sarah didn't anticipate having to resort to murder again, or so she claims, but she thought she might be able to get Miss Rawson rattled, scare her out of town."

He glanced at me. "So she went up and pounded on your door that first night. And the day you worked in the Hazlitt cabin she secured the doors from the outside with those wedges across the screens. When she heard Dahlberg and Mrs. Greenfield approaching, she released the doors and beat it. She hoped that if mysterious things, threatening things, kept happening, you might get cold feet, call the whole thing off. She misjudged you, of course, and she learned that she had. After Dahlberg was killed, even though you yourself were under suspicion, you kept asking questions, prying into the past, insisting everything went back to 1921, a year that Sarah felt the less said about the better.

"You told the reporters your ideas, and you were constantly becoming more of a threat. You figured out that Dahlberg had found tangible evidence pointing to someone and had hidden it. You, as well as Sarah, were hunting for that evidence. And because you had been closer to Dahlberg, your chances of finding it first were excellent. So Thursday night when you went to the lookout Sarah had already decided to deal with you. She was on her way to your cabin when she saw your flashlight coming along the road. She slipped inside Tuckerman's yard and waited, not knowing who you might be. But then you made things easy for her by calling out Jeff's name. She didn't want to kill you right there, so near the inn, but all she had to do then was follow you up to the marker. She waited to see whether you found the object you were both seeking before she attacked you. If she hadn't been disconcerted by your failure to find the letter, she probably would have done a better job."

Sawyer smiled, a wry smile.

"Sarah Walker talked freely last night, Miss Rawson. And of all the things she admitted, she showed regret over only one. She keeps reproaching herself for carelessness because she didn't knock you out before shoving you off that ledge. You were right, of course, in deducing that, having made an unsuccessful attempt, she would be impelled to try again. So when the lightning showed you last night, running toward Dahlberg's cabin, she knew that was her opportunity. By the way, Miss Rawson, how did you happen to think of the letter's being hidden in that old musket?"

"If I tried to explain that, you'd never believe me. Call it woman's intuition. But masculine intuition also helped with my story. It was Jeff's idea that Hazlitt had been murdered and that Luella's clue was in Morse code. And he had a lot of other good ideas."

Sawyer looked grave. "Which of you had the inspiration that the crux of our present situation was B. J. Tuckerman's murder?"

"We worked that out together. Why?"

"I want to give credit where credit is due," Sawyer said. "You thought I didn't pay enough attention to your theorizing, Miss Rawson, that I was negligent about looking into all possibilities. You gave me a lot of trouble with the press and with the D.A.'s office. Do you want to hear what really happened the night of June 10, 1921?"

"I certainly do."

"B. J. Tuckerman shot himself."

"How do you know?"

"I, too, can spin tales, Miss Rawson. After her husband was killed in the narrow-gauge wreck, Amanda Plumb was, as might be expected, extremely bitter. She used to take long walks at night, brooding. The evening Tuckerman killed himself Amanda was on such a hike and she had worked herself up to a fine pitch of indignation. She decided to go on to Tuckerman's place and give him a piece of her mind. She had reached the exploding point and she meant to march in and accuse old Tuckerman of being an outright murderer. She had no intention of killing him, although she hated him enough. Just when the thunder and lightning were worst, she reached the Tuckerman house, hurried up on the porch, opened the door without knocking. Through the open door to his study she saw B. J. Tuckerman in the act of pulling the trigger of a gun held to his head. The gun went off simultaneously with an especially loud thunder-crash, but she saw Tuckerman slump over his desk. She closed the door, went home. And if old Charlie saw her leaving, as you implied, she never knew it. Now what do you think?"

"I think she shot Tuckerman herself," I said. "Where did you learn all this? Amanda told you? Why didn't she tell it years ago? I think that when we started going into Tuckerman's death she got her wind up and fed you that yarn to cover herself."

"Okay," Sawyer said wearily, "here's the rest. When you first started yelling about B. J. Tuckerman's being murdered, you thought I was ignoring you. There's no law that I have to tell excitable gals everything I do. The man who was sheriff in 1921 is still living. Yates, his name is. He has a little acreage down in Granger. He's getting along, but he remembers the Tuckerman suicide right enough. After you first mentioned the subject I looked up old Yates, asked him a few questions.

He told me there was never any doubt that B. J. Tuckerman committed suicide. The evidence all pointed to it: position of the body, powder burns, direction the bullet entered and traveled, everything. And when I wasn't completely satisfied he gave me the information about Amanda Plumb's being a witness."

"She had told him?"

"She had told him. Within two or three days. Right at first she hadn't said anything to anybody because she felt guilty. Not guilty of killing Tuckerman, but of having hated him so strongly she was glad to see him dead. However, when people started gossiping about St. Vincent's gun being used she went to Yates and told him what she'd seen. And she asked him not to reveal her story unless he had to because she still felt conscience-stricken about her bitterness toward Tuckerman. But a murderer, Miss Rawson, wouldn't have gone to the sheriff at that time with such a story, would she? It would have been too easy then to cross her up. She wouldn't have dared do that if she had been guilty. So now you see why Sarah Walker wouldn't admit killing Tuckerman."

"Well, what about Milt Evans? Why didn't he go to class night?"

"He was sick. He came to the mountains that day to get the family's cabin ready for summer. He intended to return to Granger before evening. But for lunch he ate odds and ends of food he found in a cupboard and became violently ill. Food poisoning. Herman Tuckerman treated him and put him to bed. Milt was much too sick to go back to Granger. Dr. Tuckerman corroborates the circumstances."

I remembered that the newspaper account of Herman Tuckerman's activities the day of his father's suicide had included mention of such a call, although without giving the patient's name. I said:

"But if B. J. really shot himself—and I guess I'll have to admit that's what happened—and there was nothing mysterious about it, why was everybody so concerned over Axel's book on the narrow gauge?"

"Where's your imagination, Miss Rawson? Tired from working overtime? Take Dr. Tuckerman. If B. J. Tuckerman had been your father, would you be happy to have his crookedness expounded? Take Miss Fay St. Vincent. What if your father had been B. J.'s business associate and people were inclined to talk about birds of a feather? And if in addition you had always entertained a sneaking suspicion that your good friend, Herman, might actually have killed his father? Or take Milton Evans—what if you had been employed by one of the principals of the narrow gauge and discharged for dishonesty? And what if you had probably been involved in other sly dealings that had never come to light? Would you be eager for the subject to be re-opened? I've gone into the matter more thoroughly than you realize, Miss Rawson."

"Nevertheless," I said, "if I hadn't gone off on the wrong track—the narrow-gauge track—probably I never would have arrived at the right destination in the end."

Grudgingly, Sawyer agreed.

Jeff had been increasingly restless. Now he got to his feet, pulling me up beside him.

"What do you think, Sawyer? Will getting married and settling down with a quiet conservative guy like me keep her out of any more mischief?"

Dan Sawyer smiled, the first friendly smile I had ever seen on his stolid face.

"I shouldn't wonder, Calhoun," he said. "Might be worth a try."

They didn't bother to ask my opinion. That was all right, too. I was ready and willing to be kept out of more mischief. And I must say for Jeff that he's pretty well managed it.

Mr. and Mrs. Tom Duncan and their dog, Jeff.

ABOUT THE AUTHOR

Carolyn Thomas was the pseudonym of Actea Duncan (1913-1990). Born Actea Carolyn Young in Kansas, she met her future husband while a student in his adult education class in Des Moines, Iowa. She and Thomas William Duncan (1905-1987) married in 1942. Tom, a struggling author, taught for the next two years at Grinnell College, but his health problems led to their moving west to warmer climates. The couple lived in a trailer, supporting themselves with their writing and by performing as a traveling magic show. (In addition to working on his novels, Tom wrote numerous detective stories for a variety of mystery magazines throughout the 1930s and early 1940s.)

Actea's first mystery novel, *Prominent Among the Mourners*, was published in 1946, though it was Tom's circus novel, *Gus the Great* (1947), that became a Book-of-the-Month-Club hit, with Universal Pictures buying the film rights (though a movie does not seem to have been made). The windfall allowed the couple to settle in a ranch house in New Mexico. Tom went on to write other well-received novels, though none were as popular as *Gus*. Actea continued to write mysteries, publishing *Narrow Gauge to Murder* in 1952, *The Hearse Horse Snickered* in 1954, and *The Cactus Shroud* in 1957. (A 1958 gossip column notes that Actea had sought inspiration for her next mystery while the couple vacationed in the Virgin Islands, but no further mysteries appeared.) The couple had no children, but publicity photos during the 1940s prominently feature their beloved dog, Jeff, who was named after Geoffrey Chaucer.

Sadly, the couple's later writings do not appear to have provided sufficient financial stability toward the end of their lives, as they were buried in unmarked graves in Las Cruces, New Mexico. A fan who found inspiration in Thomas Duncan's last book, *The Sky and Tomorrow*, wanted to show his appreciation to the author, and was shocked to find out what had happened to them. He paid for a headstone to be placed on their gravesite, which was dedicated by a small group of book lovers, historians, and distant relatives in 2015.

ADDITIONAL INFORMATION

Catterick, Donna. 'Thomas W. Duncan & "Gus the Great."' *Always Back Roads* (blog). https://alwaysbackroads.wordpress.com/2011/07/17/thomas-w-duncan-gus-the-great/

Catterick, Donna. 'The Sky and Tomorrow.' *This I Leave* (blog). https://thisileave.wordpress.com/2015/07/29/the-sky-and-tomorrow/

Natte, Roger. 'Duncan, Thomas William.' *The Biographical Dictionary of Iowa*. University of Iowa Press, 2009. (Online, 2018.) http://uipress.lib.uiowa.edu/bdi/DetailsPage.aspx?id=105

COACHWHIP PUBLICATIONS
CoachwhipBooks.com

FRANCIS WALLACE

Little HERCULES

A *Detective Novel* CLASSIC

A FULL LENGTH NOVEL

COACHWHIP PUBLICATIONS
CoachwhipBooks.com

A JUDGE MASSIE
MYSTERY

THE CORPSE IS
INDIGNANT

DOUGLAS STAPLETON
and HELEN A. CAREY

COACHWHIP PUBLICATIONS
CoachwhipBooks.com

The Serpentine Club Investigates
Murder in Washington, D.C.

THE CAPITAL
MURDER

James Z. Alner

COACHWHIP PUBLICATIONS
CoachwhipBooks.com

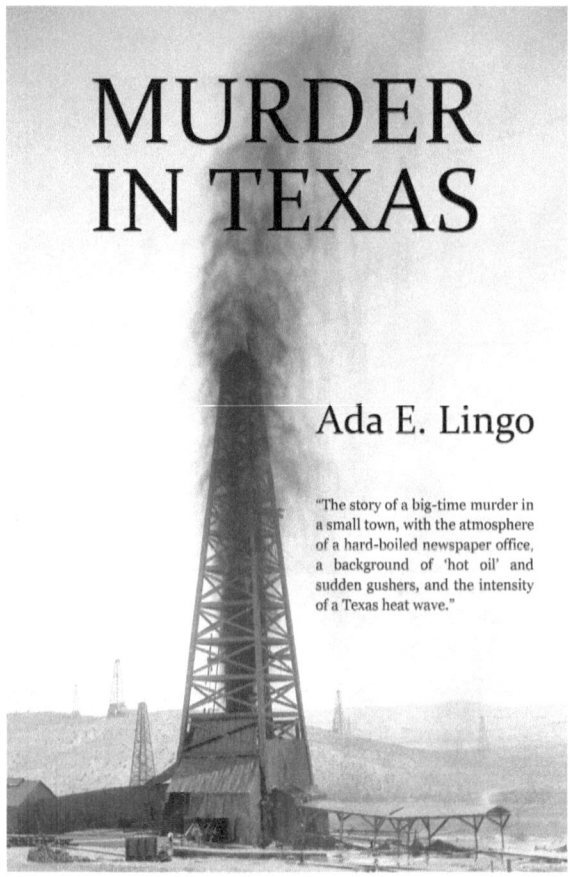

MURDER
IN TEXAS

Ada E. Lingo

"The story of a big-time murder in a small town, with the atmosphere of a hard-boiled newspaper office, a background of 'hot oil' and sudden gushers, and the intensity of a Texas heat wave."

COACHWHIP PUBLICATIONS

CoachwhipBooks.com

COACHWHIP PUBLICATIONS
COACHWHIPBOOKS.COM

MURDER ENDS THE SONG

ALFRED MEYERS

COACHWHIP PUBLICATIONS
COACHWHIPBOOKS.COM

MURDER
IN A WALLED TOWN
KATHERINE WOODS

www.ingramcontent.com/pod-product-compliance
Lightning Source LLC
Chambersburg PA
CBHW020635260626
47157CB00008B/2752